PHOENIX RISING

LEGENDS OF THE MOUNTAIN BOOK 1

ALI INGS

ALI INGS

This book is dedicated to martial artists everywhere, whether you study European and western arts, Asian arts, Medieval arts, Jedi arts, or something else altogether.

Also, to all the teachers who have shared their knowledge with me, through the many arts I've learned, thank you.

CONTENTS

CHAPTER I

It's Her

W here was she? I glanced over at the students, but she wouldn't be among them. The young men punched, yelling with each strike, following Master Holin's counting. No, she'd be tucked away somewhere. I scanned the walls, up high where the lattice covered openings let the sun into the courtyard.

A flicker of movement pulled my attention to the corner. The shadows were deep. A shadow moved, just briefly, but I saw it. Good, she hadn't missed it. She hasn't missed a lesson in weeks. I eased along the wall, silent as the shadows I moved in. From this corner opposite her, I could see her curled up, leaning against the lattice and staring down at the young men below her.

Master Holin clapped his hands twice. The students shifted as one, standing tall with their hands at their sides. He waved, and a young man stepped beside him. Master Holin glanced up at the corner, his brow furrowing. He shook his head, just a tiny motion, and turned his attention back to the boys. Had he seen her?

"Who can tell me what the fourth move in the form does? Anyone?" Master Holin shifted into a fighting stance. He bent his knees and stepped back, his right arm up at shoulder level, his fist coiled. His left arm was bent in front of himself, forearm up and fist to the sky.

I slipped from the courtyard, passing through the halls like a ghost. Once again, she'd gone unnoticed. The Master's Hall was silent, most everyone teaching or tending to their duties. I didn't see anyone as I entered a room in the back corner.

"That was fast, Kai. Is she there?" His hand was steady as he poured his tea. He sat on the velvet cushion at the low table, his one concession for comfort.

"Yes, she's back. I think she's the one."

He raised a white eyebrow at me. "Indeed. How long?"

"Days, maybe weeks. I'm sorry, old friend." My heart felt squeezed, like a hand gripped it.

"No need." He smiled and swirled his tea in the little cup. "Life moves in cycles. The years march on. I'm ready. I can feel it approaching."

"It's been a joy to work with you." I lowered myself to the cushion opposite him. Just the thought of our long friendship warmed me through.

"Are you sure about her? Women don't make good warriors." He sipped his tea, his gaze down on the table.

"How can you say that? You, who fought beside so many fine women. What would Soth, or Onni, or Lillin say?"

He stared at a scroll on his wall, a map of the Seven Valleys, tears forming in his eyes. "They would tell me I'm a fool, while they pointed their blades at my neck, but they are all long gone. I have met none like them since." The old man set his teacup on the woven placemat. "We've had many grand adventures. Go. I know you want to check on her."

"I'll be back soon."

He lifted the teapot lid and the smell of chamomile wafted through the air. So many memories in a single aroma. I shook myself free of the cascade of emotions, of memories of friends long past we shared the tea with. No, it was time to look forward.

***

The mist gathered on the leaves, large water drops falling to the ground around her. She shifted her weight, drawing her hand up and back, her other hand before her in defense. Her shoulders slumped, and she frowned. She stood straighter and tried the move again.

I eased between the trees, silent and unnoticed. She was close, nearly remembered the move, but one detail was missing for her. "Lift your elbow higher, all the way to shoulder level. It's a strike behind you, too. That arm should be parallel to the ground and coiled by your shoulder."

Her brow furrowed. She practiced the movement, slow and deliberate. Her face relaxed with each attempt, her eyes brightening. "Oh. Oh, I see. That makes sense."

"Now, do that movement, and step forward into Dragon Rises Diagonally."

She stepped back and drew her hands up towards her shoulder, her elbow high and her other arm in front. Her knees bent and she crouched, smooth and graceful. She extended a leg out and rose, moving her front arm out and up with her body.

"It's a throw?" Her eyes widened.

"It can be."

"Wow." She stared at her hands, still outstretched. "Is that combination from a different pattern?"

"Yes, it is. How do you like the movement now?"

She grinned and shifted, trying the combination again. "I like staying low like that."

"You root to the ground well. You'll thrive in lower stances. A style that keeps you under someone's balance point might work best for you. You'll need to watch for kicks, but you can be trained for that."

She dropped to the soft soil and sighed, her head in her hands. "No, I can't. They don't teach girls, or small men, or anyone who's not a large warrior type already." She raised her head to the sky. A drop of water landed on her forehead and rolled down her face. Another landed in her damp hair.

"You need training. You're good. I will train you myself out here if I have to, but give me a chance to arrange things."

She leapt to her feet and wiped her forehead with her sleeve. "I don't belong there." She bowed, hands by her sides, like she was addressing the royal court. "Thank you, Teacher, but I must go."

"Wait."

She disappeared through the trees, her dark clothing blending into the shadows. My heart felt heavy, like something was crushing my chest. She wanted to train, and she was willing to work hard. Anyone who would climb walls and sneak into a school of warriors just to learn had bravery like I hadn't seen in ages.

I spent a moment beneath the trees, letting the wildness of the mountain wash over me. Each day for the last couple of weeks, I met her here. She took corrections well and already was stronger and more confident. Each move, each new bit of information. She soaked it all in like a sponge that holds more. How much faster would she learn at the school, with so many warriors to learn from?

The sun began its slow descent as I returned to the school, casting the familiar warm glow on the surrounding forest. Light filtered through the leaves, speckling the ground with bursts of sunshine. I left the warmth of the sun behind and entered the Masters' Hall. Everyone was back in lessons or working after lunch, waiting for the approaching evening meal. I had the halls to myself as I returned to the Grandmaster.

He sat on his cushion, a pot of steaming tea before him. The bowl of vegetables smelled of ginger and sesame, balancing out the sweet tea. "How did it go?" He selected a sliver of carrot with his slender two-pronged fork and bit into the bright vegetable.

"She refused." I slumped to the cushion across from him. "She's scared. It's the best thing for her, though."

"For her, or for you?" He sipped his tea. "Isn't too much fear a problem?"

"Warriors often feel fear. They act despite the fear, and she's already done that sneaking in."

He speared a celery slice and chewed it, taking time to savor the spices. "It won't be easy. They won't welcome her quickly. She's too small to train with most of them and won't fit well into regular lessons. She'll be an outcast of sorts."

"Grandmaster, she's not from here. She's already an outcast. Would she spend so much time in the forest if she had anywhere else to be, or anyone to spend time with? Some people would welcome her. I can think of three masters who would help her. Please?"

He poured another cup of tea. Steam rose in delicate curls from the little cup. "I will see this girl for myself. If she agrees, we'll make a space for her. You will be responsible for her when I am gone. My time is drawing near."

I felt that squeezing around my heart. No matter how many friends I've said goodbye to, it always hurts. "Yes, Grandmaster. If you feel up to it, she practices just down the mountain every day. I'll take you there."

"I must meditate and conserve my energy. We'll discuss this in the morning."

He eased himself from the low table and rose to his feet, each movement a growing effort. Would he make it down the mountain to see her? It hurt to see him so frail, the young man I once fought with and travelled far beside, so I left him to meditate.

She'd be in the village by now, but which one? If she practiced in that spot, it was closest to the village of Winby. I left through the main gate and headed down the road. What did she do when she wasn't sneaking into lessons?

The trail was worn and tended, and I nearly flew down the mountain.

Farmers gathered the last of their crops in the fields around the village. They nearly harvested the pea fields, with workers carrying baskets overflowing with plump pods. The carrots would be ready next, the greens reaching for the sky. They harvested the spring onions weeks ago, and the leeks were a couple weeks away from ready yet.

The wheat field was empty, golden stubble all that's left. The miller had his donkey out, grinding the flour and bundling it into sacks. I stopped in the shade of an apple tree and watched. A miller worked these stones for centuries, the individual changing, but the process remaining nearly identical through the ages.

I passed the tanner, his knives scraping the stretching hides with a swishing clatter. Where was she? The women did laundry closer to the river, across the town. I headed there first, but she wasn't with them. What would she be doing here? Who would have taken her in? Think, what might she do here? Her hands didn't have heavy callouses.

Was she back in the forest? I stopped at the blacksmith's forge at the far end of town. With a heavy heart, I turned to go back. A small motion pulled my attention, not from the blacksmith, but past him. She sat curled up in the corner, a sword across her lap, rubbing oil on the blade with a cloth. He was letting her help? A girl?

She took her time stuffing the cloth into the fullers and being careful of the edges. I followed her gaze as she glanced at the smithy wall. A carving hung there, a stylized bird with wings outstretched. This smithy had ancient ties to the legend of the Phoenix. That carving had been here all this time, as long as stories went back.

She gathered the sword in her hands, wrapped in the protective cloth on her lap. Every inch of the gleaming blade was lightly oiled. Did he teach her that? She bowed and handed the sword to the blacksmith.

"Good work, girl. There's a bowl of porridge for you in the shop." He took the sword and lay it on the bench.

She bowed her head. She darted into a lean-to against the main workshop. Two bowls of oats and vegetables steamed, waiting atop the workbench inside. A pot of tea sat near the food, little teacups resting upside down, waiting for use. She cradled the smaller bowl in her hands and settled onto the wooden bench against the wall.

Glasses lined a small shelf above the workbench. She selected one and poured some water for herself, draining the glass twice with a sigh. Her ceramic spoon clattered against the wooden bowl. She ate steadily, her eyes on the carving.

The blacksmith wiped his hands on a cloth and stepped under the lean-to roof. "That's the Phoenix, that is." He picked up the larger bowl and sat on a high stool at the workbench.

"The bird of legend?"

The blacksmith raised an eyebrow. "Aye, but he's more than a legend. He protects this entire mountain, and all the surrounding valleys. He's the very essence of martial arts, protecting any who needs him and fighting for peace."

She frowned, still staring at the carving. "How can fighting bring peace? Does he live at the school?"

"Probably. He's been around an incredibly long time. Every hundred years, sometimes more or less, he's reborn. It'll happen any time now. There might be some chaos and danger until he's strong enough to restore order. Best watch yourself, girl." The blacksmith poured two cups of tea, drinking the hot steaming liquid in one right away.

She picked up the other little cup, holding the edges. She blew on the tea, sending a curl of steam towards the blacksmith. "One day I'm going to learn. Learn to protect people and learn to use a sword."

The blacksmith laughed, his head back. He coughed, spilling porridge from his cheeks. She curled up and shifted back as he pounded his chest, his foot beating on the ground as he choked down his food. "A comedian, are you, girl? Nobody will teach a woman to fight. My woman already glares at me for letting you touch the swords at all, never mind learning to use one."

Her face pinked at his renewed laughter. She rose to her feet and set her bowl on the workbench. "Thank you for the work and the meal." She blinked back tears and bowed her head again.

"Come back tomorrow and I'll have some daggers for you to polish." He bowed his head in return.

Her eyes widened. She stood completely still. I admit, I felt surprised as well. To show a woman such respect, even one he just laughed at. What was going on here?

She walked from the forge, head held high, even as she wiped a tear with her sleeve. What did she know of the Phoenix? I knew from my own travels how fast a story could change with each telling, and there were many variants on the Phoenix tales, not all accurate. She walked down the middle of the packed dirt path, heading towards the laundry house and meagre market.

Where was her home? How did she keep warm? I glanced up at the sun, dropping behind the mountain already and turning the sky red. It was the school's mission to train protectors and help people. If anybody needed help, it was her.

With daylight disappearing, I headed back up the mountain. The path was well defined, easy to follow in the light or dark, but the Grandmaster would miss me. I didn't stop until I reached the gates.

The air was crisp and cool. Fewer birds sang, most settling down for the night already. The mist from the waterfall rolled down the mountain. It would soon reach the village below, peaceful as I looked down on it. No matter how many years I stood and looked out of these gates, the view was almost unchanging.

The gates stood open, as always, in times of peace. A man and woman shuffled past, arm in arm, her other arm in a sling and her hand wrapped in bandages. He smiled down at her. I shifted aside and let them pass.

The fading sunlight streamed in through the paper-lined windows of the Masters' Hall, giving the wooden walls a reddish glow. I glanced at the windows as I passed. The paper was freshly replaced. I liked the privacy it gave from the rest of the school. That, and the building stayed cooler in the summer without the direct sun heating the halls.

He was already asleep when I slipped into the room. Morning would come early enough. I settled onto the meditation cushion and waited. In the morning, I'd learn when he saw her. I'd learn how long she has to prepare. I'd learn her fate.

CHAPTER 2

THE SWORD

I shook myself from my rest. The smell of chamomile pulled at my sleepy brain. Daylight streamed in through the open slats above us. He already sat at the low table, a bowl of millet and berries in front of him. He stared at the scroll on the wall, his eyes barely blinking. That image made me shiver. How could a picture make a battleground look so peaceful?

"I will come see her in three days." He picked up his teacup. "Did you find her?"

I straightened up and moved to the cushion opposite him. "I did."

"How is she?" He scooped up some millet and blew on it.

"She's getting by." She could do more than get by. She could thrive, but not there. Not where she was just a woman and outsider. She needed help. "I'll be back soon."

"Kai, you can say it. I already know."

I paused at the door, my back to him. "I want her to learn. You can help me. That's your job."

He sighed. His spoon clinked against the table despite the woven mat. "I know. Go see her. I need to set my affairs in order, and you'll just be bored."

His words shot through my heart. "I'll stay and help with anything you need. You're more than just a friend."

He smiled and shook his head. "No, I know what I need to do. You need to get ready, too. I'm fine. You know it."

I did, too. "I'll be back soon."

I've never made it to her practice spot so quickly, speeding past masters and students in the courtyard and nearly flying down the mountain. She could already be there. We had little time to prepare, and I wanted her to have every moment possible.

She stepped with each block and strike combination, barely visible through the trees as I approached. Each strike lashed out with speed. She needed more strength, though. I could fix that with time. She only learned this combination last week, from spying on the intermediate class, and already she had it down.

I slipped between the trees. She raised her leg and kicked out, her clothing snapping with the strike. Strike, kick, strike, kick. She moved between the trees. She stepped across and spun, her leg coiling and lashing out behind her. Her arms flailed, and she toppled to the ground.

She twisted and landed on her backside. Her face scrunched up; her brow wrinkled. Her pink skin turned red. She worried her lip between her teeth.

"That happens. Try again."

"Is there any point?" Her voice was a whisper, barely audible over the breeze. Her head dropped, her chin to her chest. "They'll never let me learn. This is as good as I'll get."

"You know, students in the school go through this stage as well. Everything feels awkward when you start." I sank to the damp soil beside her. "Martial arts aren't just about the combat and the techniques. They're also about getting back up when you fall and working until you achieve your goals."

"Really?" She relaxed back on the ground, her hands under her head. The sun reached her face in little speckles, filtered through the leaves.

"Really. Always remember to keep looking up ahead to your goals. There's nothing wrong with falling down. You might even want to quit, in that moment, and feel you lost your spark. When you get up, and you will, rise like an inferno. The brightest flame you can imagine. Fuel that inner fire with dedication."

She rose to her feet and brushed the dirt from her clothing. "I don't even know if I'm doing this right."

"Your skills are excellent, but you need a sound foundation to build on."

"I'm doing the best I can," she whispered.

"You're doing well. Let's start at the beginning."

Her face scrunched as she rubbed her chin. "Beginning? I don't understand."

"You've seen the blocks and strikes from class. I'm going to teach you the first form. It'll give you a more organized way to practice. Stand straight and tall. Close your eyes and relax your body."

She took a deep breath and closed her eyes. She shifted her feet together and let her arms hang at her sides.

"When you're ready, turn left and step into the front stance with your left foot. Low block with the left hand."

She followed each direction, slow and deliberate, taking in every detail I gave her. I guided and corrected, giving her time to adjust.

"There. You did it. That's the first form. Now, we'll do it again."

She stood straight and quiet without me telling her to.

I waited until she opened her eyes again. "First movement. Step left with low block. Go."

She kept her blocking arm out better this time, her stance strong.

"Where is your attacker, and what are you defending against?"

"They're here in front of me. They could be kicking or striking low." Her eyes fixed on her invisible opponent ahead of her.

"Excellent. Next move. Step and strike. Why?"

"I blocked their attack and want to move while they're recovering." She stepped and struck. A straight punch to the solar plexus. "If I threw their balance off, I could turn the strike into a push and step into a heel hook."

I froze. It took a moment to recover. "How do you know that?"

Her lip trembled. "Was I wrong?"

"No, you're correct, and you're doing great. How do you know, though?"

"The advanced class talked about it."

Not at the school, they didn't. I was sure of that. Watching her for only a few moments, anyone could tell she wasn't a total beginner. What was she hiding? Should I press her, or would she take off? Some moves were new to her, but others she had learned already. No, it's not the time yet.

"Kai?"

I blinked and shook my thoughts free. "Do you remember what's next?"

"I spin behind, right?"

"Do it."

She shifted from a front stance to a back stance, her body turning to face behind her. Her arms crossed in front of her at chest height, palms facing her.

"Purpose?"

She stood in position, silent and unmoving. Would she answer?

"It's a block against a straight strike, or I can catch a kick and step back."

"More advanced class wisdom?" Why didn't she want to tell me? Is she afraid I won't teach her?

She nodded. Her eyes never wavered from her imaginary opponent, her face staying blank as she stared ahead.

Alright, keep your secrets. I know you're a beginner in this style, or you'd know this form. I led her through, move by move. Something tugged at my memory, something familiar about how she'd use these moves. The downside to living so long and training so many styles was they sometimes blurred together for me.

"Excellent. Take a break."

She stretched her body, arms up high, before folding down and grabbing her ankles. This girl was flexible.

"Before this school, have you seen martial arts before?"

She sat under a tree on the moss, her back to the trunk. "We had them back home. They weren't this common and were different."

"Did you train?"

She stared up through the branches, silent again as she blinked slowly. "My parents didn't want me to."

A non-answer if I ever heard one. Was she training in secret there, too? Was that why she didn't want to say? Here, family honour and obedience were values everyone shared, and it was shameful to disobey parents. Still, she wasn't from here. Would she feel the same?

"Have you ever heard of the Phoenix?" I already knew the answer, but she didn't know that. Maybe I could get her to relax and open up a bit.

She cocked her head to the side. "The immortal bird? The blacksmith said he protects the mountain."

"Yes, that's the bird. What do you know of it?"

"They said it dies and is reborn. Where did it first come from, though? Was it hatched like a normal bird, or how was it born?" Her fingers traced the rough fabric of her pants over her knees, the patches firmly fixed in place with thick thread.

I blinked. That's not usually what children here ask about. Had anyone ever asked that? "It was born from a martial artist many ages ago. He was a lot like you, actually."

"What, like me?" She shook her head and smiled. "Born how?"

I settled beside her on the soft moss. "When he was a teenager, like you, he would sneak into the forest and train. This forest, as the legend goes. He developed the first ever martial art here, instead of just fighting randomly. He protected the village from bandits many times, nearly single-handed. Over time, he refined his skills, began using a sword, and even trained others."

She stared up the mountain at the mist from the waterfalls. The water tumbled a great distance over the largest fall, not far up from here. "And?"

"This man grew old and knew he was going to die one day. Bandits no longer attacked because he had a reputation, even as an old man. If he died, he knew they'd be back, and no one would be safe. His desire to protect his home and his people transformed him."

"Into the Phoenix?"

"That's right. Legends say his spirit is still here, protecting the people."

She smiled. Her hands went still on her knees. "That's a delightful story. It must be so reassuring, having someone to watch over you."

"Maybe it's more than a story? Maybe there's something special about this place?"

"It feels like it," she whispered. "Like any moment, a warrior of old days might march out between the trees, still in his armour."

"You live here, too, right? Maybe he's protecting you as well. Ready to try again?"

She leapt to her feet, a smile on her face. "Absolutely."

I couldn't help my grin. Her enthusiasm was infectious. She's just what I was looking for.

***

The clearing was empty when we arrived, like I hoped it would be. Lessons were still winding down. We hadn't heard the bell yet. Even the nearest towns could hear the bells and followed school time, their daily routines following the distant chimes that rang through the valleys.

"She's coming. I can hear her."

The Grandmaster slipped behind some bushes. I could sense him, feel his life force, but he hid from sight. Would he still see her?

She passed through the trees like a moving shadow, quiet and confident. Her toe stepped into her practice space, but she paused, her gaze scanning the area. "Kai?"

"I'm here. Ready to practice?"

She smiled and her shoulders relaxed. She stepped to the middle and nodded, her eyes closed.

"Alright, what did you learn today? Think you can show me?"

"Well," she paused, her eyes opening again. "I go down low, slowly, with balance. My hand slides down. I rise and shift forward like Dragon Rises Diagonally, but with different hand motions." She moved through the sequence, slow and fluid, no breaks between the parts.

"Yes, the two moves are closely related." I smiled at her balance. She got as low as some masters did, and they'd been practicing for decades. Did she stretch regularly? Her balance was exceptional, too.

I moved closer. "That's good. We're going to make a few minor adjustments and make it better. Turn your foot out just a hair, right there, and let your hips lead you up instead of your hand. Try again, nice and slow."

She moved again, adjusting her position with the advice I gave, and rose, confident. "That takes all stress off the knee. Thank you."

"You're welcome. Have you been practicing the first form?"

She smiled. "Yes."

"Show me what you've done."

She stood straight, her eyes closed and breathing slowing. Her eyes opened, and she stepped, turning just like she practiced with him. Her movements were crisp and snappy, striking and blocking, stepping and turning. Her gaze was sharp and always aimed at her pretend opponent. She stepped and pursued, attacked and subdued, before stepping into the closing position. She stood straight; her hands low in front of her with fingers touching.

"Where did you learn that?"

"The pattern? Her brow wrinkled. "You taught me."

"No, the hand movement at the end. That's something the Royal Guard do."

Her head dropped, her chin almost at her chest. She chewed on her lower lip. After a long breath, she looked up. "I used to be friends with a guard."

Really? Things were making sense, except for a few details. "What else did he teach you? Will you show me?"

She nodded, blinking back a tear. Water dripped from the leaves over her, but she ignored them and straightened up again. She didn't wait, moving right into a flowing pattern, slow and precise, her hands and feet moving in circles and partial circles as she moved among the trees.

No wonder she picked this up so quickly. She had been training for a while, with how smooth her motions were, each movement leading into the next one. Still, only guards learned this style. Her friend risked death to teach her. What would cause him to risk everything for a girl from another land?

She stretched her arms out, one curved high and the other low, one leg bent up in front of her. I knew that move, and she had it perfect, nearly. This guard really knew what he was doing with her. She flowed down, lowering herself into a partial crouch, and turned to block someone behind her. Her leg stretched out, and she dropped nearly to the ground, rising again in a movement similar to the one she just learned.

I could work with this. Every motion she did, she did with purpose. She needs to know what she's doing, not just the movements, but why. I smiled to myself as she settled back into the quiet stillness.

"There's someone I'd like you to meet."

"Oh?" She raised an eyebrow.

The Grandmaster stepped from the bushes. She leapt forward at the sudden movement, hands out and ready to fight, feet spread for balance. Her eyes were on him, but did she know who she faced? Still, I had to smile at her instincts for defense.

He held his hands up, moving slowly, a soft smile on his face. "I won't attack. You have good reflexes."

She blinked at him, her hands dropping a few inches. Everyone from here would know who he was, though he seldom left the school anymore. Would she recognize him? She blinked again and straightened up, dropping her hands.

"Grandmaster." She bowed with her hands in front of her, like a guard would.

"Kai told me of the brave young warrior who was training with him." He winked at her. "I'm pleased to see you doing so well. It has only been days and you've already learned the first form."

"To be fair, Sir, the forms are short." She bowed her head again.

He laughed, his white teeth flashing in the light. She glanced up at him, wide-eyed.

"The ancient forms are, yes. You will find the later forms longer and more complex. They may offer you a challenge these ancient forms do not. Would you care to learn?"

"Oh, yes, Sir." Her little body nearly vibrated.

"Why do you train? Boredom?" He cocked his head and waited.

She shook her head, her eyes on her feet again. "I just have to. I feel complete when I train, and empty when I don't. I dream about it." Her voice trailed off in a whisper.

Did she know what he just offered her? My heart skipped a few beats, or so it felt. I've been trying for weeks to get her to come. Please, accept, I whispered to myself.

"Come with me." He held his hand out to her. I glimpsed the gentle father he could have been, not the usual commanding head of the school.

Her hand raised, stopping at her side. Please say yes, I pleaded inside my head again. After impressing the old man, she couldn't stop now. He waited for her to reach out, his expression steady and unchanging. Find that inner courage, I pleaded. She took a slow breath and slid her hand into his.

CHAPTER 3

A New Beginning

"There is something I want to show you." The Grandmaster guided her through the trees, towards the path. "Something an old friend gave me. He's a warrior, too. You'll probably find it interesting."

She walked in silence beside him, her eyes ahead on the mountain. The school was just visible through the trees, glimpses through the branches of the high walls, the painted buildings a splash of colour on the mountainside.

"How did you make friends with a guard?" He turned on the path, still leading her by the hand.

"When I first arrived here, I didn't know anyone but my parents. I snuck into the gardens to play. They were training, so I watched from behind a hedge." She wiped a tear away. "He caught me watching. He could have beaten me and turned me in, but he talked to me instead. When he got off work that day, he let me join him for a drink of juice. Most people avoided us, as foreigners, but not him."

"An unfortunate thing, that tendency." The Grandmaster shook his head. "We can learn much from each other if we remain open to differences. Why aren't you with your parents?"

She stared at the path as she walked, the well-trod dirt packed hard and free of stones. She stepped over an indent from centuries of wagon wheels. "I lost them," she whispered.

"In the revolution."

She nodded. "I don't know if they lived. A laundress found me wandering the halls and got me out before the crowd arrived. She brought me here, to her sister. She said I'd be safe, and I am, but it's so lonely."

Her toes touched the bottom step as she froze. Her eyes followed the carved stone steps up the mountain, to the massive archway with the open gates. She glanced to her right, where the packed path continued on, wagon tracks leading up to the gates on a winding route.

"It's wonderful inside." I moved beside her. "Think of all the history, the warriors who trained here."

She walked with us up the steps, under the archway with writing over the gate. The School for Martial and Spiritual Development. Underneath, the virtues were printed for all to see as a reminder. How many years, decades, have I looked at those very letters?

"Kai's right. If you like martial arts, you'll see a collection of history unequalled in all the country. Come inside."

The Grandmaster led her into the courtyard, the floor paved with tightly fitted stone blocks. Large wooden buildings lined each side, high roofs to shed snow easily, all safely within the high stone walls. A young man stepped from the building to our right, bandages around his shoulder and arm, and a bottle of medicine in his hand. Open windows let fresh air in, and we could see healers tending to the sick and wounded, bandaging wounds and wiping fevered brows with soft cloths.

She bumped into the Grandmaster, her head swiveling around as students drew her attention to another corner. She cringed and glanced up, relaxing as he smiled down at her. He headed for the Masters' Hall, in the far corner of the courtyard.

He took her up the steps, unwavering and strong despite his years. She glanced back at the students in the corner, wearing the padded gloves and body protectors for sparring. They stared back, frozen in mid-fight. I laughed to myself. They'd never seen a girl here outside the Healing Building, and never going into the Masters' Hall.

"Dedication is the key to mastery," the Grandmaster called, his voice carrying across the open air to the boys.

They blinked at each other before turning back to their fight. A boy threw a wild strike, and the other ducked, nearly falling over. I chuckled, and he laughed lightly. She glanced up at the Grandmaster, hurrying up the steps to stay with us.

She scurried inside, through the door he held for her. What must it be like to see this place fresh? The wooden beams and walls had a warm glow, golden in the light filtering in through the paper-lined windows. Some windows stood open, letting in the brilliant sun, warming the stone floors in the halls.

"How long has that been growing here?" She walked to a potted tree tucked in an alcove across from an open window. Her fingers traced the leaves, wide and thick, like leather.

The Grandmaster stopped beside her. "It has been here longer than I have. I was just a tiny boy when I first came here."

"Who looks after it?" She touched the trunk, the thin bark crinkling under her fingers.

He smiled and gazed at the tree. "So delightful, the inquisitive mind. We all do, everyone here. You can, too, if you like."

She stared up at him, her fingers trembling against the tree trunk. I had trouble reading her expression, so blank most of the time, but her eyes held a world of emotion inside.

"Come." The Grandmaster continued down the hall.

She fell into step beside him, her short legs moving nearly twice as fast as his. He stopped at the next alcove. She stared up at the battle worn leather-lined armour, metal plates and rings fastened to protect the warrior who wore it long ago. A long slash marred the front chest plate, denting the metal plates up at the shoulders, down to the nicked leather belt at the waist.

"That belonged to a most mighty warrior once. He nearly died from that wound, but his desire to protect another allowed him to stand long enough to strike his foe down. He received healing here, in this school, centuries ago."

I shivered. I pushed back the sound of metal on metal, the smell of dust and blood, the cries of the wounded that coursed through my memories. One day, there would be no more battles, only peace. Would the Phoenix still exist, with no one to protect? Would that be a bad thing if he wasn't needed?

The Grandmaster led her around the corner and to a door. He slid the door along the track and stepped aside, his hand out in invitation for her. She stepped inside the room, and I followed her in. She stood there, her eyes darting everywhere, her body stiff.

"Sit here." The Grandmaster patted the edge of the bed.

She stepped over and sank to the mattress, her body tense and her eyes barely blinking. The Grandmaster walked to his meditation alcove and pressed against the wall. A panel slid aside. I sighed and relaxed at the sword and book sitting in their hidden compartment, safe and secure.

Her eyes flicked to the shining gold decorating the book's cover. The sword's scabbard was a simple, plain black wood, but the hilt was carved like a bird, delicately worked metal with intricate detail. You could almost see the details of each feather. Despite its appearance, that sword had been through many battles, surviving every one with no damage.

The Grandmaster cradled the sword in his hands, lifting it from the wooden holder. He sat on the bed beside her. "Have you ever held a sword before?"

She nodded, her eyes wide and fixed on the sword. "Not to use, but I help the blacksmith clean weapons sometimes." She reached out, her hand stopping inches from the sword.

"You can touch it," I assured her.

Her fingers brushed over the hilt, the bird's tail splitting and making the guard, its head at the pommel.

"Draw the sword and look at the blade," I encouraged.

She glanced up at the Grandmaster.

He nodded, smiling. "Go ahead."

Her small hand wrapped around the hilt. I smiled to myself. If she wanted, she could grip it in both hands and swing it that way. The sword slid free with a swoosh as she pulled it from the scabbard. No, she does not know how to hold it properly. That means she has no bad habits and is starting from scratch. I love a blank slate when training.

She held the sword up and peered at the blade. The blade sparkled; the many layers fused together scattered light differently. "Is it–moving?"

Her arm muscles trembled. The blade slipped, and she caught it in her hand. Blood dripped down her arm and collected on her sleeve. She stared, unmoving.

"Let me take that." The Grandmaster lifted the blade from her hands. "We'll get you taken care of."

He wiped the blade clean and slid it back into the scabbard. With two steps, he tucked the sword back into the compartment and pulled a cloth and bottle from inside. He kneeled in front of her and wrapped the cloth around her hand, pressing firmly. She stared at her hand, cradled between his, as he took some deep breaths. I felt his healing energy pouring into her wound.

"I'm sorry," she whispered. She wiped a tear away with her clean sleeve. "I didn't mean to."

"Quietly now. It happens." He lifted a hand and showed her his palm, a long scar across the skin from his index finger to his wrist. "It can happen to anyone."

I leaned against the wall. A flood of emotions poured into me: sadness, hope, fear, and more, all fighting for a place in my heart. How could one person feel so much?

"Is everything alright?"

I glanced up. Master Morlin stood in the doorway, his eyes narrowed at her wrapped and bloody hand.

The Grandmaster smiled at her. "Just a slight accident with a blade. I'll have her fixed in no time."

"May I assist?" He stood quietly, scrolls in his arms, unmoving.

He may be masterful at healing, but I sensed her discomfort. The link was open between us, her as the wounded, and me, the sword's protector. She shifted on the bed, drawing her legs up and crossing them before herself, her other arm wrapped around her knees.

"We're alright for now. It's a minor cut and I have something here for it." The Grandmaster curled her fingers over the cloth, holding it to the wound.

"As you wish." Master Morlin bowed his head and backed from the doorway.

The Grandmaster pulled a cloth from his bed table. He dabbed some oil from the bottle on the cloth, a greenish yellow smear with small bits of herbs in it. He peeled the bloodstained cloth back from her hand and wiped her bleeding wound with the herb infused cloth. She stared at her hand, the oil coating her wound and stopping the bleeding, and colouring her skin yellow.

"Now a bandage and you're all set." He returned the bottle to the compartment.

She returned his smile with a tiny one of her own. Her arm relaxed and her legs dropped to the mattress. I could even feel her heart slow. The cut must hurt, but she showed no sign of it, watching him in silence as he retrieved a bandage from a drawer.

He wrapped her hand snuggly with the bandage, tying it closed. "There. A few days and it'll be good as new. Keep it clean and dry until then, alright?"

"I should go," she whispered. "It's getting late, and I help make supper."

"We can prepare a room for you. You want to train, don't you?"

She blinked at him. "Here?"

"The student goes to the master, not the master to the student," I explained.

She stared at her knees with unfocused eyes. She stood, blinked at the room, and stared at the door. My insides felt squeezed, like someone had an arm around me. If that's how she felt, how was she still standing? She took slow steps, stopping at the door.

The Grandmaster set his hand on her shoulder. "Allow me to escort you to the entrance."

She nodded, barely moving.

"She needs to stay," I whispered to him.

"She needs time. Surely you can feel that."

"I can."

He took her hand and led her back through the school. She didn't say a word. The Grandmaster chose the quiet halls, those reserved for masters and apprentices, out a side door and to the main gates. I noticed the sidelong looks, the open staring from younger students hurrying back to their rooms to wash, but nobody would say anything. Nobody questioned the Grandmaster.

"Are you sure you can make it back safely?" He turned her hand over, checking her bandage.

She nodded, her eyes down.

"I'll go with her, make sure she's safe," I offered.

He kneeled in front of her. "You take care." He rested a hand on her shoulder. "Tomorrow there will be a celebration here for everyone who lives in the valleys around the mountain. I'd like you to come. I'd like to meet with you again."

"Thank you," she whispered, finally lifting her gaze to meet his.

He smiled and stood. It really was a shame he never became a father. He'd have made a good one, but service so often involves sacrifice. Mind you, he looked after all the valleys and villages around the mountain. Many villagers were still alive today because he stood down bandits in his younger years, chasing them from the valley borders.

She held her wrapped hand to her chest and looked up at him. The corners of her mouth turned up a fraction. She turned and walked through the gates; head held high. I kept pace with her, staying at her side.

"What happened to the Phoenix when he first died? How did he become the Phoenix and get reborn?"

The mist gathered in the cooling air, bringing a chill to the bone.

"At first, he was a new spirit, with no idea how to work with his new form. He floated around the valley, lost and uncertain, just an insubstantial being in the mist. Another spirit found him as he sank into the sacred pool, despair clouding his being. She taught him many things, like how to interact with people while in his new form, and what he could and couldn't do. He was a beginner again, learning things anew."

"I wonder if he still remembers what it's like, starting fresh like that. It's been centuries, right?" She stared down at the village below, little people moving around and preparing for the night. Lanterns sparked to life, a few at a time.

"Maybe you should ask him?"

She laughed. "Nobody takes notice of me unless they need me. Why would he be different?"

I hesitated, my heart aching. Was I any different? The Grandmaster's words stung my soul.

"How do you know all these stories? Are they shared a lot here?"

I sped up, falling beside her again. "Of course. Every village shares them, and the school keeps them in scrolls. They've shaped everything from what people value to how they behave. Surely you've heard them in the village?"

She shook her head. "Not like you tell them. Just little bits I overhear when they tell their own children. You speak like you were there."

"I'll share more stories as you practice. You won't become a great martial artist if you don't practice."

She pressed her lips together, her eyes on the lights below. The sun disappeared behind the mountain, casting everything in deep shadow. Was I still using her, if she got what she wanted, too?

CHAPTER 4

THE CIRCLE OF LIFE

He breathed out, shallow and quiet. I waited. His chest didn't rise again. His soul separated from his body, disentangling from his corporeal form. I watched the silvery mist rise and curl around me, before fading into the night. He was on his way to his final destination, where his soul would reside for eternity.

His last instructions and wishes were there, sealed in envelopes on his desk. I could only hope they would follow his wishes. He'll have chosen the school's temporary guardian, among other matters. My gaze flicked over the second letter; the name hidden behind the first envelope.

Had she ever been to a funeral before? She'd seen death, or at least the mourning, if she survived the revolution. I'd seen death more times than I cared. I knew how to mourn, but did she?

***

Master Morlin slid the door open and stared at the bed. My old friend lay ashen and motionless, gone, only his soulless body remaining. Was Morlin in mourning? He was so somber at the best of times; it was hard to tell. He stepped beside the bed and leaned down, his fingers feeling for a pulse.

"He's gone," he whispered.

Master Enlan stopped at the doorway. He stepped inside and raised an eyebrow at Master Morlin, who nodded. "I'll inform the others. Prepare him."

Master Enlan noticed the envelopes. He picked them up and examined the names, his own, and that of another master. I waited quietly in the corner as he opened it and read the contents. I knew it was instructions for the school, what he wanted done while they awaited the next Grand-master.

He reread the bottom notes twice. The Grandmaster left instructions about her, who her Master was to be, and to waive the rule preventing her from training. "As you will it," he whispered. "I hope you know what you're doing."

Master Enlan left the room, envelopes in hand. He needed to deliver the second one right away. I wanted to go, to see who else he wrote to, but the sword and book need-ed my protection now more than ever. Master Morlin knew about it, saw the compartment open yesterday. He wouldn't know how to open it, but alone in this room, he might try. I wasn't giving him that chance.

Master Morlin wrapped clean cream bedsheets around him, moving with care and reverence. Healers appeared with a board and blankets, usually used to move the wounded. They finished wrapping him, lifted him, and slid the board under him. My friend left the room one last time, carried by those who cared for him throughout his life, never to return.

Could I protect the sword and book, and still do everything I needed to? She needed training. Could I do it all before word got around and my time ran out?

***

"He wanted you to come. He invited you directly."

She sat curled up under the tree, the water dripping down on her, rolling down her face and mingling with her tears. "He's dead. There's no chance to talk to him again."

I wanted to wrap her in my arms and rock her gently, let her cry her tears and feel cared for. My heart squeezed me tightly, punishing me for something I couldn't help. I stuffed the feelings down and focused on her. "How do you know? He might surprise you. Please, the ceremony begins soon. I'll stay with you. I won't leave if you don't want me to."

She dropped her head into her hands. Tears rolled down her arms, soaking her sleeves. Grief rolled through my body. Was it mine? Hers? Both? Through it all, I could sense her fear.

"Come. It's time." I kept it a suggestion, soothing her with all the warmth I could put in a few words.

She sank her hands into the grass and pushed herself up. After a moment to sniff and wipe her eyes again, she turned and headed to the path. The school stood above us, visible from everywhere, angular roofs glinting in the sunlight. Her shoulders tensed and her hands balled into fists, clenching and relaxing.

"Did he know? Will he hear me? Are spirits safe to talk to? Will he even be there still?" She worried her lip between her teeth.

"Do you think he was a good man?"

She nodded. "He was so kind to me."

"His spirit will be just as kind. It's still him, just without his physical presence. He was a good man, and he cared about people. He won't want to scare you."

Her blank expression faded, the corners of her mouth fighting between a frown and a smile. She let out a deep breath and her shoulders lowered. I remained beside her as we walked up the path, just as I promised.

We caught up to a group of older women, walking slower than the girl who played on the mountain every day. Villagers walked along the path, all heading to pay last respects to the man who served them and guarded them.

"Aviva," Minda greeted, still wearing her washing clothing under her faded red cloak. "What a sad day. You journey with us?" Minda held out her hand, reaching for the girl.

She nodded. "I met him yesterday," Aviva whispered. "He wanted me to come." She slipped her hand into Minda's wrinkled hand, slightly twisted with arthritis.

The women glanced around at each other, crossing their arms over their chest and brushing their fingers down their noses. All but Minda stepped back from Aviva.

"Come. Walk with me. I knew him when he was just a boy. Would you like to tell me about meeting him?" Minda linked her arm with Aviva's and steered the girl up the path. With her stooped back and hunched shoulders, Minda was the same height as Aviva.

"No," I whispered. "It's not for others to know."

Aviva shook her head. "It's hard to talk about." She wiped a tear away.

"No matter. When you are as old as we are, loss is a part of life. I imagine it is fresh for you, and probably overwhelming." Minda patted her hand, holding it against her arm.

Aviva nodded, her eyes down on the path.

The small group climbed the path and passed under the archway, following the gathering crowd. I was grateful Minda gave her the hug and attention I could not. She always was a caring old soul. She might have been one of the Grandmaster's oldest friends, playing with him as a child.

"Kai?" Aviva whispered.

"Pardon, dear?" Minda turned to face her.

"I'm here," I whispered back. "Right behind you."

Aviva nodded; the motion was barely visible as she walked.

Drums pounded a steady rhythm. A singer chanted, the valleys themselves amplifying the musical sound. The crowd pressed closer, their attention on the far corner, on the raised stonework. Everyone wore something red, a scarf, a cloak, or an apron.

Aviva stared up at the pedestal. A body, his body, lay wrapped in red cloth atop it.

Masters and students filed into the courtyard, a procession all in brilliant red clothes with bright yellow trim. They lined the walls, the masters closest to the pedestal, the students around the remaining perimeter.

The drums stopped, their sound echoing through the valleys a few beats longer. The crowd was silent. Not a sneeze or single voice disturbed the peace, not even weeping. Even the birdsong was absent, like they also felt the loss somehow. She stood frozen beside me, barely blinking.

Master Denneth moved behind the pedestal and faced the crowd. As the Grandmaster's last apprentice, it was his right to speak. He spoke of the Grandmaster's many deeds, of his kindness and strength, his abilities and accomplishments. How was it, no matter how many eulogies I heard, they never really captured the full essence of someone?

Despite being beside me, she seemed miles away. Was she here, or off in the revolution in her memories? Grief rolled through me, stronger than just my own. How many people had she lost? Did she get to mourn any of them? Had any had a proper funeral? Not likely, if they died in the fighting.

Her eyes grew wider with each battle Master Denneth listed, each person he saved and knew by name. Yes, the Grandmaster was quite the warrior in his younger days, and I'd been there at his side for all of it.

Could she imagine the kind old man as a young warrior in full armour, sword held high as he defended those who needed him? Master Denneth stared down at his mentor, silent, wrapped in cloth. Tears rolled down her cheeks, silently splashing on the stone floor beneath her as she stared up at the pedestal, seeing Master and apprentice together one last time.

Wait, she can feel it. She's sensitive. I guessed as much when we first talked, but she could feel it all, the people around her and what they felt, everything.

The red linens burst into flames, orange light glowing and dancing high over the courtyard walls. The crowd ducked and covered their eyes. When we looked again, the body was gone. Not even a pile of ashes remained.

Master Denneth got to his feet and touched the stone pedestal. The crowd rumbled, people staring around, everyone looking for an explanation. Students stared at the pedestal, mouths open, their normal calm shaken. Legends spoke of this.

"The Phoenix will be reborn," Master Denneth whispered.

I smiled. He knew. Did the crowd hear him over their own mutterings?

"I'm here. Wait quietly with me and we'll say goodbye once the crowd has gone. He still wants to say goodbye. Over here, by the building. We'll be out of the way."

She followed me to the shadow of the Healing Hall. She weaved through the back of the crowd, her small size helping her squeeze through tight gaps. Was she usually that pale? I remained beside her as she leaned against the building, her arms tight across her chest, a hand over her mouth.

The crowd lined up and paraded before the empty platform. Each person took a few moments, kneeling if they could, head bowed, hand over their heart. She watched it all with a furrowed brow, head cocked to one side. What were funeral customs like in her homeland?

I glanced around at the masters, standing tall and still along the raised platform. Master Denneth was scanning the crowd. Please, notice her, I pleaded silently. His gaze passed over her. He narrowed his eyes and looked again, stopping at her.

He slipped along the back edge of the platform, down the few steps, and along the outer wall. Students straightened up as he passed. She noticed him walking along the buildings towards her and kept her attention on this new stranger. Her body twitched. Fear welled up in my throat, fear that wasn't mine.

Master Denneth stopped and kneeled in front of her. "I'm glad you came."

Her eyebrow twitched. She took a slow breath, opening her mouth a fraction to let it out again. Her fingers gripped her tunic, turning white.

"You impressed him. He liked your spirit." Master Denneth smiled at her, a smile very much like the one the Grandmaster gave her.

She twitched and the corners of her lips rose.

BANG! She startled, her elbows pushing her from the wall. Master Denneth wrapped an arm around her, steadying her as she panted for air.

"Fireworks. They start here in celebration of a life well lived. All the villages will send some up before morning." Master Denneth took her hand and gave it a light squeeze.

She looked out over the courtyard, her hand over her heart. Most of the crowd said their goodbyes and left without a word. Only a few stragglers remained.

"Take a moment, and we'll go say goodbye. He's been waiting for you." Master Denneth's dark eyes met hers and he smiled again.

She glanced up at the platform, her gaze falling away again, only to snap back to the pedestal. The Grandmaster's spirit sat on the pedestal, legs crossed, in full form of his elder self. She blinked, rubbed her eyes, and blinked again.

"You can see him?"

"Can you?" she whispered.

"Yes, I'm sensitive to the spirit world. He and I go way back. He was my Master, once."

"I'm not imagining things. I'm seeing a ghost?" Her shoulders shook.

"Spirit," I corrected. "He'll move on once he's seen you. He wanted to talk to you today, didn't he?"

The last few villagers paraded past the pedestal, unaware of the spirit sitting on it. The students had already filed back into buildings, the last few moving slowly and somberly to their duties. Only we and the masters remained.

"Come. Let's go see him." Master Denneth stood, her hand still in his, and pulled gently towards the pedestal.

Her body was rigid as she stared at the spirit. She let out another breath and followed, her eyes wide, staying behind Master Denneth's arm as she peered around at the spirit. He walked her up the stairs onto the platform, stopping in front of the pedestal.

"Master." Master Denneth bowed his head, his free hand over his heart.

"My favourite student." The voice didn't come from the spirit so much as simply fill the surrounding air. "Welcome, Little One."

She gave a shaky smile, tears threatening to spill from her eyes.

"I'm pleased you came. I'd like you to meet Master Denneth, your new master."

"Wha—" Her jaw dropped.

"He will teach you and guide you along your martial arts journey." The spirit held his hands out, palms to the sky.

She sputtered. The spirit grinned and winked. He was every bit the young warrior I fought beside all those years.

"Yes, Master." Master Denneth bowed his head again.

"She'll need to settle in. Take her as an apprentice fully now. You won't regret it."

"Yes, Master."

"Always my favourite. Just don't tell the others." The spirit winked. He faded, a wisp dissolving into the wind.

She stared at the empty pedestal, barely moving to breathe.

"Come. You'll want time to settle in before supper." Master Denneth set a hand on her shoulder.

She blinked. "I'm not ready," Aviva whispered.

"Are any of us really ready for a big change in our lives?"

"I'm with you," I reminded her. "You're not alone."

She closed her eyes and nodded, tears streaming down her cheeks. "My things?"

"Where are they?" Master Denneth wiped her tears with his thumb.

"My room, behind the noodle stand." She stared at the main gates, out into the forest.

My heart dropped. She'd been living there? That was the edge of the village, and sometimes wild animals strayed that close. She'd be better off here, safer, but I felt that sensation, like my stomach fell to my feet.

"Why don't we go get them, and you can relax fully when we're back." Master Denneth nodded at the gates.

The masters were moving around again, going back to their duties. He led her down the stairs and across the emptying courtyard to the tall main gates.

"Master Denneth?" Stern Master Foril stood at the gates.

"I need to make a trip to the village. I'll be back shortly."

CHAPTER 5

MOVING DAY

Master Foril nodded. We passed through, an unlikely group, and headed down the mountain together. The sky was a rare clear and bright blue, and the air was as dry as it could get. I doubted she even noticed, though. She stumbled occasionally, recovering fast, but where was her attention?

The fear inside was gone, replaced by a numbness, a fatigue of sorts. Under that all I felt hope, a warmth inside my heart, a tiny flame of desire. I wish I knew what she was thinking. Was she an Empath, able to feel other's emotions, or just sensitive to energies? I'd need to find out. It would affect her training long term, but for now, that could wait.

"Have you trained before?" Master Denneth kept his voice calm as he broke the silence between them.

She glanced up at him, her gaze falling to her feet again quickly. "A little," she whispered.

"I only ask, so I know. We work with all students where they're at, and if there are things you've missed, we'll teach you." Master Denneth squeezed her hand gently.

We walked down the mountain in silence together. What did she see as she looked around? I let my gaze roam over the mountainside. The trees stood tall, their leaves damp with the humidity from the rivers. No direct sunlight reached us, not even on the path, except as tiny speckles as the leaves blew in the slight breeze. Birds flitted above us; their voices were nearly lost with each burst of fireworks.

She watched the little birds, tiny brown specks among the bright green leaves. "It's so beautiful here."

"I love walking the mountain every day, seeing the animals, and feeling the breeze." Master Denneth took a deep breath, his nose lifted. "That is the smell of life."

She looked up at him, meeting his gaze fully, with no hesitation.

"Walking the mountain is excellent training for fitness, and it strengthens the legs. More students should venture out while they're still young, and not wait until they're old like me." He chuckled.

She smiled and ducked her head. "You're not really old, like ancient old. Not yet."

He threw his head back and laughed, his mouth wide open. "Hush, child. One day you'll be old, too."

The villagers were on the main road among the houses, sharing tankards of ale and sharing tales of the Grandmaster's youth. The blacksmith roared with laughter, hot poker in his hand, as he lighted the fireworks. Sparks sprayed over the road and the small rockets flew into the sky, bursting high overhead with a blast of colours.

"May we see another warrior as capable and honourable in our lifetime." The blacksmith held his tankard out, hand waving with enthusiasm, and ale splashed over his hand as they refilled it.

Master Denneth nodded to the people we passed. People respected and honoured Masters, who often came into the villages to help the sick and teach the young, or even help after tragedies like a fire. I didn't think Master Denneth was from this village, but he'd been here before.

She led him by the hand through the wide streets, between the spread-out houses with gardens around them. Low stone walls marked each plot, protecting the delicate plants from being eaten by the chickens that roamed the streets. Each dwelling had only one or two rooms, walls of wood, and a roof of thatch. They penned the animals in the middle of the village, protected from the wildlife that roamed the mountain. She stayed towards the outer edge of town, leading us to the far end.

Aviva stopped beside a small house, in front of a thin-walled lean-to in the back vegetable garden.

"Preita has been looking after you?" Master Denneth looked around, taking in the cracks between the boards, sealed with scraps of wood and nails that stuck out.

Aviva stopped, her hand on the lean-to door. "Yes."

She opened the door and stepped inside. It was an old tool shed, barely large enough for her to stretch out on the floor in. Her blankets sat piled in the corner, a worn pillow on top. Someone had sewn old hay into bats of insulation and fastened it to the walls. Despite the appearance of the outside, it was dry in here, and warmer than I expected.

"How long have you lived here?" Master Denneth stood in the doorway, giving her more room.

"A year? No, that's not right. Maybe more? I came after the palace fell, when she couldn't hide me anymore. They made space for me here, since inside is so crowded."

She kneeled in front of a small bookshelf, made with spare materials, but put together with skill. The edges were smooth, and the corners were tight. Little wall hangings embroidered on scraps of cloth with thread remnants gave the room some colour and warmth. She might have done them herself, from the looks of it. A small pile of thread scraps still sat on the bookcase. One shelf held battered books, and another held some clothing.

"That was kind of them. Is it warm enough here?" Master Denneth kneeled beside her.

"If it gets freezing, the blacksmith lets me sleep in the workshop, where the forge keeps it warm. They also give me an extra blanket."

A small pile of cloth sat in the far corner, near her blankets. I peered at it. Wool mittens and a hat, from the looks of it, knitted with a felted lining. A generous gift for a girl with next to nothing, from a people who were just comfortably getting by themselves.

"Do you have a bag or something to carry everything in?" He scanned the little room, stepping just inside to see better.

Aviva shook her head. She pulled a winter coat from the pile, worn and patched, and lay it open. She took her clothing from the shelf and lay it inside, along with her hairbrush and books. The little wall hangings joined her other belongings, and she tied the coat closed.

"I'll talk to them. Would you like to come, or wait here?" Master Denneth stepped back through the doorway and straightened up to his full height.

She hugged her bundle of belongings to her chest. Her lip quivered.

"Wait here. I'll be back." He gave her shoulder a squeeze before stepping from her little home.

"Tell them thank you?" Her voice was barely a shaky whisper. She wiped her eyes with her sleeve.

"I will."

She settled on her pile of blankets, her legs giving out. Aviva stared around her space, now empty without her few belongings bringing colour to the shed.

I settled beside her. "You'll be okay. It's scary, though, isn't it?"

She nodded, her head down. "What if I fail?"

"You keep trying. Failing is part of learning. As long as you keep trying, you'll get it. Don't give up and you won't fail for good."

Her arms tightened around her bundle of belongings. "I can do that."

"Some students learn quickly. Others take years to learn some things that may normally take a few months. Nobody is turned away just because they need more time. You'll be fine."

She leaned back against the rough wooden wall. "What's he like? Master Denneth?"

"What does your gut tell you? What do you feel about him?" She's looking ahead. Great.

She smiled, even as she blinked back a tear. "He's kind, like the Grandmaster was. Did the Phoenix ever go anywhere new like this?"

"He's been to many distant places over his many lifetimes. Each new regeneration is like a fresh start for him."

Master Denneth appeared in the doorway, casting deep shadows into the small space. "Would you like me to carry that?"

She glanced around her little space and sniffed. Aviva stood and handed him the itchy bundle. He tucked her belongings under his arm and took her hand. Fresh grief rolled through me; every bit as strong from her as at the funeral. Her home might not have been fancy, but it was hers. Still, she needed a proper home.

I followed them back up the mountain, honouring her need for silence. The walk back seemed longer somehow, with her so quiet. She didn't focus on anything until we reached the front gate.

She stared up at the archway, the gold lettering catching the setting sunlight. Could she read the symbols there? I'd lived here much of my life, moving from the student dormitories, through the Masters' Hall, and into the Grandmaster's room. Many people had come and gone through that time. Nearly all stared up at those same symbols when they were new.

"What do they mean?" She followed him through the archway, her small hand still in his.

"What does what mean?" He slowed and gave her his full attention.

"The writing over the entrance?" She gazed up at the back, where the same symbols were carved.

"They list the traits of a true warrior. Perseverance, honour, loyalty, wisdom, and more. I know you read, since you have books. Do you not read that?"

"I can't read your language," she whispered, her eyes on her scuffed and tattered boots.

"You will learn." He guided her through the quiet courtyard, to the Masters' Hall at the far corner. "You've been here before?" Master Denneth waved at the doors.

"Once. The Grandmaster invited me."

"This is the Hall of the Masters. As my apprentice, you'll have a room next to mine. You'll have your own space, and if anyone bothers you, come to me immediately. If I am busy or you can't find me, this place is full of masters. They will assist you." He led her up the thick wooden steps.

"Do other apprentices live here?" She followed him through the doors and inside.

"Yes, they do. They are all older and more advanced students. Your situation is unique, so don't compare yourself to them." He led her in the opposite direction to last time, down another hall.

Lanterns glowed high along the walls, coloured paper covers tinting the light like a rainbow. The wooden floor reflected the light, polished to a shine beneath their feet. She glanced at the wall carvings as they passed, trying to catch as many details as possible. They framed scenes of famous battles with scrolled borders. Pillars carved with stories and images of ancient trees supported the building. The gold paint reflected the light and brightened the halls.

Master Denneth turned one last time. "Our rooms are down this hallway. It's easy to find." He took her halfway down the hall and stopped at a sliding door. "This one is mine. Yours is right there." He pointed to the next door down the hallway. "The first thing I'll teach you to read is my name, as that's what this says."

He pointed to the carved nameplate beside the door, a dark wood contrasting with the walls. She examined it, her fingers tracing the lettering. He gave her time, waiting for her to step back and look at him.

Master Denneth walked her to her door and slid it open for her. He stepped aside and let her pass. Her eyes were drawn up to the ceiling, where a wooden section rose high above her. He pulled a lever at a pillar and slats opened, letting the fading sunlight stream down on them.

"This operates the wooden blinds. In nice weather, you can get plenty of daylight in here. Keep them closed when you're not here, as the weather can change quickly." Master Denneth set her bundle on her new desk. "Close them at night, too, when it's cool."

She nodded.

"You say yes, Master," I prompted.

"Yes, Master."

Master Denneth smiled at her. "Give yourself time to learn the etiquette. I know it's all new to you."

She smiled shyly, her gaze down at her desk.

"Place your belongings where you like later. Supper is in a few minutes, so we need to wash and prepare. Your wash basin is here, but it's empty." He waved his hand at a wooden stand with a bowl and glass pitcher. "Come and use mine. I'll show you how."

Master Denneth slid her hallway door closed and opened a door on her side wall. He passed through into his own room. Just inside against the wall, he had an identical wooden stand, with a bowl and pitcher on it, a bucket on the bottom shelf, and folded towels and cloths on the middle shelf.

He lifted the clear glass pitcher and poured water into the basin. Master Denneth took a cloth from the shelf and dipped it in the water. He washed his face, hands and feet before dropping the cloth on the bottom shelf beside the bucket. Master Denneth emptied the basin into the bucket and poured clean water in it.

"Go ahead. Face first, then hands, then feet, just like I did."

He stepped aside. Aviva moved in front of the basin. Her hand shook as she took a cloth and dipped it in the water. She submerged the cloth and lifted it, squeezing the water out with both hands. Aviva wiped her skin, refreshing the cloth and wringing it out as she needed, until the grime of the day was gone.

She cradled the basin in her hands and lifted. Her eyes widened, and the basin clunked back on the wooden stand. She took a breath and lifted again. Master Denneth steadied the basin for her as she lowered it over the bucket and poured the dirty water out.

"It's heavy, so we stay strong. Soon you'll move it around like it's as light as a feather. If you spill, get a towel and wipe it up. It happens to everyone sometimes." Master Denneth set the basin back on the stand for her.

She squirmed, shifting from foot to foot. "What about other–umm–needs?" Her face burned red.

Master Denneth smiled and waved at her room. "The last door is your bathroom, complete with running water. We use this washstand before meals, for tradition and washing up, but everything else you need is in your bathroom. I'll get you a change of clothing and we can eat after that."

He left through his own door to the hallway, sliding it closed behind himself. She stood still, only her head moving as she took in his rooms. I glanced about, trying to take the room in like she did, like I'd never seen them before.

Compared to her little lean-to, this must seem like a luxury, but she said something about the palace once, too. Each room had a bed, desk, and dresser, a meditation cushion, and masters had a low table they could write or eat at or sit around with others for company. Her room was identical, without the low table.

"Why don't you unpack as you wait? You don't have many things, so it won't take long."

She smiled and nodded. "Right."

Aviva returned to her room. Her bundle was still on her desk. She untied the coat and unfolded it. Her clothing fit all in a single drawer, but the school would provide for her now. Her dresser would soon have training uniforms and everyday clothing for all seasons. She set her hairbrush on her dresser for now.

She picked up her books and held them close to her chest. There was something about her smile. She really loved those books. She ran her fingers over the letters on the top book, writing I didn't recognize. What was in this book that it meant so much to her? Did someone special give it to her? She set her books on the corner of her desk.

A knock echoed around her room. Her head whipped around, her eyes on the door. She stared at it, unmoving. Was she even breathing?

"Go see who it is."

CHAPTER 6

NO LONGER ALONE

S he took a slow step, and another.

I was so glad the rooms weren't big, or this would take forever. "Go on." I chuckled to myself.

She grasped the handle and pulled. The door shifted but didn't slide open. She wrapped both hands around the handle and pulled with all her might, her feet braced against the floor as she leaned back with her entire weight. The door slowly slid open with barely a sound. Aviva straightened up and wiped her forehead with her sleeve.

A tall young man stood in the hall, a friendly smile on his face. "Welcome. I'm Garin. I thought I saw someone come in here."

She rolled her shoulders back and stared up at him. "Thanks," she nearly whispered.

"Are you coming to dinner?" He waved down the hall, his dark eyes focused on hers.

Aviva nodded. "Master—"

"You can call him Master," I whispered. "Everyone will know who you mean."

"Master is getting me clothing." She looked down at her dark, worn shirt and pants, patched with any materials she could get her hands on.

"I'll see you at supper. If you need help or can't find something, my room is that one right there." Garin pointed across the hall and two doors down.

"Thank you. It's all so—"

"Overwhelming?" He arched his eyebrow.

Aviva nodded. "This morning I was just another person in the village. Now—"

He laughed, low and warm. "I doubt you were just another anything. Not if you're here on the Grandmaster's personal invitation."

"Garin." Master Denneth walked down the hall towards them, a bundle of clothing in his hands. He nodded a greeting, that hint of a smile on his face.

"Master Denneth." Garin bowed his head.

"If you'll excuse us, I have a student to prepare for supper. Thank you for welcoming her warmly."

Garin brought his hands up, fingertips together, and elbows at his sides. He bowed his head again. "Of course, Master Denneth." He stepped back.

"Come, child." Master Denneth stepped into her room as Garin left. He closed her door for her, moving it with one hand, her clothing tucked under his arm. He set the clothing on the bed and unfolded it. "You'll be wearing the same clothing the others wear. It's not cut for a woman, I'm afraid, but it'll work until I can have some made for you."

"Thank you, Master." She sat on the edge of the bed beside the clothing, her fingers sinking into the soft fabric piled for her.

"You learn etiquette quickly. You're doing well." He opened the tunic, showing her the ties inside. "Here, you slide it on and tie these together." Master Denneth showed her the different ties inside, explaining which ones went together. "Got it?"

She nodded. "Yes, Master."

"I'll step out and wait. Open this door when you're done." Master Denneth walked to his room, closing the connecting door behind him.

"What about you, Kai? Privacy?"

I laughed. "I'm gone. Say my name when you're ready, or if you need help." I slipped into the hallway, the door posing no obstacle to me.

I listened and waited. Cloth rustled. Something dropped to the floor. More rustling. A faint squeak, maybe? Should I help? No, she'd call if she needed me. What if she was strangling herself, and the squeak was her last breath? Don't be silly, Kai, I scolded. You'd feel her distress. She's fine. Just a bit flustered.

"Okay, Kai." I heard her clearly, as if the door wasn't there.

Moving back into her room, I looked her over. "You did fine. Any questions?"

She fingered some ties on the side of her pants. "What's this for?"

"That's for rolling your pants up in hot weather, or if you're crossing shallow water. You don't need it right now. Let your master know you're ready, like he asked. Normally you'd knock, wait a few moments or for a verbal answer, and slide the door open, but he said just open it."

She crossed to the door, her hands gripping the wood. The connecting doors weren't as heavy, and it slid for her without her working so hard.

He sat at his desk, writing with a quill. Master Denneth turned and saw her. He set the quill on the stand and stood, looking her over. "You have any trouble?"

"No, Master, thank you."

"The Dining Hall is this way. Follow me."

He led her into the hallway and through the Masters' Hall. She scurried along behind him. He wore the same style of clothing she did, a simple wrap tunic and loose pants, though his were black and hers were light grey. He had an over-robe that flowed in the breeze as he walked, cut close to his body, that gave extra warmth when he was sitting quietly. Students never seemed to stop moving, and she was warming herself up, running to keep up with him.

A side door connected directly to the main hall, where the library and Dining Hall were, among other rooms. The wooden buildings looked similar inside, only the colour changing. The Master's Hall had wood with reddish tones and thin red paper over the windows. The main hall was a golden wood with white paper blinds.

He slowed for her, letting her stay beside him without running. A set of double doors stood open at one end of this new hall. We could see long tables set up, made of dark polished wood, and benches lined up along each one. The far end of the room had a raised area, with another long table overlooking the others.

Students in all colours of clothing, from light grey like her to dark brown, darted around the room and gathered on the benches. She drew back at the sound, her steps slowing as we approached. They'd get quiet once the masters assembled, but until then, they could socialize and be boys.

He placed a hand on her back and encouraged her on. "It'll be quieter inside at the table you'll sit at. Come."

Master Denneth walked her down the center aisle to the last table before the raised area. Students stopped talking and stared as she passed. She kept her eyes ahead, though her shoulders tensed. As the only woman, she'd stand out. As a foreigner, she'd stand out more. Her fingers gripped her tunic.

"This table is for apprentices. You may eat here. I'll be right up there, nearby, if you need anything."

"Thank you, Master." She stared at the table.

"I'll walk you through it," I promised. "I said I'd be here for you, and I meant it."

"Pick any seat you like. If you have problems, come to me right away." Master Denneth gave her shoulder a light squeeze.

She walked to the far end of the table, near the side wall. Aviva was as close as she could get to the edge of the room, and her back was to the masters, so Master Denneth could watch her easily. Apprentices were supposed to be of the highest character, but would they accept a girl among them?

Aviva lowered herself to the smooth wooden bench. Her feet barely touched the floor unless she perched on the edge. She stared down at the white bowl and ceramic spoon in front of her, everything already set for the meal.

"It'll be fine. You'll get to know people soon. You've already met Garin."

"Yes, but he already has friends," she whispered.

More boys and young men streamed into the room, darting to tables and sitting with their friends.

"Hey." Garin eased himself onto the bench across from her. "May I join you?"

"Hi." Her smile was shaky, and she blushed. She nodded.

Garin's companions sat beside him, leaving her alone on her bench. More young men sat at their table, all older teens or early twenties like Garin, though the space beside her stayed empty.

"Where are you from?" Garin tapped the table with his fingers, barely making a noise. His attention was fully on her.

"Winby." She fidgeted with her spoon, turning it over and over. At least she was making eye contact.

He grinned. "You weren't born there, though."

She lowered her eyes to the woven placemat in front of her. "Grat Sharon."

Garin raised an eyebrow. "How did you end up here, in Niflfjall? That's across the ocean."

Aviva shook her head. "That's a long story. Are you from nearby?"

"I am. My village is Mornby. It's only a valley over. Have you been there?"

"No. I didn't go far from the village."

The gong rang, drowning out voices. The hall fell silent. She noticed everyone looking up behind her. Aviva turned and saw Master Enlan standing, his hands held out over the long table full of masters.

"A moment of silence, blessings for the food, and for all those who grew or prepared it for us." His voice carried through the otherwise quiet room.

Everyone bowed their heads, their hands resting folded on the edge of the table. Aviva copied them. She didn't know the prayers yet, but we'd teach her. She sat quietly, glancing around with her head bowed.

"You may eat."

Garin stood. "Wait here. I'll be right back."

She looked around. A few students at each table stood and walked to serving carts, where massive bowls of food rested, steam rising from them and curling, as it rose into the air. Garin and another young man carried the serving bowls to their table, setting them down for everyone. Students ladled food into their bowls, a rice and wheat mixture with bright vegetables and nuts mixed in.

Garin heaped food into his bowl. "Would you like some help, since it's your first meal and all?"

"Yes, please." Her voice nearly disappeared under the sound of wooden spoons scraping against the serving bowls.

She passed him her bowl, and he filled it part way. "You can have more after, but it's best to only take what you need, and not too much. Here you go."

Aviva cradled the ceramic bowl in her hands. "Thank you." She set it back on her placemat and picked up her spoon.

I had to smile. Shy little Aviva already is making friends. Maybe this wouldn't be as hard as I thought? Garin was one of the oldest apprentices, close to becoming a master himself. With him helping, the others might accept her more readily. Maybe not, but she might need all the friends she could get. Maybe they'd overlook her being a woman, but an outsider?

She stayed quiet through most of the meal, only talking when Garin addressed her. She listened when they talked about training and lessons, paying close attention. If I couldn't sense what she was feeling, I'd never have known how overwhelmed she felt inside. Could they tell?

"Kai?" she whispered.

"You're doing well. It's almost over."

She set her spoon beside her empty bowl.

"Would you like some more?" Garin nodded at the serving bowl, still partly full of food. "We're allowed as much as we want."

"Thank you, but I got plenty." She smiled, her eyes down on her bowl.

"We'll be excused soon. Your bowl and spoon go in those baskets by the doors." Garin pointed to the tables on either side of the doors, holding large woven baskets.

Aviva nodded. "Thank you."

"Happy to help. We were all new once, even the masters."

The students all turned to the head table again. Aviva shifted and watched Master Enlan standing at his place again.

"You may go when you are ready. Live in balance." He raised his hands, palms up, and lowered them to his sides.

Master Denneth slipped from the bench and down the steps, stopping beside her. She looked up at him, waiting.

"If you've had enough, come and finish settling in. It's been a long day, and tomorrow starts early."

Aviva nodded. She shuffled from the bench and stood.

"Don't forget to say thank you," I whispered.

"Thank you, Master." She ducked her head.

Master Denneth took her hand. "You're welcome. You know how to clean up?"

"Yes, Master." She finally looked up at him, her face still pinker than normal.

"Go ahead." He gestured to her dishes.

"I'll see you tomorrow." Garin took another helping of food.

Aviva smiled as she picked up her bowl and spoon. "Thank you for your help."

She followed Master Denneth along the side of the hall.

"Garin has a girlfriend."

Her fingers clenched her bowl and spoon, but she didn't slow her step. I spun, but Garin was talking with his friends again, and nobody stood out to me. No matter. If a master knew who called that out, that student would receive extra lessons in etiquette and manners.

She relaxed the instant she left the Dining Hall, trotting beside Master Denneth through the connecting passages. He stopped at the end of their hallway.

"Do you remember which door it is?" He raised an eyebrow and waited, calm and unmoving.

She closed her eyes and raised her hand, her fingers tracing out the letter symbols in the air before her. Aviva walked down the hallway, slowing around the halfway point. She examined each name plate. "It was about halfway. Not this one—"

We followed slowly.

She closed her eyes and made the symbol in the air again. Aviva scurried to the next door down and stopped. "These two?"

"Excellent. You have the evening to relax. Most students study or practice skills after the meal. I'll be arranging lessons for you tomorrow. The first week can feel–tough, physically, so you can always return here and rest."

"Yes, Master." She bowed her head.

"I'll get you more clothing for tomorrow." Master Denneth gestured to her door. "Rest."

"Thank you, Master." She gripped the door handle and pulled with all her might.

CHAPTER 7

NOT STRONG ENOUGH

Once inside, she fought the door closed again. Aviva turned and looked around her new room. The walls were a calming light beige, with plenty of space for her wall hangings. The furniture wasn't new but was in excellent repair. She had plenty of space, compared to her lean-to.

Aviva walked to the bed and sank onto the mattress. Her eyes widened, and she grinned. Compared to some blankets and a straw pad, this must seem luxurious.

"Is this real?"

"It sure is." I settled onto her meditation cushion in the corner. "Was that your first big meal?"

She stretched out on her bed. "No, I started going to the fancy parties with my parents when I was ten. They weren't like that, though. So many young people–"

I chuckled. "I went to a fancy ball once. It was organized for all the people there."

She sat up and blinked back a tear. Aviva looked around again, her gaze slowly circling the room. Everything was polished and cared for, warm and comfortable. "The Phoenix built all this?"

I leaned back against the wall. "In his fourth lifetime. He knew protecting everyone was a massive commitment, and he needed help. They chose this site. The villagers all pitched in and worked together. Anyone with useful skills helped."

"Many helpers make tasks lighter." She shifted on her bed, her back to the wall.

"That's right."

"Was it all built at once? It looks like it. The stone floors are too uniform, with no long seams."

She noticed that? Some students were here for years and never really looked around. "It was all planned at once and took many years to build. They thought ahead. Remember, the Phoenix had a few lifetimes of experience to help decide what they needed. He wanted it to be for everyone, and not just those who trained, so they included the library and the Healing Hall."

Her head dipped lower and lower, her shoulders slumping. I let the room go quiet. She needed rest.

Master Denneth knocked lightly on the connecting door and waited. She didn't respond, didn't even look up or twitch. After a few moments, he slid the door open and glanced in. He noticed her slumped against the wall.

He left her new clothing on her desk and walked to the bed. Master Denneth lay her down, supporting her head in one hand as he stretched her out on the bed. He slipped her boots from her feet and set them under her bed.

Her blankets were still under her. He passed back into his own room and came back with a spare blanket for her. Master Denneth draped the blanket over her and tucked it around her. He pulled on the lever, confirming her slats above were closed, before he extinguished her lamp.

Her breathing was quiet and rhythmic in the dark. She'd need her sleep. Tomorrow her new life begins.

***

The gong pulled me from my meditation. She rolled over, her eye cracked open and slammed closed again. The gong faded. That was her only wake up call, the start of a morning for students and masters alike.

"None of that now." I put as much cheer in my voice as I could. "Up you get. Your new life begins. Up, young lady."

Her eyes opened a crack and stared ahead, unseeing. I shoved the lever up, letting the cool air and bright sunlight stream down over her. She leapt from the bed, blanket wrapped around her, and yanked down on the lever. The cool breeze stopped, and the room seemed warmer right away.

"Get changed and washed up. You have chores to do. It's a way of giving back to your master. Go. Your fresh clothing is on the desk."

She stared down at herself; her clothing rumpled from sleep. I'd have suggested she change last night, but she fell asleep so fast.

"Take that into the bathroom and hang it on the radiators as you wash. It'll warm the cloth and ease out any wrinkles."

She smiled and grabbed her fresh clothing from the desk. "Thanks."

"You're not the first to forget to prepare for the next morning. Now go. You have chores to do."

I relaxed on the meditation cushion and waited. Meditating to the sound of running tap water wasn't the same as being near a flowing river, but it worked. She was fast, and came back in minutes, scrubbed and changed, her hair brushed and tied back.

"You and mornings don't get along, do you?" I chuckled.

She blinked at me.

"Your tunic is fine, but swap the ties on the pants or you're going to lose them when you bend down. Those side ties aren't right."

Her fingers fumbled with the cloth ties. She worried her lip between her teeth, her brow furrowed, as she focused on retying her pants.

"That's it. Now, knock quietly. Go get his glass pitcher from the stand. We fill it with water from a ceremonial fountain in a nearby courtyard. It's not far. He's probably meditating already, so try not to disturb him."

She stepped beside the door, her body curled up and hunched over. Aviva knocked. Would he even hear that? I wondered. After a few quiet moments, she slid the door open and stepped inside. He sat in the alcove on his cushion, eyes closed, and hands folded in front of him.

Aviva turned and faced the washstand. She stared at the pitcher, the glass reflecting the dim lamplight. Her hand grasped the glass handle. She grunted under her breath and cradled the side in her other hand. Aviva slid it from the shelf and hugged it to her chest, her knees bending from the weight.

She waddled back to her room and slid the pitcher onto the desk. Once the connecting door was closed, she opened the hallway door. She returned for the pitcher and held it to her chest, supported by both arms.

Aviva frowned at her door. A glance around showed nothing in the hall she could set the pitcher on and still lift it again. She shimmied up against the wall and put her back to her door, shuffling and shoving until it was closed again. *She's a thinker, all right.* I had to smile.

"Now, down the hall, turn left, and head for a door on the back wall. The fountain is in a courtyard behind the hall."

The back door was already open. Sunlight filled the courtyard, warming the stones. She leaned against the door frame and looked out, sheltered by the overhanging roof. A carved stone fountain stood in the middle of the space.

Garin, Merek, and Drefan gathered around the fountain, their own pitchers on the stone floor beside them. Garin held a cleaning brush. They watched the fountain as Merek pumped hard on a handle. Water spurted from the fountain. Another spurt. Water burst up and flowed freely, pouring down into the deep basin below.

Garin set the brush in a small basket and looked up. "Good morning, early riser. We're almost done. You can put that down while you wait."

"Maybe. What are you doing?" She walked over and squatted, dropping close to the ground. The pitcher clinked against the stone. She wiped her forehead with her sleeve.

"We clean this every morning. As advanced apprentices, it's our honour." Garin peered into the basin and nodded.

"It's flowing well." He leaned down and picked up her pitcher for her.

"She's supposed to do that herself." Merek leaned against the fountain, glaring down at her.

"And she will." He turned the pitcher's handle towards her. "It gets easier."

She took the handle and supported the base with her other hand. I heard her grunt from my place at the door, her muscles tense under the heavy glass. Garin kept his hand at the top of the handle, taking some weight for her. How long would it take her to build the muscle she'd need?

"We fill ours first, since we clean it." Garin picked his own pitcher up in one hand and held it under the streaming water.

"Thank you," she whispered.

He set his full pitcher down, still using only one hand. "You're welcome. You know, most people don't become apprentices until they've been here a few years, and they're already strong from training. It takes time to build this kind of muscle."

"You make it look so easy," she mumbled.

Merek and Drefan filled their pitchers and stood back. I wandered out to the small group.

"I've had years to build my strength doing this. The glass is heavy, so we stay strong. It's one more opportunity to keep ourselves in fighting shape, should we ever need to act."

"It's supposed to weed out those not strong enough," Drefan muttered.

Her eyes narrowed, but she said nothing. He felt something inside, like a tightness around his heart. Wasn't someone going to say something?

"You do it. I'll help steady it." Garin still held her pitcher, though she gripped the handle, too.

She cradled the bottom in one hand and eased the pitcher under the flowing water. The water flowed into the glass container, sending little musical splashing sounds into the courtyard. She shifted her grip when her hand slid, the glass bottom becoming slippery with the dripping water. She strained under the weight as it filled, her knees bending and her body leaning. Garin took more weight from her until she could stand straight again.

"It's getting heavy," she whispered.

"It'll be okay," he whispered back. "It'll be hard at first, but you'll get stronger fast. Give it time."

Her body shook as she brought the pitcher back over the edge of the fountain, though he kept it from tipping or hitting the stone basin. She cradled it to her chest, her arms around the damp glass. Garin leaned down and picked up his own full water pitcher, not letting go of hers for a moment.

"How did you get so strong?"

"I'll see you guys at breakfast." Garin nodded to the others.

"Later," Merek called. They turned and left without another word.

"Most of our chores and tasks give us a chance to get stronger. This one will build muscle faster than any other, but take each chance you get. I wasn't always this strong. I worked at it, too."

He walked her back to her room. She waddled under the weight, though I saw him take more weight as she got tired. Her clothing was damp with sweat when she stopped at her door.

"Set it down. I'll put mine away and be right back to help you." Garin eased her pitcher to the floor against the wall.

"Will Master be mad at me?" Her voice shook. She stared at the floor.

"Not him. He's wise and fair. Any student would love to have him for a master." Garin took her hand and lightly squeezed it. "I'll be right back."

She stared at the water, still rippling in the pitcher, the small waves calming as it rested on the floor. Garin disappeared into his room. She wiped her forehead with her sleeve, wrinkling her nose at the scratchy outer cuffs.

Garin returned within a minute. "Ready?"

Aviva nodded. She bent down and gripped the pitcher, giving him space at the top of the handle to help her again. She stared at the heavy door and sighed. Garin moved with her as she set her back against the door edge and shuffled, sliding it open with little footsteps.

"We put some in your smaller pitcher. Set this one down, put yours beside it on the floor, and I'll help." Garin nodded to her washstand.

She lowered her pitcher to the floor, the glass clinking on the wood. Aviva reached up for hers and smiled at the smaller, lighter glass. She set it beside the large pitcher and wrapped her hands around the heavy glass.

"You guide it. I'm just steadying it for you."

She lifted the pitcher, though Garin had most of the weight, and tipped it over her smaller pitcher. Water flowed, making the glass sing as it poured. She set the heavier pitcher down and replaced hers on her stand.

"Now we take this to your master."

She lifted the pitcher and held it close to her chest. With it only half full, she mostly moved it on her own, though he kept a hand on it to help. Garin knocked softly on the connecting door and slid it open. Master Denneth still sat on the cushion, unmoving from earlier. Garin helped her ease the pitcher into place, barely making a noise. They returned to her room, where I waited.

She slid the connecting door closed again. "Thank you. I really needed help."

Garin grinned. "It will get easier. Until then, come early like that, and I can help you. See you at breakfast." He left her room, sliding the heavier hall door closed for her.

"You handled that well. You should change."

She glanced down at herself, the rumbled and wet cloth draping from her body. "Yes, I think I will. How often do my clothes get washed? Will I run out, or do I get more somewhere?"

"They do laundry daily, so if you need things washed, you don't have to wait. Toss dirty clothes in the hamper in your bathroom."

She looked over at the faint knock. Master Denneth slid the door open. He glanced over at her, taking in her rumpled appearance. "I'll get you more clothing now. You did well. Wash again and I'll leave the fresh clothing on your desk." He smiled and retreated into his room, the door sliding closed behind him.

"Go. You need a wash," I teased.

"Kai, out." She pointed at the door.

I slipped into the hallway. Master Denneth and Garin were talking outside Garin's door. Was he heading for breakfast already?

"I appreciate how you're helping her. It speaks well to your character. You'll make an excellent Master someday."

Garin bowed his head. "Thank you, Sir. She's a hard worker. With a little help, she will, too."

Master Denneth chuckled. "Yes, I think she will."

They parted, Garin going one way and Master Denneth the other, leaving me alone in the red-tinted halls. The sunlight streamed through the paper blinds and cast a warm morning glow on the wood. At least she has three of us so far. Would that be enough?

CHAPTER 8

RESPONSIBILITIES

How long would it take her to get ready? I should have time, I figured. I sped down the hall and around the corner. The door stood before me. My heart squeezed with my own emotions this time, grief and pain that were still too fresh.

The room was dark and lifeless, the plants he cared for gone already, though his other belongings were here. I felt for the book and sword and smiled. There they sat, nestled in the hidden compartment, the panel still in place. Their existence wasn't a secret, but their current hiding place was. Unless Master Morlin shared it with anyone. It might be awhile before I can move them, though.

Did I have to worry about him? He and the Grandmaster had been friends since they were Aviva's age, mid-teens, if I had to guess. Honestly, I was horrible at guessing ages, especially with girls, no matter how old I got.

I felt calm, so she was fine. Was Master Morlin a threat? I might have time to find out. I left the silent and dark room, my heart lifting to be back in the light again. Master Morlin's room was right nearby. If I was lucky, he was already in the dining room.

I paused outside his door. No sound came from inside. No light shone under his door. I slipped into his room unseen. I'd find nothing in the dark like this. A small ball of light flickered to life as I focused on it, giving me light to see by.

The papers on his desk were notes on herbs, a new combination he was experimenting with to fight infections and stimulate the immune system. He was a brilliant healer, even I couldn't deny it. I just didn't like him. The man had all the bedside manner of a stone wall. According to the notes, he was getting excellent results, and wounds were healing faster.

Nothing about the sword or book, or even the Grandmaster, though. His room was spotless, not a paper or anything out of place. Maybe his office? I let the light go out and left. There was nothing I'd find here, not easily, if there was anything to find.

The halls and courtyard were empty. She'd be with Master Denneth in the Dining Hall now. He'd be staying close to her while she settled in. I'd have time. The Healing Hall was quiet. No one was in the entry. With patients being given breakfast and assessed, I had the office area to myself.

I passed a small room where Master Tula unwrapped a man's hand. I could feel the heat from here. He had burned himself badly on something. My affinity for light and fire made me sensitive to such things. Most Masters had some advanced abilities, gained from their focus and meditation. Master Tula would have been my choice for head healer, despite his being younger by a few decades. He was also highly skilled.

Master Morlin's office was as tidy as his rooms. His desk didn't have any papers on it, nothing on the counter or workbench. Wooden filing boxes stacked along one wall, all neatly labeled and closed. I glanced at the labels, hoping to find one with 'evil plans for theft of sword' or something, but no luck.

Apprehension filled me. Aviva? I sped from the room, out the back hall and into the courtyard, behind the laundry. I flew past the kitchens beside it and into the main hall, ignoring the rain falling from the sky in a gentle drizzle. My inner being hummed with the heat from the kitchens and laundry warming me to my core.

My inner self calmed. She was alright, at least, but I'd been gone longer than I intended. People filed from the Dining Hall, some heading to the courtyard while others passed into the Masters' Hall. Why did she have to be short? I'd never see her in this mess of people.

I found her outside her rooms.

Master Denneth held an envelope in his hand. "I have a message for Master Ninden in the wood shop. Deliver it for me?"

"Yes, Master." She took the envelope. Her hand was steady, and she looked well, a tiny smile on her face. She scurried down the hall away from me, heading for the wood shop.

Master Denneth watched her go. He also would have made a brilliant father. What brought him here, I wonder? He shook his head. "Oh, the energy of youth." He disappeared into his room, the door closing behind him without a noise.

If she was delivering messages, I knew right where to find her. She'd learn her way around and meet more masters, while Master Denneth arranged her lessons and schedule for her. Would she find everything? Should I check on her? I promised to be there for her.

No, students would head to classes now. Nobody would bother her. The halls were already empty again. She'll be fine a few minutes more. I have other things to check on.

I headed into the courtyard and behind the main hall. The back gate was unlocked, a small and thick wooden door leading into the thicker forest, so I passed through. This was the shortest way up the mountain, and I'd left her long enough.

***

The mountain was still, and its energy flowed freely. Everything was as it should be. I stepped back into the sunlight, leaving the sacred cave behind. The rain stopped some time while I was inside. The mist still lingered from the waterfall, slowly spreading as it flowed down the mountain. I sped down towards the school, wasting no time. The sun was already higher in the sky than I realized.

A noise pulled my attention to the side. It was hollow, but not? What was that? I turned and followed the noise, passing through the trees without a trace. Something was moving under some trees ahead, something lighter coloured.

She sat under the trees, her light grey clothing making her visible from farther back than normal. Her clothing was damp from the mist. She had a pile of branches in front of her. Aviva held a branch in front of her, between her feet, as she sawed through it with a small hand tool.

Aviva cut the branch shorter and stripped smaller twigs and branches from it with the handsaw. The prepared round piece joined others in a pile, and she picked up the next branch, cutting it like the others.

I settled beside her. "What are you doing?"

"I'm working smarter." She set the final round piece down.

Aviva lashed two pieces together with a strip of scrap leather. She added more pieces and fastened them in place, all without a single nail, until she had a platform. She flexed the piece and frowned. Another layer joined the first, more leather scraps holding it together.

She picked up another round piece, this one thicker than the others. Aviva propped it up and held it between her feet. A hand drill? Where'd she get that? She lined it up on the end and hollowed it out, making a tube.

"Did you take that from the workshop?"

"I have permission. I'll return it."

Master Ninden let tools out of his sight? I almost didn't believe it. The hand drill was slow going, and she was sweaty when the drill bit poked through the other side. She made a second just like it. Aviva rustled through the bag, pulling out a cloth and a container. Grease? She dabbed the cloth in the grease and ran it through the tubes, using a stick to push it.

"Does Master Denneth know you're out here?"

She frowned. "Not specifically. He said I had some free time before my morning lessons begin and I could explore. Kai, at the funeral, Master Denneth said something about the Phoenix being reborn. What was he talking about?"

Aviva pulled a couple of smooth and round fighting sticks from the bag. They were in the trash heap yesterday; I was sure of it. She changed the drill bit to a small one and drilled holes in each end. The sticks slid through the larger tubes.

I knew what she was making now. "There's a legend here. The Phoenix protects people, but he has a flesh and blood helper, a bonded, you could say. When they get old and die, the Phoenix's connection to the physical world is diminished, and must be reforged with a new bonded."

"He said the Phoenix would be reborn, though. He didn't say anything about a bonded."

I sighed. Why did she have to ask so many questions? Sure, I'd rather see her curious about the world than not, but what was I supposed to tell her? Legends about the Phoenix were everywhere, but few people knew the full truth. And I might be the only one now, with the Grandmaster's passing.

"Most people don't know about the bonded. Can I ask you not to share this information?"

She nodded. "Is it always a man, this bonded?" She took some wooden disks from her pack and drilled a hole in the middle of each.

"No, the bonded has been women, too. It's always a warrior, though."

She slid the disks over the sticks and used wire through the holes to hold it together. "How does he protect people? The Phoenix and his bonded, I mean."

"He's the very spirit of protection, of being a guardian. He can act directly through his bonded, who benefits from his knowledge and skills. Also, people will flock to the Phoenix and aid him, rallying to his side."

"Can the bonded be any capable warrior, or is there more to it?" Aviva lashed her axel and wheels to the bottom of the platform. Now she had a small wagon. While it didn't steer easily, at least it could carry a load with more ease while she got stronger.

"There's a lot more to them. They need to share his desire to protect, to die for someone if they must. They also will gain his knowledge, acquired over centuries of learning, and must be smart enough to use it well."

"The book?"

I had to smile. "The book."

"What kind of knowledge?" She took a length of old rope and tied it to the front of the platform. Aviva stood and wrapped it over her shoulders. She doubled it back and tied the other end to the other front corner. Now she could pull it behind herself, keeping her hands free.

"Is this for the water pitcher?"

She nodded. "Until I get strong enough. I'll still need to pick it up to fill it, and turning corners will be an effort, but I won't need to carry it farther than I can. Well? What kind of knowledge?"

Persistent little thing, she was. "It depends on who the Phoenix bonds with. They store everything each host learned in the book. One was a great healer, so that's in there. Another was an inventor, a bit like you. Another had a gift with languages, and another knew people well and understood human nature. It's all added in the book."

"Is that why it looks so thick?" She gathered her tools and set them back in the canvas bag.

I chuckled. "Yes. It's not an ordinary book, though. It's special."

Aviva tossed her backpack in the wagon. She draped the rope over her shoulders, under one arm so she didn't choke herself.

"Let's get back and dry off. I think he's planned a reading lesson for you, and he should be ready soon."

She perked up, bouncing on her toes as she walked, the wagon rolling behind her. "I can't wait. Later, will you tell me more?"

"I promise. First, you have lessons."

We headed back through the forest, the wagon trailing behind, the wheels rolling over the soft soil without a sound.

***

She wheeled the wagon into her room and tucked it against a wall. The damp trail left by the wheels was already drying. She glanced at the open door between her room and Master Denneth's. He looked up from his writing desk.

"Return what you need, and we'll begin. There's dry clothing on your desk."

Aviva bowed her head. She slid the joining door closed. "Kai, out."

"I'll be in the hall."

The trail from her wagon was already dry, not a mark was left on the floor. The humidity was still higher than normal. Rain must be coming today. The masters with arthritis have got to be feeling this. The hallway was deserted, and I had the place to myself. Students would be in lessons, and masters had their own duties.

She struggled through the door, shoving it closed behind her. The canvas bag hung over her shoulder.

"Where did you get the idea of a wagon?"

She smiled. "Villagers use them all the time."

Of course, they did. Have I stayed here too long, forgetting what life out there was like? Everyone here carried heavy things. It kept them strong and fit. I followed her through the halls and into the main courtyard.

She ducked between the laundry and the Healing Hall, heading for the workshops behind them. We paused at the blacksmith. She cocked her head and stared at the anvil, where he worked the hot steel with a hammer. After a moment, she shook herself free of the rhythmic clanging, and she headed to the next building over.

"Aviva, how did it go?" Master Ninden turned on his stool.

She bowed her head as she slipped the bag off. "Very well, thank you. I appreciate you letting me borrow everything."

He took the bag from her, his large hand dwarfing her smaller one. "One day you will show me what you made." Master Ninden smiled at her.

"One day, Master Ninden. What are you working on?"

"Come see."

We joined him at the high workbench. Small carved pieces of wood rested on a leather mat beside sandpaper. They were still coated in fine dust.

"A toy? It's a horse and rider, right?"

He chuckled. Master Ninden picked up the little horse and wiped it off. He handed it to her. "Yes, but it's not a toy. It's a meditation tool."

She ran her fingers over the carved horse's back. "It's wonderful."

"Don't you have somewhere to be?" He held his hand out. "Lessons restart in a few minutes."

Aviva set the horse in his palm. "Thank you, Master Ninden." She bowed her head.

"You're welcome, child. Now go."

CHAPTER 9

So Much to Learn

She darted from the workshop. It thrilled me she found reasons to smile, whether it's a fresh change of clothes, or a little wooden horse. Her quiet enthusiasm has won gruff Master Ninden over, and her hope. Few people dared enter his workshop, and fewer still got to borrow his tools.

Aviva returned to her room. At least she was dry this time. She knocked and waited before opening the connecting door. Master Denneth stood, talking to a small man in master's robes. She hesitated in the doorway.

Master Denneth waved her over. "Aviva, this is Master Faldor. He's the head librarian. I've been called to the village, so he'll begin your reading lessons."

"Yes, Master."

Master Faldor smiled at her. "Would you like to work in the library, or here?"

"I'm fine with either choice," she whispered, her hands in front of her, her fingers twisting. If her appearance wasn't enough to remind me she wasn't a local, her expressions and mannerisms sure were.

"We'll go to the library. There's something about being surrounded by knowledge that's inspiring, isn't there?" Master Faldor winked at her.

The corners of her mouth twitched up. She bowed her head and stared at her feet. I felt a burst of warmth around my heart, an enthusiasm that wasn't mine.

She followed Master Faldor from the room. He sped down the halls, his over-robe billowing behind him. She jogged behind him. I stayed with her with little effort. We passed into the main hall and down corridors she hadn't seen yet to a set of polished double doors near the main entrance.

He opened a door and held it for her. She stepped inside and stopped. Aviva stood open-mouthed; her eyes were wide open as she stared. I looked around, used to the sight. What would she see? They lined every wall with shelves stuffed full of books, scrolls, and manuscripts, with more shelves all around the room in bookcases. Hanging lamps cast a soft glow, illuminating everything. Students sat at tables spread around the room, studying.

"You like it?" He beamed at her.

"I love it," she whispered.

"Come. We don't want to disturb them, so we'll use a private study room."

She scurried after him, weaving between shelves and tables. He passed through a doorway in the back wall, into a tiny room with cushions and a low table.

"Sit. I'll be right back." He pointed to a thick cushion on the floor.

She sank to the floor, balanced on the cushion, and crossed her legs. Aviva folded her hands in her lap and glanced around.

"Whenever you have a quiet moment, it's always a good idea to practice meditation."

Aviva nodded. She closed her eyes. Her breathing slowed. Her shoulders relaxed. Even her foot stopped twitching. A cascade of emotions poured through me. I clearly felt frustration, that tightness in the chest from not being able to do something, and yet there was a brightness, a light of hope in there, too.

Master Faldor came back with a few thin books in his hands. He pulled the curtain across the opening and chose a cushion beside her. She fixed her gaze on the books he set on the table. Master Faldor opened the top book and slid it in front of her.

"These are beginner reading books, normally for small children, but they'll get you started."

She stared at the page, her eyes tracing the black letters over the pictures below. Her fingers twirled the ties on her tunic. Did she even know she did that?

"Do you read in any language?"

She smiled. "Yes, Master Faldor. I read Sharonese at an advanced level."

"Wonderful. Our alphabet is different. Do you know it?"

"No, Master Faldor." Her shoulders slumped.

"Well, that's a great place to begin, isn't it?"

She perked up and shuffled her cushion closer to the table, right in front of the book.

***

She rubbed her eyes and tried not to yawn. We'd been here almost an hour, and she worked the entire time, learning the sounds and practicing simple words.

"You did well for your first day." Master Faldor closed the book. "Take these with you. Practice. When they are easy, bring them back. I'll get you more, so you can keep learning."

"Thank you, Master Faldor."

"With your dedication and work ethic, you'll be reading advanced scrolls here in no time. Don't feel pressured, though. The library is always open for you. Go rest and get ready for lunch."

"I'll show you the way back," I promised.

She picked up the books and held them to her chest. Master Faldor slid the curtain back, and we left the study room together. She kept her eyes down, avoiding the other students as we passed to the doors. Aviva stopped and stared.

There, beside the doors, a scroll hung on the wall. Bright reds and golds shone from the thick paper, the image of a bird with open wings staring at her. Its feathers were painted to look like flames. She gasped.

"Yes, that's the Phoenix." I stopped beside her. "That one is much closer to his true appearance, and nearly his identical coloring."

"People have actually seen him?"

"I see you noticed the scroll." Master Faldor appeared beside her. "Yes, some people have seen the Phoenix, and a few records exist from them. More often, people know or suspect who is embodying the Phoenix during each lifetime. There are only so many elite warriors, and not all have his qualities."

"Embodying the Phoenix?" Her gaze was fixed on the scroll, like she was memorizing each detail.

"I have some children's scrolls that tell some stories. We can begin working on those together, so you can learn more for yourself." Master Faldor placed a hand on her shoulder.

She noted his long, stork-like legs and the water painted below him, reflecting his image in ripples of colour. "The Grandmaster was him?"

"Yes, he was." Master Faldor's fingers tightened on her shoulder, just enough to wrinkle her tunic slightly. "Until the Phoenix has a new partnership, who knows who the next one is? Until then, we'll be ready for trouble. Go eat. They won't thank you for being late."

She tore her eyes from the scroll and dashed through the doors.

***

Garin wasn't at lunch today. He must have been on duty in the infirmary, one of the few posts where you ate somewhere else, so he could help with patients. I stayed with her through the meal. She sat at the end of the table, alone.

Master Denneth kept a careful watch over her. The other apprentices mostly ignored her, sitting together away from her. She almost went without food, but I saw the look Master Denneth gave them. Willin brought the bowl for her so she could serve herself. Defying a master was the fastest way to end your apprenticeship. She finished her meal in silence and set her spoon down.

"Master Denneth would like to speak to you once we're dismissed."

"Huh?" She spun on the bench. "Oh."

Master Enlan stood and dismissed everyone. She slipped from the bench and set her dishes in a basket. Aviva walked up the few steps to the masters' table.

Master Denneth stood. "The rest of your lessons officially begin tomorrow. I'm still arranging some of them. For this afternoon, Apprentice Padrig will do a fitness assessment with you." He nodded to a young man waiting at the bottom of the steps.

The young man, large and muscular, nodded to her. "I'll meet you in a private training yard in an hour." He bowed his head to Master Denneth, his arms by his sides, and his hands touching fingertips in front of his chest.

"Thank you, Padrig. She'll be there at the double bell."

Padrig left the Dining Hall, long strides covering the ground. He disappeared through the doors in the throng of students rushing out. She stood there, worrying her lip between her teeth.

"This is only an assessment. Once we know where your fitness is, we'll make a plan to get you where you need to be and help you with your weaknesses. Just do your best.

There is no standard to meet, no right or wrong, just where you're at now."

"Thank you, Master." She released her lip and almost smiled, just a hint of it there.

"Now, rest and relax. It's not good to exercise on a full stomach."

"Thank you, Master." She smiled widely.

He waved at the door. She raced down the steps, bounced down the Dining Hall, and was gone. I headed for her room. Where else would she go, after all? She was already inside, under the open slats, letting in the warm afternoon breeze.

Aviva spun and collapsed on her bed, staring up at the daylight above her. "How did he get started? When he was still human, I mean. Was he a student like this?"

I settled onto her meditation cushion. "No, he wasn't. The school wasn't built yet. He started life as a farmer. He was a villager, just like you."

"A farmer? Really? How did he become a protector?"

"It was a different time. Warlords still ruled the country, and bandits roamed freely. He was strong from working the fields and could swing a scythe with accuracy. One day, some rough men rode into the village. They stopped at the farmhouse he lived in and demanded food."

She stretched out on her bed. "Just like that? They walked into a total stranger's house?"

"That's right. He was in the field beside the house, harvesting grain. A woman cried out from inside. He didn't hesitate. Scythe in hand, he ran for the house. He burst through the door. They were shoving his sister around. She fell against the hearth and cried in pain. The hot bricks had burned her. She cradled her red hands to her chest and sat crumpled on the floor when he came in."

"What did he do?"

"He roared with anger. The entire village heard him, even those in fields away from him. One man pulled a sword and held it to his sister's throat, right against her skin. He saw the streak of blood, heard her whimper in pain. He swung his scythe, blade flashing as it lifted over his head."

"Could he save his sister in time? What happened? No, he didn't have time. He couldn't—"

"If he struck first, the bandit could kill his sister before his blow struck. He waited, fury in his eyes. That bandit wasn't leaving alive if they harmed his sister, he swore to that."

Aviva rolled onto her belly. "I thought he was a protector of life. Was she okay? Did he save her?"

"It was a different time. Today, villages are mostly safe. You walked through them, even at night, and were fine, right?"

She sat up and leaned back against the wall. "Yeah. I only had to watch for wild animals."

"He stared the bandit down. His eyes were full of hate. The bandit smirked at him. The young man swung the scythe handle up and hit the bandit under the jaw. The bandit was watching the blade and didn't react in time, since the blade swung down behind the young man instead of over his head."

"What about the sword at her neck? Was she okay?"

"She saw him move and curled up, away from the sword. The sword fell beside the bandit as he dropped to the floor. Another bandit drew his sword. The young man turned and brought the scythe blade to the bandit's throat."

Her eyes were wide, her hands over her mouth. "What did he do? Did he hurt them?"

"The villagers showed up, tools and shovels in their hands, ready to help. The blacksmith arrived first, heavy hammer in hand. He charged through the door, hammer raised, and stopped. One bandit lay motionless on the floor, the other was standing incredibly still, scythe blade to his neck."

"He helped? The blacksmith, I mean."

"Yes, he did. He was courting the young woman, and when he saw her laying there, he glared at the bandits. He took a step, hammer high, ready to strike the bandits and end it all right there."

She blinked. "What happened next?"

"The Phoenix, I mean the young man, well he was calm now that his sister wasn't about to be killed. He reminded the blacksmith the bandit couldn't change if he was dead, and that all life had value."

"Even though he nearly killed the man himself moments ago?" She rolled to her belly again and let her arm drop, her fingers running over the smooth floor below.

"In that moment, he knew how dangerous uncontrolled anger was. He knew he needed to work on managing his feelings, so he wouldn't harm someone again, unless he needed to."

"What about his sister? She's still huddled on the floor, her hands burned, right?"

I chuckled. "Okay, hang on, and I'll tell you. The blacksmith lowered his hammer and looked at her. She leapt up and ran into his arms, stepping on the bandit with the broken jaw. The blacksmith tucked her under his arm and took her out, where the village healer could tend her hands. The other villagers arrived and helped the Phoenix tie up the bandits. They took them to the middle of town."

"Was there a law and guards, like now? What happened?"

"There was a law given by the local Warlord, but nobody was around to enforce it. The villagers were on their own. The blacksmith and his apprentice strengthened a shack and added bars and locks. They made a prison to hold the men. The healer fixed the man's jaw, and they stayed and worked until they'd repaid the village, helping the farmers for an entire year."

"Everyone was okay with that? Them just being there like that? Did they live in the prison that whole time?"

"They were let out to work under supervision and went back when they were done. What would you have done with them?"

She curled up. "I don't know."

"Most people don't become bandits for fame or fortune, not even back then. Some did it for the money, that's true, but most are desperate and just trying to feed themselves. Maybe a family, too. Stealing is easier than working desperately hard in fields, hoping the harvest will get you through the year. With no one to stop them, many became bandits."

"Until the Phoenix?"

"Right. Until the Phoenix. Now get ready. You've got somewhere to be."

She sat bolt upright, her eyes darting about the room. Had she forgotten?

"Fitness assessment? Training yard?" I prompted.

She smacked her forehead with her palm. "Of course. Thanks."

CHAPTER 10

TOO MUCH, AND NOT ENOUGH

Aviva leapt from her bed and darted for the door. She slid it enough to slip through and shoved it closed behind her. I followed. The door was no barrier to me. She charged down the hall, only to slow and stop. Aviva looked both ways.

I chuckled to myself. "Out the side door to your left and down the hall. He'll be in one of those training yards. Let's find out which one."

She grinned and charged ahead, straight for the door. Aviva leaned hard against the heavy door, shoving it open. Her hand gripped the handle, and she hauled it closed again. Her hair floated behind as she darted down the corridor between the high stone walls.

The stone was warm from the sun, the light high overhead beaming down into each training yard without casting shadows. She passed the first yard, empty and quiet, the wooden slatted curtain closed over the entrance. Aviva stopped at the second doorway and peeked inside.

Padrig waited in the middle of the large stone training yard, his body straight in a perfect handstand. He glanced up at her. His body folded, and he lowered his feet, righting himself with full control over his movement. He opened his mouth.

The bell rang, drowning out all noise and echoing off the stone. Padrig smiled and waited as the echoes slowly died, leaving them in the wind's silence and birdsong once again.

"Whenever you're ready, we'll begin with a standard warmup from the beginners' classes."

She twisted her fingers together and looked at her feet. "I haven't had a class yet," she stammered.

His brow wrinkled. "Follow me. Just do your best."

He stood straight and tall, waiting. She shifted, copying his position. I smiled and eased myself into the corner. She should be okay. The basic fitness assessment wasn't overly taxing, and I knew she was fit from her time in the village and training with me.

Padrig stretched his arms out and turned his body at the waist. He crouched until his knee touched the stone floor. She followed without strain. Her slow martial art had given her balance, not a wobble or tremor in her movement.

He twisted and rotated, stretching his entire body gradually. She kept up, not sweating or straining. Padrig stood. He jogged to the wall and started doing easy laps, just fast enough to get the heart pumping harder. She followed, quiet as his little shadow, silent and focused. After a dozen laps, he moved back to the middle.

"If you're ready, we'll begin the assessment."

She nodded. She wasn't even breathing hard.

"Since you haven't trained, don't worry about technique. Just follow as best you can. We'll start with thirty fast punches, in bursts of three. Copy how I stand." Padrig settled into a horse stance, his legs spread, and his knees bent. He held a fist out, the other coiled by his side.

He blinked when she lowered into a stable horse stance, her fist out and ready. I couldn't help but smile. His brow furrowed for a split second, before his face returned to the relaxed expression from moments ago.

"Go."

Padrig threw three fast punches, pausing after the last. He aimed at the mid-belly, a basic middle punch. Each time, his other first came back to his side. I grinned. She knew why we did that, the smart little minx.

His eyes widened as she threw her strikes, each as fast and accurate as his. She got the rhythm in the first few bursts, learning his speed. She held her back fist higher than his, on her lower ribs instead of at her hip, but her technique was solid. She even twisted her fist right before the end, adding power to her strike.

He stopped after thirty punches. "You sure you haven't trained?"

"I never said that," she whispered. "I haven't done classes."

He arched his eyebrow and pressed his lips together. She remained in horse stance, without shifting or wiggling.

Padrig straightened his knees and stretched his legs. He dropped to the stone floor. "Pushups. Do as many as you can when I say go. I'll tell you when to stop."

She lowered herself to the stone and set her hands beside her shoulders.

"Go."

Even from here, I could see her struggle. She raised herself up once in the time he did five complete pushups, though she lowered herself with control. He pushed through about thirty pushups while she struggled to do four with solid form. Aviva didn't have a fifth pushup in her.

Padrig frowned. "Stop. Roll over and we'll do sit-ups."

She followed him through a whole series of exercises, including squats and lunges and other tests of strength. Some she did well, any that required leg strength, but she just didn't have the upper body strength for others, and she struggled. Physical chores gave her some strength, but not for this.

Her legs shook. She stood, breathing hard, her clothes soaked with sweat. He scratched his chin, frowning at her. Surely, he must be done by now. The bell rang.

"Go clean up. I'll inform Master Denneth of my assessment." Padrig waved at the doorway. He walked to a padded training dummy at the side wall and spun, kicking it. The dull thud filled the training yard.

She turned to the door. Her steps were slow, and her shoulders slumped. I caught up in time to see the tears she brushed from her eyes. She held her head high, though her jaw muscles clenched.

"You did well."

"I could barely keep up for most of that," she whispered. She wiped her eyes with her sweaty sleeve again. "How can I survive training if it's like this? I'm so tired I can barely lift my feet."

"That wasn't the beginner's assessment."

"What?" She stopped at the door to the Masters' Hall, her hand on the frame.

"That was the assessment for beginning apprentices. You should have had five years of training to get fit before he did that one."

She curled up, leaning hard against the wall beside the door.

"I'm not sure what he's going to tell Master Denneth, since that's not what he was asked to do. You did incredibly well for someone without the training background. Don't let anyone tell you otherwise. How about a shower? Your muscles will feel better for it."

She took a few slow breaths. Aviva pressed against the wall, straightening her body.

"He also didn't give you a cooldown. Don't stop moving yet. You need to stretch out. It'll keep you from getting sore later."

She threw her body weight against the door, leaning hard on it. The door inched open until she could squeeze through. Aviva grasped the handle and fell sideways, dragging the door with her. She stumbled down the hall and slumped against her door.

Master Denneth opened his door and looked down the hall. He walked over and kneeled beside her, taking in her panting breaths and sweaty, rumpled clothing. "Aviva, how did it go? Are you alright?"

She chewed her lip, tears forming in her eyes. "I did my best."

He wrapped an arm around her shoulders and pulled her to her feet. Master Denneth slid her door open with one hand and eased her through, closing it behind them. "Can you shower and change into clean clothing?"

She nodded. He let her sit on her bed. Her fingers fumbled with her clothing ties.

He frowned, deeper than I'd ever seen from the normally steady man. "I'll be back in moments." Master Denneth left her room.

She pushed herself up and shuffled into the bathroom. I stared between the bathroom door and her bedroom door. Would she be okay? She'd be upset if I followed her, even to watch over her. I passed into the hall.

Master Denneth disappeared around the corner. I charged after him, rushing to keep up. He marched through the hall and out the front door. I followed him across the courtyard to the Healing Hall. He headed right for the herbalism workshop, glancing in rooms as he passed.

Master Tula looked up, not pausing for a moment with the mortar and pestle. "Denneth, what can I help you with? Do you need more powder for your lungs?"

"No, thank you. I haven't had trouble since the cold went away. My apprentice is exhausted after an intensive fitness session. Do you still have that amazing liniment for muscle fatigue?"

Master Tula nodded. He set the pestle down and turned to a shelf full of bottles and jars. He selected a bottle of dark brown oily liquid and took a clean white cloth from a basket. "Your rooms?"

Master Denneth smiled. "Yes. If you can see to her, I have someone I need to talk to."

"Of course, old friend. I'm on my way."

"She's cleaning up right now. I'll be back as soon as I have answers." Master Denneth stormed from the room.

I shivered. I didn't need to feel his emotions to sense the discontent and anger rolling off her master right now. She was more important, so I followed Master Tula back to her room. Even walking quickly, Master Tula moved with a quiet calmness of a healer.

He knocked on her door and waited a moment.

"Just a minute," she called.

I heard clothing rustling. Quiet footsteps approached the door. The door slid open a crack. She grunted with effort. A quiet whimper escaped her.

"Let me help," Master Tula suggested.

Her eyes grew wide as she saw someone new through the barely open door. She stumbled back and stared up at him.

He slid her door open and closed it behind himself. "I have something to help your body feel better." Master Tula held up the bottle. "If you strip to your undershorts and a sleeveless tunic, I can help you."

She nodded. Her body trembled, just enough to see. No doubt he saw it, too. She fumbled with the ties on her tunic.

He set the bottle and cloth on her desk and kneeled in front of her. "Take a slow and deep breath. I'll help."

She nodded; her eyes fixed on the wall over his head. Her hands dropped to her sides. He unfastened her tunic and eased it off her, leaving her in a simple close fitting undertunic without sleeves. He pulled the tie on her pants, and they fell to the floor, not cut to fit her well yet.

"You can sit. This won't hurt. Master Denneth will be back any moment now." Master Tula took her hand and guided her to the bed. "Have you ever been to a healer before?"

"Not here. Back home I did," she whispered.

I sank to her meditation cushion, staying out of the way. Master Tula had the bedside manner you'd expect from a Master Healer, and I knew he'd care for her well. He uncapped the bottle. Pungent herbs filled the room with a medicinal smell. Master Tula poured some oil on the cloth.

He talked calmly to her, asking her about her life in the village, as he rubbed the oil in with the cloth. He started at her hands and worked up to her shoulders, shifting the tunic enough to get her back muscles, too.

"And then the Grandmaster asked me to come back here, but—" Her eyes filled with tears.

"He died that night." Master Tula nodded. "I understand."

She wiped her tears with her hand. "He was so kind."

"Yes, he was a great man." Master Denneth came in through the connecting door to his room. "How do you feel?"

She looked up, meeting his gaze. "I'm okay."

Master Tula chuckled. "Now, how are you really feeling?"

Aviva stared down at her lap. "I'm so tired."

"I'll bring your supper here tonight. You can practice reading if you feel up to it, or rest." Master Denneth picked up her books and set them on her night table.

"I'll leave the cloth and liniment for you." Master Tula capped the bottle and set it on her desk, the cloth draped over it. "If you need more before bed, use it. You can use more in the morning, but don't use it after that without checking with me first."

"Thank you," she whispered.

"You're welcome. Rest. You might feel normal again by morning." Master Tula bowed his head, his hand over his heart. "Denneth."

"Tula. Thank you." Master Denneth bowed his head back, returning the gesture.

Master Tula opened the door and stepped through. He gave her a warm smile as he slid the door closed.

"I'll be back with your supper soon." Master Denneth backed through the connecting door, sliding it closed as well.

Aviva stretched her arms and legs out one at a time. She sniffed the liniment. Her nose wrinkled.

I laughed. "It might smell bitter, but it works like nothing else I've ever tried. You'll feel like a new woman in the morning."

"I hope you're right," she muttered. Aviva reached for her pants and slid them on, moving slow. "Will Master be mad?" She fumbled with the ties, managing the knot on her second try.

"For what? You tried your best, right?"

She nodded. A tear fell to the floor. Aviva reached for her shirt. She groaned and stopped. "For being so tired. For not being good enough."

I snorted. "You're enough, just as you are. It's your first day. Do you think he expects a warrior already? If so, why bother coming to train here?"

"I don't know what he expects. I don't know what to expect. I don't know how things work here, or when people ask too much, or when I'm not being taken seriously. I don't fit in here, Kai." She sank to her mattress and flopped back on the bed; shirt forgotten on the floor.

"You'll learn. You think we're born knowing everything? Even knew students who were born here have to learn how things work. You'll be fine if you don't give up." Don't give up so soon, I pleaded in my head.

A soft knock on her door pulled her attention over. Master Denneth slid the door open, a tray balanced in one hand. She sniffed the air, her nose turned to the food, and smiled. He set the tray on her desk, moving the bottle and cloth.

"Eat. It'll help your body repair your muscles after such intense exercise. If you have trouble with your reading and want help, come see me. I'll be doing some work at my desk, and don't mind the interruption." Master Denneth smiled.

"Thank you, Master." Her lip quivered, and she grabbed it with her teeth.

"Each day is a new beginning." He slid her door closed.

She stared at the food, her mind spinning. What was she thinking? I wish I knew.

CHAPTER 11

UNWELCOME

A viva settled on her bed in clean night clothing, fresh from the shower. She picked up the cloth and poured some liniment on, the greenish brown oil colouring the white fibers. "Kai, why is everyone expecting trouble with the Grandmaster gone? How will we know when the Phoenix is bonded again?"

Is this what's been on her mind through her meal? She hadn't spoken a word to me the whole time she ate. "Word will spread quickly about the funeral and the fireball. Most people don't burst into flames when they die. Bandits will hear at some point, and they might begin moving in, testing our defenses."

"Tell me about the Phoenix." She rubbed the cloth over her hand and arm, working her way up to her shoulder. "What was he like? How did he really become the Phoenix, if he was once a man? There must be stories about this."

I curled up on the cushion. "There are. If a little foolish, he was a brave and determined man. He was born a man. He lived a long time, ridding the mountain range of bandits and training as a protector. Peace ruled the region and people were safe here. Even local rulers sought his opinion and protection."

She rubbed the cloth up her leg, massaging her muscles with each stroke. "He was old when he became the Phoenix?"

"Ancient. He stayed healthy for a long time, with all the walking he did, and people freely shared fresh food with him, to thank him. One night, he approached the village elder and said his time was done. He was passing into the spirit world that very night."

Her eyes widened. She poured a little more liniment on the cloth and started on her other foot and leg. "How did he know?"

"He worked so hard to protect people, he became the embodiment of protection. He wanted people to be safe, and live in peace, and he worked on himself until he was peaceful. He purified himself with the spirit's fire through his selfless actions. He was already blending with the spirit world."

"Was he sad? Knowing he was going to die?" She rubbed as much liniment into her shoulders as she could, stretching to reach under her top.

"After a long life of service? No, he wasn't sad."

"What did the elder say? Do you know?" She folded the cloth and set it on her desk with the bottle.

I chuckled. So inquisitive she was. "Yes, there are many stories of the Phoenix. The elder was worried the bandits would return once they knew he died. The man made a promise. Not just any promise, but a vow he could not break, here in this sacred valley."

"A special vow?" She pulled her blankets back and sat on the bed.

"Yes, an incredibly special vow. Anyone who needed a defender could call on him. He would be there, and he'd guard them, just like he did in life. He'd never forsake his people, and they'd always have his protection."

"Is that all it took for him to become the Phoenix?" She wriggled under her sheets and covered herself.

"All? He put his whole heart, soul, and spirit into the promise. It echoed through the valley, touching every part, all living things, from the smallest grass blade and insect to the mighty mountain itself. The people believed, and when he died, he remained in the valley as a spirit."

"What about bonding with someone? That's how it works now, right?"

"That's a story for another day. You need rest, and you're already half asleep. Good night."

Her eyes closed and her breathing slowed. She was already moving better, could pick up her tunic and fold it before bed, and her reading went well. He helped a bit, but she did well on her own.

Master Denneth knocked quietly and slid the door open. He set more clothing on her desk for her, folded neatly. Master Denneth extinguished her lamp and checked the slats, already closed for the night. She didn't stir once as he returned to his own room.

With her taken care of, I snuck out to the Grandmaster's suite. The panel remained closed. I felt the sword and book inside, safe and undisturbed. Everything was as it should be. I returned to her silent room and settled on her meditation cushion. Tomorrow was another big day, and morning would come quickly.

***

She woke and stretched, moving freely again. Her wagon helped her today. She dragged her wagon and carried the empty pitcher out, pulling it back on her little wagon, wrestling it around the corners on her own. Garin helped her fill her little pitcher and lift the large one back on the stand for her master.

Aviva looked at the liniment bottle and shook her head. She went off to breakfast with Garin and Master Denneth.

When she returned, she sat in Master Denneth's room and practiced reading as he repaired the binding on some old books and gave some books a new cover.

Master Denneth finally set his supplies down. "This morning you'll join the beginner's class. This afternoon you and I will do a private session. I can better assess where you belong, but after your workout yesterday, the beginner class might be a welcome respite."

"Yes, Master." She closed her books and held them to her chest.

"I brought your practice clothing for you." He pointed to a pile of light-coloured clothes on his dresser, a shiny sash on top. "Get changed and I'll help you with the sash."

She stood and collected her new clothes. Aviva wandered into her room. I followed. She slid the door closed. Aviva set her clothing on the bed and unfolded it, checking the ties.

"Any questions?" I offered.

"Just like our regular clothing, but a different colour?" She fingered the pale green cloth.

"Absolutely. It should tie closed the same way."

"I think I'm good. Privacy?"

I chuckled. "I'm gone."

The hall was quiet. First lessons wouldn't be out for a few more minutes, when most students would rush to their next classes. A few sweaty apprentices came back, their faces flushed from exercise. I missed my student days, more years ago than I cared to count. Getting to help her, it was like reliving them again, in an odd way.

I heard her soft knock on the connecting door and slipped back into her room. She stood just inside his room, tunic and pants on, the sash in her hands. He looked her over and nodded.

"You tie it like this." He took the long grey sash from her. "Start like this."

He wound the shiny sash around her waist. She watched everything intently. Master Denneth walked her through the knot, step by step, and had her try it a few times.

"Excellent. Now, I'll introduce you to the Master leading your class. Come." Master Denneth opened the door to the hall and let her pass through.

She hurried behind him through the halls. This time, he passed through the main door and across the main courtyard, near the large hall where most students lived. Instead of the smaller private training yards, there were larger training yards on this side of the compound. These were the very places I found her sneaking in to watch most often.

Students gathered in the beginners' yard, milling about and talking as they stretched. A man stood against the wall, arms crossed, frowning. Oh, not him. He's not teaching, is he? Master Denneth walked her over, his expression calm as he approached the master.

"Master Holin, this is Aviva. She'll be joining this class this morning." Master Denneth bowed his head, just a fraction.

Master Holin looked her up and down, still scowling. "Very well. Join the group. Follow along as well as you can."

"When class is over, clean up and change. Your other lessons begin today as well. Can you find your way back?"

"I'll show you," I offered.

"I'll be fine," she assured Master Denneth.

Master Denneth smiled. "I know you will. I'll see you after." He turned and left the training yard.

"Come near the back. You'll be more comfortable," I suggested.

She walked around the edge of the gathering students until she was behind everyone else. They were all younger and smaller, boys maybe eight to ten years old. They were stretching and moving, so she did the same. Why wouldn't she choose her regular warmup?

Master Holin occasionally glanced at her, still scowling. I suppressed a hiss. He was part of the reason no women trained here. Even he couldn't rescind a personal invitation from the Grandmaster, no matter how badly he wanted to.

"Line up." Master Holin paced slowly in front of the group.

Students snapped into place, all equally spaced, staring ahead at him. She lined herself up behind a boy and copied them, still as a statue. Master Holin frowned. Seriously, would his face break if he dared smile occasionally?

"Salute."

The boys raised their hands in front of them, fingertips touching, elbows by their sides. She tried, but I hadn't taught her this yet. She earned another frown. He started barking out commands, calling for different strikes.

I felt despair creep around my heart, a crushing like someone wrapped a fist around me and squeezed. She didn't know the names of the strikes yet. She copied, but was always a second behind the others. Hang in there, girl. You got this, I pleaded in my head.

Master Holin sped up his commands, driving the students harder. The boys started sweating, clothes snapping with each punch. She couldn't keep up, but kept going, always a strike behind.

"Breathe," I whispered, slipping beside her. "Clear your mind and follow me."

I opened myself to the sky. Feel his intentions, I reminded myself. Feel his spirit. "Straight punch," I whispered, as he called the next command.

Her fist whipped out in unison with the boys.

"Hook punch," I guided, at the next command.

Her fist circled around, swinging up at her shoulder level, just a hair behind the boys. We fell into a rhythm. The despair eased, and I felt a hardness take its place. Determination? I wasn't sure, but it was easier to handle. She focused and unleashed each strike, only a fraction later than the group. I needed to teach her our terminology.

"Now we'll practice the first form."

The students snapped to attention. Aviva shifted, hands by her sides, following the group.

I felt the bottom drop from my stomach, and this time it was my emotion. "Watch them and go only as far as they go. They learn it broken down, not fluid, like you learned it."

Aviva took a slow breath. I felt like jumping out of my skin. The last time she practiced, and I felt her, she was calm and still as a pond, reflecting peace and tranquility.

He called out numbers. The students moved as one, bowing together. She didn't know the bow yet, either, but did her best. She followed them through the form. Her technique was spot on, well above beginner level, though she hesitated on each move.

"You're doing great. Keep going." She was halfway there, but I felt nauseous.

He ran them through the form twice more. After the first round, she knew where to stop each time, and she kept up better. The nausea faded, and I felt something else, something I couldn't name. Master Holin moved around the group, walking between the boys, offering corrections. He watched her occasionally, but never came close.

"I'll help you in free time, like we used to," I promised. "Don't worry. You're doing great."

"Bow." Master Holin moved in front of the group. He returned their bow, and everyone straightened up. "Dismissed."

"Come. You need to wash, and you have another lesson soon. Back through the door and to the right."

She didn't say a word the entire way back. Sweat soaked her clothing. She pressed her lips together. Was this her first class ever? I think it was. If the guard trained her in secret, like I did, she wouldn't have ever trained with another student around.

I followed her into the bedroom. "Go have your shower. Toss the dirty clothing in the hamper and take something clean to wear after."

Aviva still didn't speak. Her clean clothing was piled on her desk. She gathered some and walked into the bathroom. I settled on her bed. The shower started, water hitting the floor in a steady rhythm. I loved that sound. It soothed the soul.

The room was reflecting her personality. Her little wagon sat in the corner, ready for morning. Some of her wall hangings were up already, bringing a splash of colour to the otherwise calming beige walls and reddish wood. Books sat on her desk, her night table, and her bed.

The shower stopped. The towel snapped and slid over her skin, audible from here. Was she trying to wipe her frustration away? I perked up at the knock on a door, not hers, but Master Denneth's. I crept to the connecting door and listened.

"She doesn't belong in my class. She can't keep up."

"How was her technique?" Master Denneth was calm and unflappable, as always. No wonder he could see the spirit world so well. This man practically embodied meditation in the daily life.

I grinned at the sputtering noises. "She's adequate. That's not the point."

"I will make other arrangements for her training. Thank you for your input."

I felt her behind me. How much of that did she hear? She wrapped her arms tightly around herself, her head dropped to her chest. A tear fell to the floor. My chest felt tight, that despair creeping back in. She shuffled to her bed and sat on the edge.

Master Denneth knocked on the door and opened it slowly. He frowned at her. She burst into tears. He walked over, his feet silent on the floor, and sat beside her on the bed. Master Denneth wrapped an arm around her shoulders and pulled her close.

"I'm sorry I failed you," she whispered.

CHAPTER 12

Healing

"You did no such thing. I'm proud of you."

Her head snapped up. She stared at him, wide-eyed.

"I'm sorry. I didn't know he was teaching this morning. Besides, you impressed him." He wiped her tears with his fingers.

"I did?"

Master Denneth nodded. "He couldn't complain about your technique. He wanted to, but he couldn't. That tells me a lot about how you're doing."

"Really?" A hint of a smile started, her lips curling up just a hair.

"Really. I don't think group classes are right for you. I have a solution."

She blinked. I felt warmth spreading through me. There's that light of hope she usually radiated. She opened her mouth, closed it again, and blinked one more time.

"Give me a few minutes." Master Denneth stood. "I'll be back. Practice your reading while you wait."

She smiled. "Yes, Master." Aviva wiped her face with her sleeve.

Master Denneth returned to his room, sliding the door closed. She picked up a book from her night table. Her hands trembled. She shifted back on the bed and set the open book down.

"Read aloud and I'll help," I offered.

"Thanks, Kai."

She started at the beginning, a simple child's storybook, reading each word slowly. I watched the pages as she read. Aviva gained confidence with each page. Soon she read at almost a normal pace, as if she was telling me the story, not reading it.

"Great. Get the next one."

Aviva set the first one on her desk and took another. Once she settled with the book open, she started reading. I had to admit, she impressed me with how quickly she was learning, with how different her alphabet was from ours. She nearly finished the second short book when the knock startled her.

"Well?" I chuckled. "Are you going to let him in?"

She moved to the hallway door and slid it open, pulling with both hands. Master Denneth stepped inside, a young man behind him. Her master settled in her desk chair and the young man stood beside him, watching Aviva. She shoved her door closed and sat on the edge of her bed again.

I had to smile. Aviva was assessing this new person as discretely as he was doing to her. She saw him at meals. They ate at the same table, though his room was in another hallway here.

"Aviva, this is Frewin. Part of his advanced training is learning to teach and prepare students. I will split your training here between private sessions with me and small group sessions with him leading and instructing."

Aviva bowed her head. "Yes, Master."

"Frewin, one day, part of your duties might be to teach villagers to defend themselves. This will include a variety of people, large and small, men and women, so this is good practice for you. This afternoon she and I are doing a session so I can assess her. Would you like to be present?"

"Yes, Master Denneth." Frewin bowed, fingertips together.

"Wonderful. It will be an educational experience for you both. Thank you, Frewin."

Frewin bowed again. He left the room.

Master Denneth nodded to the book on her bed. "How's the reading coming?"

Aviva smiled. She picked the book up and ran her fingers over the cover. "It's getting easier."

"Show me."

She opened to the first page and started reading. Most common words she recognized already, though she slowed occasionally to sound out a word. After a few pages, she looked up at him.

"You're doing well. I appreciate how hard you work."

"Thank you, Master." She looked down at her book, but I clearly saw her face reddening, and the smile forming.

"Now, it's time to start herbalism. If you're going to defend people, you need to know how to heal basic injuries and treat simple health conditions." Master Denneth stood. "Master Tula has an apprentice who will teach you today."

"Do I need anything to take notes?"

Master Denneth paused at the door, standing quietly for a moment. "That's right. You do read, just not Theirrese. They can provide you with scrolls and quills. Come."

She trotted behind him through the halls. We left through the main door and crossed the courtyard to the Healing Hall. Students and masters passed us, heading to their next lessons or duties, wherever that might be.

Aviva stared up at the writing over the doors, black paint within the grooves to make them stand out from the reddish wood. She mouthed the letters and sounds to herself, her brow wrinkled.

"That says Come, All Who Need Healing." Master Denneth stopped and let her look properly.

Her gaze roamed over the sign. She nodded and reached for the door handle. I saw her muscles tense, ready to haul on the door.

"Wai—"

She pulled hard, and the door swung wide, pulling her off her feet. She clung to the handle for balance and grunted as the door smashed her against the wall.

Master Denneth caught the edge of the door inches before it hit her face. "We get many villagers here for treatment. The doors are light enough for someone with severe arthritis or a grievous injury to move them."

She stood, still clinging to the door, her legs shaking. She took a deep breath and nodded.

"Come with me." Master Denneth took her hand and led her inside.

The door swung easily closed behind us, pulled by a light chain and counterweight. The Healing Hall was bright and airy. Windows opened wide, letting in both natural light and fresh mountain air. The walls were a cream colour and the benches in the front area had padded cushions. They stacked more cushions in a corner. A desk sat empty just inside the door.

A young man poked his head from a room nearby. "Welcome, Master Denneth."

"Thank you." He led her down a hallway, the polished wood gleaming in the sunlight.

She glanced in an open room as they passed, stacked with linens and bandages. Aviva scurried along behind him, her footsteps not disturbing the silence of the building. Some treatment rooms sat open and empty, a simple cot and a stool waiting for the next occupants.

He walked to the far end of the hall and stepped through an open door. She followed and stopped just inside, staring around with wide eyes. They lined the room with shelves, each loaded with bottles and baskets, some with powders or oils and others with flowers, and jars with cloths.

Worktables sat around the room, each with a mortar and pestle and brass scales. They spaced stacks of paper and quills around on some of them. She inhaled deeply. The fragrant flowers, oils, and bitter herbs filled the air.

A young man, maybe in his early twenties, measured out powder onto a dish on the scales. He adjusted the counterweights and removed some powder with a little metal scoop. Once he nodded, he poured the powder into a tiny bottle and capped it with a cork.

"Master Denneth, welcome," he greeted. "And you, as well." He smiled at her.

She smiled and nodded.

"Aviva, this is Eron, Master Tula's apprentice. He's most skilled for his experience, a gifted healer, and can teach you a lot."

"You're kind to say so," Eron nodded.

"Aviva is a hard worker and ready to learn. Her reading skills in Theirrese are new, so she might need some help, though she learns fast. She can take notes in her native language. She might need help with labels, at first."

Eron nodded. "Alright. We can work where she's at. We all learn at some point. Let me clean this up and we can start."

Master Denneth set his hand on her shoulder. "When you are done, it will be lunch time. Wash up, say the blessing as best as you remember, and go to the Dining Hall."

"Yes, Master." She watched every move Eron made as he cleaned up the powders and set the scales aside.

Master Denneth left, leaving her standing beside the workbench. She gripped the tabletop and chewed on her lip.

"Here, come sit." Eron placed a stool at a larger worktable and patted it.

She darted over and sat, eager eyes on him. Eron collected some bottles and containers and set them on the table in front of her. He took another stool and sat beside her.

"We'll start with the most basic healing herbs that treat a wide variety of conditions. These all grow here on the mountain, and throughout the region, so at some point you'll probably come help me collect them, too. They can save you one day."

She reached for a bottle of purple flowers, stopping inches from it. Aviva glanced up at him.

"Go ahead. Uncap it and pour some into this dish." He placed a small white ceramic dish in front of her.

She pulled the cork out. The purple flowers were still bright, even dehydrated, and the sweet smell filled the surrounding air. Aviva tipped the bottle over the dish and a few flowers dropped inside.

"A little more. You want some leaves, too, and the flowers will come first."

Aviva tapped the bottle with her fingers. Flowers tumbled out, followed by some dark green leaves, tiny and round.

"Touch, taste, and smell them. This grows everywhere. It's good for the immune system and can help with inflammatory diseases." Eron picked up a flower and bit into it.

"Can I write this down?"

He gestured to the quills and paper on the corner of the table. "Go ahead. When you can read well enough, I have scrolls on all the herbs, and you can have a copy."

She took the paper and dipped the quill in the dark blue ink. I watched with fascination as the letters took form. After something like a paragraph, she set her quill down and picked up a flower. Aviva sniffed it and touched her tongue to the petals.

"You can eat it. If you ever run out of food, you can eat this without cooking it. Blended with a couple more herbs you'll learn about soon, you can survive for weeks." He poured the herb back into the bottle using a little brass funnel. "Which bottle would you like to explore next?" Eron pointed at the collection of bottles he brought over.

***

She gathered her notes and clutched them to her chest. "Thank you." Aviva slid from her stool.

"You're welcome. I'll see you later." Eron moved her stool back to another worktable and collected the bottles.

She slipped from the room and down the empty hall. "Kai, do all warriors learn to heal?"

"They should. Here they do. Not all are as talented at healing, but any warriors from here can handle basic wounds and illnesses. You never know when you'll be called to help a villager, or injured in a battle, yourself."

She snuck out the front door, careful not to swing it hard. "Can the Phoenix heal?"

"Absolutely. He can renew himself or heal his bonded with a thought, and through his bonded he can heal others. Still, herbs are the easiest way to heal, if it's not a life-or-death situation."

"Why does he have a bonded, again?" She gripped her papers as the breeze rustled the pages and dashed across the courtyard.

"Well, the bonded gives him direct access to the physical world, and two people working together can do more than one person alone, right? How long would it take you to learn without the help of teachers?"

Aviva grinned. "It would take longer if I had to figure things out on my own."

"One day you'll teach others what you know, as part of the great circle of teacher and student. We also teach villagers how to defend themselves and heal. It's one way to bring about a more peaceful world."

"Through learning to fight?" She slipped through the doors and into the Masters' Hall.

"By learning how to stop bullies."

"How does the Phoenix and bonded work together?" She scurried down the halls to her room.

"The bonded warrior becomes like a physical host to the spirit of the Phoenix. Their spirits work together to bring peace through both the physical and spiritual realms. The Phoenix can even fight through the bonded, once the process is complete."

She slid her door open and wiggled inside, closing it behind her. Aviva set her notes on her desk with her books.

"Now, wash up. You remember how?"

She poured some water into the basin and set the pitcher down again.

"Do you remember the prayer?" Master Denneth stepped through the open joining door. "It's carved there, but I know you can't read it yet." His fingers brushed over the prayer carved at the top of the washstand.

"No, Master," she whispered.

"No matter. I don't expect you to know after one day." Master Denneth led her through the prayer of appreciation.

I joined along with them, adding my blessing to theirs. She repeated the words after us as she washed her hands in the basin. We waited as she dried her hands on the cloth and folded it, setting it to hang on the holder.

"Let's go eat." Master Denneth led her from the room.

She settled into her usual spot at the dining table, at the far end by the wall. The hall was still quiet. We were early. A few other apprentices clustered in the middle, talking about some advanced training technique. She sat quietly with closed eyes, meditating.

Merek and Drefan dropped to the bench across from her. She opened her eyes at the noise, the bench shifting on the floor. Her shoulders tensed, but she didn't move. They smiled at her, though I bristled at the wolfish nature of their grins.

"I need you to do something for me." Merek slid a piece of paper across the table to her. "Deliver this to Master Enlan."

Aviva picked up the paper and stared at it. "Why can't you do it?"

"My master isn't here yet. I'm not allowed to approach the table."

She slid the paper back to him. "You can wait, then."

"I'm senior to you. I told you to do something. You're supposed to do it," Merek snarled.

I scanned the page, reading the words despite them being upside down. "He's lying," I whispered. "You don't have to listen to another apprentice outside of lessons, unless Master says so. Hold firm."

Merek glared at her. She stared back, her face blank. I could feel the churning inside my heart, her fear and resolve and distrust.

"Is there a problem?" Master Denneth appeared beside the table.

"No, Master Denneth." Merek grasped the paper and crumpled it up, stuffing it into his pocket.

"Aviva, come and sit with me today." He set his hand on her shoulder. "Bring your dishes."

"Yes, Master." She slipped from her seat and followed him up the steps to the Masters' table, bowl, spoon, and cup in hand.

Master Ninden shifted over and made room for her on the bench. "So, smart one, any new creations?"

She lowered herself to the bench, her eyes down, though I saw her smile. "I'm still working on some plans." Aviva set her dishes on the table.

"The figurine is ready. Next time you stop by, I'll show it to you."

"Thank you, Master Ninden." She bowed her head to him.

Students and masters filed into the dining hall. Master Morlin walked up the far steps. He stopped and stared when he saw her there. She noticed his gaze and stared down at her bowl. He continued up and sat in his usual place on the other side of Master Enlan.

Master Enlan said the blessing, leading the group through it. She whispered the parts she remembered. I scanned the room, watching the people. A few apprentices accepted her, Garin even smiled at her from his place at their usual table, but most students stared at the foreign girl sitting where she didn't belong. I'd heard their whispers in the hallways, how it wasn't fair, her coming in like that.

Once Master Enlan sat, Master Ninden filled her bowl with the rice, millet, and vegetable dish. "Eat up. Someone as little as you need to grow big and strong." He smiled down at her.

She smiled shyly back up at him. I'd never seen him take to anyone so quickly before, but he was a good man to have looking out for her. Even other masters wouldn't challenge the man. Knowing she was safe during this meal, I snuck from the room.

Everyone who wasn't in the Healing Hall or on watch was in the Dining Hall. I had the hallways to myself. The Grandmaster's room was dark and silent, eerie after being so full of life recently. I placed my hands on the panel. The book and sword rested inside. All was well. I returned to the Dining Hall.

Aviva was rising from the table with the masters when I returned, dishes in her hands.

Master Denneth placed a hand on her wrist lightly. "Return to our rooms. I'll teach you meditation today, and tomorrow we'll meditate with the group. I'll be there shortly."

She nodded. "Yes, Master."

"Merek." Master Denneth's voice cut through the noise of the Dining Hall.

"Yes, Master Denneth?" Merek paused in the doorway.

CHAPTER 13

MEDITATION

S he didn't wait around. She set her dishes in the basket and slipped from the Dining Hall. I followed.

She walked briskly, heading straight for her room. "Where do you go when you disappear? You didn't stay for lunch."

"I have something important that needs my attention occasionally. I'll only go when I know you're fine. When you need me, I'll be there."

"Thanks, Kai." She entered her room. Aviva moved to her bed and sat; legs crossed. "Everyone meditates together?"

"Every day. The younger students do it in the morning after they clean up from martial classes. Since you're an apprentice, you'll meditate with the masters and other apprentices in the afternoon instead."

She nodded. Her fingers played with her sock as her eyes wandered over her room. "It still doesn't feel real."

"Give it time. You're not the only one to show up like this, going from humble beginnings to becoming a warrior. Are you ready to learn some new ways to meditate?"

"New ways?"

"There are many ways. Some are fun, others are restful, a few are more active."

"Fun and restful sound good. I'm active enough." She laughed. "I never thought I'd say that, either."

Master Denneth knocked and opened the joining door. "Come over here."

She rose and wandered over to his room.

He sat on the large meditation cushion on the small platform near his bed, his back to the wall. He gestured for her to join him. "Sit like this, facing me."

She shifted onto the cushion, sinking into the soft padding. Aviva crawled into place. She tried to cross her legs like him, one stacked on the other.

"It'll get easier. You need to build flexibility in the hip. Now, hands on knees, fingers relaxed, thumb to your index finger."

She wrinkled her brow. "Index finger?" She looked at his hands and copied what he did.

"That's what we call the first finger. I sometimes forget you're not from here. You've adapted so well." He straightened his spine. "In group meditation, you can choose any method we cover today, as long as you're quiet. You can even do the walking meditation, or join the group making art."

She grinned. "Art?" Aviva sat straighter.

He chuckled. "We'll get to that. First, we'll sit. Count your breath. If your mind wanders, simply bring it back to your breathing. Your purpose is to focus on each moment, calm inside like a reflecting pool."

She nodded.

"We'll sit for five minutes before we try another style. Begin."

Aviva closed her eyes and took a slow breath in. I settled behind her, where I could feel her energy more easily. Her breathing deepened and her body relaxed. Master Denneth was also feeling her energy, a skill all masters had. She calmed inside, especially compared to lunch. All I felt from her was peace. I brushed my energy up against hers, touching her heart. She felt warm and opened herself to me just a little more.

"That was a great start." Master Denneth opened his eyes.

He told her about a few more ways to meditate and let her try them, answering all her questions as she thought of them. She did okay with some methods and better with others. She was getting tired, though, and I felt her focus falter with each additional attempt.

"Now it's time to try some more active methods. We must allow the mind to settle and focus on the body. Come to the small table."

Master Denneth moved to the low table and settled on the small cushion, his legs crossed and folded under the table. She moved across from him, easing herself into place. Master Denneth set a large sheet of paper in front of her and another before himself. He gave her a quill and inkpot and kept one for himself.

"With this one, we sit quietly, quill on parchment. Let whatever comes to you flow out onto the paper. Don't control it. Just breathe and let what's inside you out. It might be a picture, or spirals, or circles, or even an unbroken line that wanders across the page. Whatever comes, let it out. It helps to close your eyes a bit, so you can see the paper, but aren't trying anything specific." He picked up his quill.

She gripped the quill, her hand trembling slightly. "Is there a chance to draw outside meditation?"

"There are art and calligraphy classes. We can talk about that after."

She bowed her head and nodded.

"Begin when you're ready."

Aviva took a slow breath in and dipped her quill in the ink. With her exhale, she touched the quill to the paper. I watched the lines forming on her page, her hand skating above the paper as long sweeping lines appeared. She definitely wasn't trying for anything, and the lines weren't connected.

Her breathing slowed incredibly, but I felt her energy surging inside her heart. I brushed against her again. Just a fleeting moment.

The quill kept moving on the page, lifting and settling. More black ink appeared. Lines formed, some crossing those already there, and an image started taking shape. Some formed curls and spirals, others were long curves. Her hand slowed, and she set the quill down.

"Open your eyes fully. Look."

She blinked at her paper. "What? But I—" Aviva stared at the image of a bird, staring back at her. "I didn't try."

"Calmly, child." He placed a hand over hers on the table. "I told you to let whatever was inside you out, and you did. Now I understand why the Grandmaster brought you here, and why I'm your master."

Her lip trembled. "What does it mean?"

Master Denneth sighed. What would he tell her? What questions would she have for me? What would I tell her?

"Why do you study martial arts?" Master Denneth held her gaze.

"Because—"

He waited. She gripped the table with her fingers. Did she even know?

"Because I have to. I don't know why." She worried her lip between her teeth.

He smiled and nodded. "Let this dry. You can hang it on your wall, but don't tell anyone how you made it. You can say you drew it, but don't mention the meditation."

"Yes, Master. I don't understand."

"I know. You will. For now, I must advise you not to use this form of meditation around anyone but me."

"Yes, Master." She stared at the image, the bird with long feathers she drew without knowing it.

"There's one last meditation to cover today. We'll walk and meditate." He explained walking meditation, how to move slowly and deliberately, and how to open her senses to the world around her. "Let's go."

He led her from the room and through the Masters' Hall, with slow and deliberate steps towards the side courtyard. Were we joining the group? The door slid open without a noise and the fresh breeze ruffled her hair. The fountain made the only noise, the water splashing into the basin below.

Master Denneth walked along the edge of the courtyard with her, around people sitting on cushions near the fountain, or those at the small tables doing drawing meditations. She smiled as she walked, her eyes half-closed. This wasn't too different from the way she relaxed to the martial art the guard taught her, so I wasn't surprised at how easily she sunk into a meditative state.

She matched his slow pace, step by step. Following behind like this, I could feel her energy building and swirling around inside her. Now I just needed to teach her how to organize and use her energy. She had some idea from her training with the guard, but she was capable of so much more.

After minutes of walking and a few laps, the bell sounded. Masters and apprentices stood and gathered anything they might have, cushions or papers, and folded the tables.

Master Denneth placed a hand on her shoulder. "You did well. Come, and I'll show you everything."

He walked her over to the middle, beside the fountain. "They set the tables out each time for drawing meditations. See how they fold up and put them in that shed?"

She nodded.

"They're brought out, and they set paper and ink out for anyone who wants it. See the big bin beside the shed?"

Aviva nodded again. People tossed meditation cushions into it and an apprentice wheeled it into the shed.

"You can take one and sit, if you feel like it. You're welcome to sit anywhere near the group, here in the middle. Sometimes meditating with experienced people, like the Masters, it can give you a better feel for how to circulate your own energy."

"Do I choose one type and do it for the entire hour?" She watched a few apprentices sweep the courtyard, now that they put everything away.

"You don't have to. Sit with me for the first bit, as long as you can manage, and you can walk or try another meditation if you like after that. Leave the cushion and clean it up when we're done, so you don't disturb the others. Move quietly and don't talk, and you'll be fine."

Aviva smiled. "What about other forms of moving meditation?"

Master Denneth held her eye contact. "We haven't discussed those yet. What do you know of them?"

She stared at her feet. Was she squirming? Her fingers played with her pockets.

"No matter. We'll go over those soon, and you can do them, too." He touched her chin. "Let's go back. It's time for your assessment, and first session with me. You need your training clothing."

She looked up at him, a half-smile on her face. My heart burst with warmth, though I felt the fear, too. Fear for what? She trotted along beside him back into the hall, her body trembling. Excitement? I felt jittery, but warm and happy.

"Change and wait in the hallway for me." Master Denneth opened his door.

Aviva slid her door open and stepped inside. "Privacy, Kai." She slid the door closed on me.

"Gone." I leaned against the wall, across from her door.

Clothing rustled and quiet little feet moved around her room. I tuned in, listening for her. It was only a minute or so, and she stopped moving around.

"Kai?"

"You need help with the sash?"

"Yes."

I slipped into her room and moved beside her.

She had it wrapped around herself, but only fastened the first part of the knot. "What's next?"

I talked her through the knot, letting her do it. "There you go. You got it."

She beamed, and I felt that warmth again. Interesting. She wasn't that happy when she made her wagon, and she did a great job with that. This girl adored martial arts and learning them, even wearing the clothing brought her to life somehow. We stepped into the hallway.

Master Denneth was closing his door. He looked up and smiled. "Frewin is meeting us in the training yard. He's mostly watching today, so focus on me and what I ask. If he asks something of you, do it, and I will watch. Do your best. Today is about learning what you know already."

"Yes, Master." She followed him down the hall. Aviva hurried along behind him, her body already warming up.

We left through the door to the private training yards. Frewin was waiting in the second one, stretching and moving to warm up. Master Denneth closed the curtain behind them and guided her to the middle of the yard.

He faced her. Frewin stepped beside Aviva. Master Denneth bowed. Frewin bowed back.

"Please, Master," she whispered. "I don't know your way of bowing yet."

Master Denneth smiled. "Frewin?"

"Like this." Frewin faced her. "Follow me slowly."

He stood straight and tall, his arms by his sides. Frewin kept his elbows by his sides, but circled his hands out and up until his hands were in front of his heart. He held his palms inches apart, facing each other, and bowed from the hip.

"The forearms moving represent gathering everyone together. We hold them between our hands and protect them. We bow to show we serve them, not the other way around."

"That's lovely." She smiled. "It means something."

"Everything we do has a reason. It's mostly a reminder of our purpose and duty." Frewin turned back to Master Denneth.

"Thank you, Frewin." Master Denneth nodded slowly to him. "Now, we'll go through the techniques you know, one at a time, so I can see how your technique is. The Grandmaster left a note, and he mentioned you had been studying independently. We'll organize what you know and see what you need help with."

"How would you like me to start?" She stood still, her body stiff.

"Do you know any of the forms? The first one, right?"

"Yes, Master."

"Show me each form that you know. We'll explore any additional moves you've learned after that. Start whenever you are ready."

Aviva stepped back. "Do I bow before each one, every time?"

Master Denneth nodded, stepping back to give her more room. Frewin moved beside him, staying quiet and back a bit more.

She bowed. After a moment of stillness, Aviva stepped into the first form. She did it just like we practiced, each move flowing into the next. I grinned. She remembered each correction we worked on, and her technique was excellent. She finished and stood quietly, bowing once more.

"What do you think, Frewin? Speak freely."

Frewin wrinkled his brow as he stood watching her. "Her technique is what I'd expect from someone who's been practicing at least a year. There are a few differences, little things she does, that I'm curious about, though."

Master Denneth waved her closer. "When did you start learning the form?"

"Just over a week ago, maybe?" She squirmed under his gaze.

"That's all?" Frewin's jaw dropped.

Aviva nodded. "Yes. I'm sorry, I don't know how to address you here."

"When he's teaching and helping, call him Teacher." Master Denneth rubbed his chin.

"Yes, Teacher."

Frewin arched his eyebrow. "Have you ever studied another style?"

She bowed her head. "Yes, Teacher."

"Show us." Master Denneth pointed to the open area.

Aviva stepped back and stood quietly. I felt her energy build. Which form would she choose? What would she show them? She knew a half-dozen forms, maybe more. Even I didn't fully know what she could do.

She raised her hands to shoulder level. Aviva stretched her arms out and shifted her weight, stepping to her side. I picked out the strikes and blocks as she flowed through the form, her motions slow and deliberate, her power moving towards her imaginary opponent. Aviva stepped and crouched, lifted and kicked, never stopping completely. She settled back into the starting position, her hands by her sides, her body still.

"Where did you learn that?" Master Denneth waved her over again.

"What was that?" Frewin stared at her. "I saw some strikes and blocks and such, but some of that was completely new to me."

"It's the style of the Royal Guard," Master Denneth explained. "How did you learn such a style?"

She twisted her fingers together in front of her. "I became friends with a guard before the revolution," Aviva whispered. "He taught me."

Sharp pain surrounded my heart. I nearly staggered and braced myself against the wall. A tear splashed against the stone courtyard floor at her feet.

"What happened to him?" Master Denneth gave her shoulder a light squeeze.

"He didn't survive." Her voice shook. "I practice to honour him, and for myself."

"Take a deep breath." Master Denneth kept his voice quiet.

She lifted her chin and breathed in; her eyes closed.

"It's the parent style to ours," Master Denneth explained to Frewin. "Our style is more direct and forceful, focusing on strength and technique to defeat others. Her style is about redirecting force, so her smaller size won't be a hinderance. Even royal ladies are fierce fighters, using that style."

"How would that help her learn our style, if they're that different?"

"They share a common root, even if they look different sometimes. Did you recognize any strikes or techniques she used?"

Frewin smiled. "Many. Some were quite advanced."

The pain receded, and I straightened up. I moved beside her. "Are you okay?"

She nodded, barely, but I saw.

"I'm still here for you. Can you keep going?"

She nodded again.

"We'll keep practicing that in our free time together. I might know a few more forms from it, though it's been a long time since I've practiced them."

She smiled.

"Can you show him another form? Do you know more?" Master Denneth met her gaze.

"Yes, Master, a few more."

"Show us?"

CHAPTER 14

So Much More to Learn

Aviva moved back to her place. She collected herself and began moving. The forms all started the same, but this one used a lower and longer stance. Her leg strength was remarkable. She was also flexible.

She closed the first form and stopped for moments, before flowing into the next, and the next, until she shared all she knew. One included a lot of kicking, another was about turning and striking all directions, each was different. Another had her balance on one leg a lot.

"Excellent. Come and take a breather."

She walked over and stood in front of Master Denneth.

"Alright, Frewin, what are her strengths? What does she still need to work on? Where would you start with her?"

Frewin crossed his arms over his chest, his chin in one hand. "Well, this is new for me. Her balance is impressive, and she's flexible. She won't have the power of her opponents, so we'll help her use all she's got, and she can work on her speed to help with that. I guess I'd pick the fourth pattern, going back to the others later, so she can work on the speed. Practicing with targets and the padded striking bags will help her develop power."

Master Denneth smiled. "That is a thorough plan. I will leave notes about what she and I work on, and you can keep me informed about how she does in sessions with you. Remember, new students go through periods where they seem worse as part of their growth. You did, too."

Frewin smiled, and his face turned red. "Yes, Master Denneth." He bowed.

"Why don't you start the fourth pattern with her? Give her a few moves to work on before your next session."

"Yes, Master Denneth. Ready?"

Aviva straightened up and nodded. "Yes, Teacher."

"We start like this."

***

"Are you ever going to tell me what happened after he died?" Aviva slid her door closed and headed into the bathroom.

"After who died?"

"The Phoenix, silly," she called through the open doorway. "You promised."

I heard her undressing and moving around near the shower. "I did, didn't I? Well, the village went into mourning. There was peace for a while. He'd protected the valley for so long there were no bandits around, but they started coming closer again after a few months. They'd target farms and businesses at the edge of the valleys, getting bolder and moving further in."

Her clothing hit the laundry basket near the door, sailing into view briefly. "What about his promise? Didn't the farmers know about it?"

"They did. They weren't sure he was still there. They didn't call out to him, so he couldn't hear them. He was a new spirit, you see." I settled on her meditation cushion, where I could still speak to her without yelling.

"Hear them? Where was he? In the spirit world?" The shower curtain moved, hissing on the rail holding it. Water splashed.

"His vow tethered him to this world, though he was partly in the spirit world as well. He could wander into the spirit world, but he couldn't stay long. He mostly dwelled at the top of the mountain, waiting for them to call him if they needed him."

171

The water went silent. I heard the distinct sound of soap being lathered, the swishing squeak of soap and skin. "They called eventually, right? He heard them, or he'd not be here."

"Yes, someone called. Many people doubted, but one person believed. She went looking for him, despite him being a spirit, and he felt her desire. The bandits had threatened her sister and mother, and she was ready to do anything to save them."

Water flowed again, and I waited as she rinsed off. It was only minutes, and the shower opened, and she pulled the towel from the bar with a swish. "What happened next? Once she called him?"

"He flew down the mountain and touched her heart. Her desire, need, and bravery combined with her belief in him, and they formed the first bond."

"His first bonded was a woman?" She appeared in the doorway, her hair still dripping. Aviva wrapped her belt around her tunic and tied it closed.

"Yes. There have been many great warrior women through the ages, and many more women of great courage living ordinary lives, despite the dangers they faced. Her desire to protect her family blended with his desire to protect everyone. They both became stronger. Now, supper is ready. Don't be late."

***

Tiny beams of sunlight shone through the shutters. She mustn't have closed them completely, but I didn't mind. We'll need to have Master Ninden check them before winter, in case it's the latch or lever, but for now, I'd enjoy it. She slept peacefully on the bed. I waited on her meditation cushion. She needed all the rest she could get.

Her first week had passed swiftly. Garin kept her company at meals. She used her wagon less each day, lifting the pitcher more easily, though she'd need it for a while yet. Frewin was patient with her, and she learned well from him. He never made her feel like she didn't belong. She enjoyed the sessions, though not as much as when she and I worked together.

It was her lessons with Master Denneth where she thrived. He knew many styles and blended them for her to suit her strengths. Master Denneth played with her with movements and drills, doing a lot of partner exercises so she could learn pace and timing. I doubt she knew how quickly she improved.

I glanced at the pile of wood shavings on the floor near her laundry sack. She piled scrolls from the library on her desk. A few pictures hung on her walls now, creations from her art classes. Most were of the mountain, images made with water-based inks.

The bell rang, a calming, deep sound that echoed many miles in the valleys. She rolled over and stretched, her eyes scrunched closed as she yawned. Aviva huddled under her blankets, pulling them over her shoulders tightly.

"Morning."

"Morning, Kai."

"Up you get. It's a big day for you."

Her eyes popped open. She stared at the room for a moment. Aviva pulled her blankets back and sat, her feet landing on the cool floor. She winced and lifted her feet again. Her slippers sat over here, by the meditation cushion.

She sighed. Aviva minced across the floor on her tiptoes, darting for the warmth of the bathroom. She spun and grabbed her clothing from her dresser, dancing on her toes, before dashing out of sight.

"After breakfast, before your reading lesson, you and I have a special training session in your free period."

The rustling of cloth stopped. "Are we going into the forest? Should I dress for a run?"

"We are going into the forest, but not for a run. Your everyday clothing is fine. I'll be waiting here in your room for you. Get moving."

Garin would be with her at the meal, so I knew she'd be fine. He didn't have shifts in the infirmary again for a while. No, I needed to go up the mountain. Something shifted in the energy up there, and I needed to find out what.

I slipped from her room and through the empty halls. The back gate was unlocked, as expected, and I passed into the trees. Mist hung heavy over the mountainside, flowing down from the waterfalls not far away. Who thought to put the school so close? Oh, right—

Shadows were deep, and the bears were out, looking for berries before winter. They wouldn't be close, but I might see one soon enough. I sped along the path up the mountain, making no noise on the soft soil.

Nothing. I stopped and opened myself, listening to the surrounding nature. Birds were waking and calling, a wolf howled in the next valley over, the breeze rustled the trees, but nothing unusual. That strange energy I thought I felt was gone. Did I dream or imagine it?

I turned off on the dirt track we ran the other day. I darted around the trees and rocks, speeding ahead for the bridge. Mice darted back into the undergrowth. Birds flew overhead, calling to me. Still no sense of anything unusual.

I stopped on the bridge. This was where I first felt it yesterday, or I thought I did. I looked out through the trees and up the river. I could see all the way to where it branched out, flowing as multiple streams across the mountainside.

Water carried energy more easily than the rest of nature, but the river was clear, as it should be. Could I have been mistaken? I shook myself and took a breath. Where did it go? For now, the forest was untouched. I'd come and check it again, but I had somewhere I needed to be. Today was a big day.

I raced back down the mountain to the school I called home.

***

"Should I be in here, Kai?" She hovered in the doorway, the light behind her illuminating the room.

"Yes, now step inside and shut the door before someone sees you."

She stepped through and let the door close behind her. "If it's okay that I'm here, why would it matter if someone saw me?" She was crouched and pressed against the wall.

I sighed. "Open the window across from you for some light. That's a girl." I waited until light flooded into the small storeroom. "You're okay to be in here, but usually students get special permission before taking a weapon. You have permission, but it's not in writing yet. Now hush and do as I say."

She stared at the racks of weapons lining the room, the metal shining in the light and reflecting it in every direction. She clasped her hands in front of her, her fingers twisting around each other.

"It's time to find your practice sword."

Her jaw dropped and her eyes widened. "Really?"

I chuckled. "Really. We need one the right size for you, and light enough, too. Try the third one from the left, there in front of you."

She stepped to the rack and reached for the sword. Her hand hovered inches from the hilt. She paused.

"Pick it up. It's not going to help you with it hanging on the wall there, now. Reach out and grasp it with your fingers pointing up towards the pommel. Hold the blade along the back of your arm, tip to the sky, arm by your side."

"Like this?" She cupped the guard in her palm, her thumb and fingers wrapped around the handle. Her index finger lay along the handle, not quite reaching to the pommel.

"Yes, exactly. Lift it carefully and lower your arm. Let the blade rest along the back of your arm."

She moved slowly, her hand shifting on the sword as she lifted it from the rack.

"You're fine. Keep going."

Yes, the sword tip was just below the top of her ear, held like that. The next size up would be too long. Short was easier to learn with, so this would do.

"That'll work for now. If you grow, we'll get you a bigger one. Grab a scabbard from over there. Fourth bin, for a sword that size."

She stepped near the window and to the bins. Scabbards stacked neatly in the bins, sorted by size. Aviva reached her empty hand in and grasped one.

"Now make sure it fits. We don't want to come back if we don't have to."

"Are you sure I'm allowed to be here, and can take this?"

I snorted. "Have I led you wrong yet?"

"I don't think so. I don't actually know. Maybe I haven't been caught yet?" She gripped the scabbard between her knees and gradually swung her arm around, bringing the sword in front of her. Aviva gripped the handle in both hands.

"Try this. Sword in one hand, scabbard in the other. Guide the scabbard over the sword tip and push the sword inside. If you try and sheath it like that, you'll skewer yourself."

She frowned. "I'm doing what I can. This is new, okay?"

"I know," I soothed. "You're doing well, and you work really hard. It won't be long, and you'll use that sword like a real fighter. Just don't cut anything off before I get you trained, okay?"

The corners of her mouth twisted up. "I'll do my best."

"You always do. Now, let's get into the forest, where we've got room to swing that."

She cracked the door opened and peeked out. It was silent outside. We were deep in the back corner of the compound, where few people went regularly. She slipped through the small space and down a narrow gap between the kitchen and the outer wall.

"Through this door, and into the trees."

"Aren't these locked?" She turned the handle and pushed the door open.

"The kitchen staff use this one to dump wastewater in the trees after meals. The water can do some good out here. Plants like the extra nutrients from the cooked food."

She darted into the trees and through the bushes.

"This way." I guided her up a game trail, deeper into the trees.

She climbed without a word. Our daily runs were strengthening her legs. We crested a small rise and stopped on some flat boulders below a branch of the waterfall. The mist was heavy here, cooling us in the midday sun. Trees between us and the school hid us from view, though we could see down the valley to the village below with ease.

"Draw your sword. You can set the scabbard aside for now. We'll get you a sword belt soon."

She grasped the hilt and pulled the sword free, a metallic swish covering the noise of water cascading down over the rocks. She set the scabbard on a large rock and stood there, waiting.

"Remember the grip you did in the storeroom?"

She shifted her grip on the sword, using both hands to steady it. Within moments, she had the blade behind her, fingers wrapped around the guard and hilt. I smiled. That was much smoother than the first time.

"Excellent. We'll take it slow and work on the first four movements. Are you ready?"

She grinned; her eyes focused ahead of her. Aviva shifted her grip, and the sword settled back against her arm. "Ready."

I got to work teaching her the first sword form.

CHAPTER 15

DISCOVERIES

Aviva turned, her blade whirling through the air. She froze. Her eyes met Master Denneth's. He stood at the edge of the boulders, tall and still, watching her.

"Your form is already good. Release the tension in your wrist." Master Denneth walked across the rock and stopped in front of her. "Where did you get the sword?"

She lowered the blade. I felt my insides churn as she squirmed before him, her eyes on her shoes. "Kai chose it. He said it was okay."

"Kai did, huh?" Master Denneth stroked his beard, silent for a long moment. "I'll arrange some time in a private training yard each day, so you won't be late for your other lessons. I know how much you love your reading sessions."

She glanced up, her mouth open, her eyes wide.

"I'll bring that back for you and leave it in your room. If you run, you'll make it on time. Master Faldor will wait, and you don't want to disappoint him when you're progressing so well." Master Denneth smiled and held out his hands.

She scampered over and grabbed the scabbard. The blade tip wobbled, and she tried a few times before it rested in the scabbard. She slid the sword into the scabbard fully. Aviva walked over and lay the sword in Master Denneth's hands.

He nodded to her. "Go. Learn. You're doing well."

She grinned and spun. Aviva was down the path, out of sight in moments as she shot down the mountainside. The bushes rustled as she tore off through them.

"Why her, Kai?" he whispered. "Don't let her come to harm." Master Denneth followed her, his long legs carrying him over the rocks with ease.

She may not be an obvious choice, but she was a good choice. I knew it when I met her, and I still believe it now.

***

"Come with me."

She looked up from her desk, her eyes on the Phoenix drawing hanging over it. Aviva glanced over. Her sword stood in the corner, where she stored it when she wasn't training. "Where are we going?"

"Into the forest. Time for more training."

Her chair slid along the floor, and she stood. In the last week, she'd added sword lessons to her training with Master Denneth, and she loved every moment of them. Her eyes lingered on her sword. "More sword training? The boulders?"

"No, somewhere new and special. You're ready for something more advanced. I think you'll like the challenge. Out the back gate. We're going up the mountain."

"Of course," she whispered.

She moved through the halls, silent as a shadow. We left through the back gate together. She nodded to the watchman over the gate, and he nodded back. Aviva smiled. Did she miss the game of sneak, now that Master Denneth gave official permission for her to leave during the day?

I took her up the normal path until the little bridge. We stopped for a moment, and I felt around me. Still no sign of that energy. I was doubting myself.

"This way."

She turned up the side path. The path was steep and rocky. Her legs worked hard as she followed me up the slope. We could rest at the top. Today she didn't have any lessons, it was her rest day, so we had all the time we needed.

"What's in the cave?"

"You can see the cave?" I smiled. Of course she could. She was as tied to me now as I was to her.

"It is a cave, right? Through the trees there?"

"Yes. We're going in."

I led her inside. With a thought and a gesture, torches flared to life along the wall. She peered down the tunnel as far as she could see. Aviva took a deep breath and straightened up. She marched down the tunnel and around the bend.

She gasped, wide eyed as she stared at the cavern. Part of the waterfall flowed through an opening in the ceiling, pouring over the far rock wall. Water filled a pool below, before flowing out through a gap in the rocks.

Aviva walked to the edge of the pool and looked down. Little life forms glowed beneath her, bioluminescence making the water sparkle. Water grass and algae clung to the many pillars of rock that jutted up from the water.

I focused, and the torches around the cavern flared to life, casting a warm glow over the water. The smoke drifted up, pulled by air currents, out through the top opening. She stared up at a tiny sliver of blue sky, visible through the cracks overhead.

"How did you find this place?"

"Martial artists have been coming here for ages to train. Open your heart and breathe slowly. Listen for them. Can you hear them? Can you feel them?"

She relaxed her shoulders and slowed her breathing. I moved behind her, my energy brushing against hers. Echoes of footsteps on rock and the occasional splash reached her, energy from previous warriors who trained here, still imprinted on the mountain and in the rock. Faint shadows moved around the room, leaping from rock to rock.

"Wow. That's—" Her voice trailed off, though it still echoed from the rocks.

"Step onto that first pillar. Calm yourself and balance. Center yourself. Feel the rock below you. Find your balance."

She stared at the water below her. Aviva shifted her gaze to the pillar. Her foot reached out, and she touched it to the pillar. Aviva slowly shifted her weight. Her arms waved as she wobbled. Aviva took a breath and straightened her spine, her eyes up on the waterfall across from her. She brought her second foot to the pillar and stood tall.

"That's it. Now, walk around, from pillar to pillar. Go smoothly and calmly. Find your balance. That's all you need to do. Do a lap around and come back."

She looked around her. The pillars were all different heights, different distances apart. Some tilted, and others were flat. I waited at the edge of the pool, letting her make her own choices. She reached her foot out to another one close by and stepped. Within a few pillars, she moved fluidly between them.

Aviva eased her way around, her eyes up and ahead, feeling for the pillars she sensed with her peripheral vision. As she approached the waterfall, the spray made the rocks slippery. Aviva took her time, sometimes stepping up, other times stepping on lower pillars, and occasionally stopping to balance, crouched low with her hands on the rock.

She stopped at the waterfall, on a pillar only a couple of feet away. Aviva reached out and touched the falling water as it flowed down the rock wall. Her balance was steady on the tilted slippery rock. She reached out with a foot and stepped up, shifting her weight. Her foot slipped on the rock below and she gripped the new pillar with her hand. I smiled as she pulled herself up with ease.

"The water comes from the sacred pool above. When you are ready, I'll take you there."

She turned on the wet pillar, crouched low as she reached down for the next one. "How long have people been coming here?"

"An incredibly long time. Over a thousand lifetimes. Keep walking. You're not back yet."

She looked ahead, picking her path. Aviva stepped from pillar to pillar. Her toes touched first, landing lightly beside me in a low crouch. The smile on her face as she stared over the water was one of confidence and achievement.

"That was great. Now, go around again, but this time, you must step using the stances and movements from the forms the guard taught you. Manage it without falling in, and I'll teach you another form from that style."

Aviva trembled beside me, bouncing on her toes. She stepped into a long bow stance, arms stretching out to block and strike. Aviva pivoted to the next pillar, and she stepped into a short cat stance, landing toe first. Her arms stretched up and down, blocking and redirecting her imaginary enemy. Her balance was spot on. Time for the next form. I smiled to myself.

She flowed from pillar to pillar, tiger stance, horse stance, punch and strike, block, empty step, low stance, snake in the grass, and more. I noted her angled hip in tiger stance. I'd need to correct that, and free up her stepping for her. It's an easy fix.

The sound of her feet echoed softly around the cavern as she moved, nearly lost in the rustle of her clothing. Even her breathing magnified in here, a perfect resonance chamber. I smiled at the gentle thud when she leapt back beside me, her fighting stance absorbing the landing with ease.

I took in her sweaty clothing, damp from the spray, and the moisture beading on her forehead. "You did well. Ready to begin the next form?"

She grinned, straightening up. Despite her breathing hard and the slight tremble in her legs, she nodded. Did this girl ever quit? I'm not sure she knew the meaning of the word.

The cavern went dark as we left, the torches going out behind us. Daylight greeted us, the warm sun drying her clothing. We walked down the mountain part way, to a clearing where the sun would reach us fully. This would do nicely. She leapt up on a boulder pile and stood, looking down on the valley below.

"What do you feel?"

"I can feel the rock beneath my feet. The breeze is warm and like a hug. The sun is—invigorating." She turned and looked up the mountain, at the first waterfall high above.

"Close your eyes. Now, what do you feel?"

She crouched down on the boulder, her hands on the rock. Aviva closed her eyes. "I feel," she took a deep breath in, "old. Full of life." She opened her eyes and stared up at the mountain peak.

"This part of the forest is older than the part right near the school. It's older than most of the mountain's forest."

"Most?" She leapt down and moved to the nearest tree. Aviva touched the rough bark with her fingertips.

"You'll see it soon enough for yourself. Ready?"

She nodded. Aviva scampered over to the middle of the clearing and stood tall.

"This form is about shifting balance quickly. Practice it slow to start, only speeding up when you feel comfortable. You already know the first six moves."

I named the moves and guided her through them, though she knew them well. I could tell she'd never done them in that order, though. Aviva turned slowly from the bow stance, all the way around to a cat stance, drawing her foot in for balance.

"Good. The first new move is in the sword form you're learning. Dragon scoops up water. Lower down into snake in the grass, with your hand reaching forward, rotating your palm up. Imagine scooping someone's ankle in your hand and standing, throwing them off balance."

She moved slowly, giving me plenty of time to correct her form. We went through these first seven moves a few times together.

"For now, you can practice those. We'll add more moves soon. It's time to go back. You don't want to miss supper, and you could use a good wash first."

***

She slid open her door and stepped into her room. Something seemed off. I could feel it. Could she? Aviva glanced around her room, her hand still on the door. Something on the bed moved, just a little flicker I barely noticed.

I moved to her bed. "You have a note." The writing was scrawled in a hurry, almost illegible. "Show this to Master Denneth. He needs to see it."

She picked up the paper and stared at it. Some words she knew, but many she didn't. She glanced down at her bed and paused.

Aviva pressed lightly on her pillow with a fingertip. "Ouch!"

I brushed my energy against hers and sent a little soothing into her. Her finger was throbbing, but it eased for her. She kneeled beside her bed and lifted the pillow cover, moving it as little as possible. Aviva peered inside.

"What's that?"

Little brown things were scattered on her pillow, just under the cover. She lifted her hand to reach in.

"Don't touch those. Go get Master Denneth. Let him take care of it. He knows how to handle that safely."

She drew her hand back. "What is it?"

"I think it's crushed up walnut shells. They'll be sharp. I smell something, though. They might have been coated with a powder, and you don't want that near scratches or open wounds. Even on bare skin, it'll cause some burning."

Aviva stepped back and stared at her pillow. Her brow wrinkled. She stood and went to the connecting door, knocking softly. After a few moments, she slid the door partly open.

"Master?" She peered around the door.

Master Denneth was sitting at his desk, writing. He looked up. "What can I do for you?"

"I think someone is trying to play a trick on me. There's something wrong with my pillow, and someone left a note."

He stood, his chair sliding back with the force, and strode into her room to her bed. Master Denneth stood a step back and sniffed. He frowned.

"It's under the pillow cover," she whispered, still across the room at the door.

Master Denneth crouched and picked up the note. He read it twice before folding it and tucking it into his tunic. Master Denneth picked up one of her paintbrushes from her desk and used it to lift her pillow cover to see inside.

"Go wash in my room. Shower thoroughly, paying careful attention to your hands. When you're done, go to supper. I'll bring you fresh clothing in a moment and leave it just inside the bathroom door. Go to supper without me. Tell Master Enlan I have something urgent to do, and not to wait. I'll see him as soon as I can."

"Yes, Master." She bowed. Aviva backed into his room.

Master Denneth went into her bathroom and washed his hands thoroughly with the soap at the sink. He dried his hands and left. He was probably getting her clean clothing and possibly fetching a healer. I passed into Master Denneth's room and waited.

"Kai?" Her voice was barely audible over the shower noises.

"Yes? I'm here."

"What did the note say?"

How was I supposed to tell her that? That someone wanted her gone, and will hurt her to do it? That someone will give her chemical burns and scars if she didn't leave? It was bad enough she had few friends here, but the friends she had were good friends. No, I couldn't tell her.

"How much did you understand?"

"Just the go home part. Kai, what did it say?"

Master Denneth returned with fresh clothing in his arms. "Your clothing is here inside the door when you're ready." He reached around the doorframe, setting her clothing on the floor inside the bathroom.

"Thank you, Master."

Master Denneth returned to her room and slid the connecting door closed.

"Kai?" The water noises stopped, and I heard the towel slide from the bar.

"They threatened you. If you don't go home, they'll hurt you."

CHAPTER 16

TROUBLE FINDS HER

C loth rustled as she dressed. Aviva didn't say a word. She emerged from the bathroom, freshly scrubbed, her hair still damp and in a braid.

"Wash at the basin and we'll go to supper."

She stared at the glass pitcher. A tear formed at the corner of her eye. She looked at her finger, still red from the powder. After a long moment, Aviva poured the water into the basin and said the blessing. She went through the motions, though her eyes didn't fully focus on anything, and she didn't look around.

"Come. I'm with you."

The dining hall was already busy when we arrived. She focused on the table at the head of the room. Master Enlan sat in the middle chair already. Aviva took a deep breath and walked down the hall towards the table, past the tables of boys talking and joking and laughing.

Her legs shook as she climbed the couple of steps at the front of the room. Aviva walked behind the table until she reached his spot on the bench. "Master Enlan?" Her voice trembled. She bowed her head and brought her hands up in respect, fingertips touching.

"Yes?" He turned and faced her. His expression was stern, but it usually was. I sensed her hesitation, a pit in my stomach.

"Master Denneth has something urgent to see to. He will see you as soon as he is able."

Master Enlan nodded. "Thank you. Take your seat."

She scurried from the platform and down to her usual spot at the end of her table. Garin wasn't here yet. Did he have duty again? She curled up on the bench and stared at her bowl. Was that a glimmer, a reflection from the inside?

"Change your bowl with the one beside you. Do it now and don't touch the inside."

"Kai?" she whispered. Aviva cradled the bowl in her hands. She swapped it with the one beside her.

"I'll explain later. I'm not leaving you today. You'll be okay."

Merek and Drefan dropped to the bench across from her. Another young man she hadn't met sat beside her. I didn't know him well, either. Still, they never sat with her. She glanced up at them and they smiled. Her insides twisted. I could feel it, and mine were in knots.

Master Enlan stood and offered the blessing. Boys and young men gathered the serving bowls and set them on the table. Aviva stared at the bowl set just past her, near the young men surrounding her.

"Take your bowl and get food from the bowl in the middle of the table. Take your teacup and spoon," I whispered.

She tucked her teacup and spoon in her tunic pocket and picked up her bowl. I watched her place as she went for the food. They watched her go, open-mouthed, as they scooped food from the nearest bowl into their own smaller bowls.

Aviva settled back into her place on the bench. She took her spoon from her pocket and began eating. Even though her eyes were down on her bowl, I could see her watching them.

The young man beside her, what the heck was his name, scooped up some veggies from his bowl and stuffed them in his mouth. His face went red. Tears streamed from his eyes. He clutched at his throat.

She stopped eating. "Help!" She turned to the Masters' table with pleading eyes.

He spit his food out and panted, his swollen tongue hanging out. He clawed at his mouth. She picked up her bowl and stepped away, watching with wide eyes. Master Enlan and Master Morlin were at his side in an instant.

"What happened?" Master Enlan stared at Merek, Drefan, and Aviva, piercing them with his gaze.

Master Morlin sat him up, holding him so he could breathe better. He signaled, and another master walked down to his side.

"What did you do to him?" Merek shrieked.

"Nothing," she whispered, backing against the wall.

"You three, follow me. Everyone, back to your meal." Master Enlan marched from the hall.

Merek and Drefan slid from the bench and followed. Aviva set her bowl and teacup back on the table and walked along behind them, back a few feet. Master Morlin and the other master carried the boy from the room through another door.

"I'm with you. If you can't answer their questions, don't say anything until Master Denneth is here." I slipped beside her, keeping pace with her.

Master Holin caught up to her and walked behind Aviva, just as she was leaving the Dining Hall. She looked around as she followed the others. Of course, she'd never been in this part of the Main Hall before.

Master Enlan opened a door. The young men walked in. Aviva followed, staying more than an arm's length away. I stayed beside her, as I promised, and brushed my energy against her heart. She gripped the tunic over her heart.

Master Holin stood over the students. She kept her eyes down and waited, standing as still as the statues of warriors in the Masters' Hall.

"What happened?" Master Enlan stared down at the group, his arms folded over his chest.

"She did something to him. She made him sick." Merek waved a pointed finger at her.

Master Elan stared down at her.

"I don't know what happened. He was okay, and then he wasn't," she stammered.

The door opened. Master Denneth walked in. He stopped beside Aviva and rested his hand on her shoulder. Master Denneth raised an eyebrow at Master Enlan.

"Master Denneth, there was an incident at supper. Pedar has taken ill, and they have accused her of making him sick."

"Oh? How did she do that?"

Master Enlan stared at Merek. "You're certain she did it, so you must know how. Care to share it with the rest of us?"

"She must have done something to his bowl. Maybe she used Corbinite Powder or something." Merek puffed his chest out.

"Interesting. The same powder I found covering nut shells under her pillow cover? That would have made her incredibly ill and seems a poor place to store a toxin. When you consider the threatening note left in her room, it doesn't seem likely, now, does it?" Master Denneth pulled the note from his tunic and handed it to Master Enlan.

Master Enlan read the note, his brow furrowing deeply as his eyes scanned each line.

"The powder was on her blankets as well. She will require all new bedding before nightfall." Master Denneth gave her shoulder a light squeeze.

"Please, Sir. I don't know what Corbinite Powder is. Eron can tell you which herbs we've covered," she whispered, tears forming in her eyes.

"Corbinite Powder isn't an herb. She wouldn't find it in the Healing Center." Master Enlan tucked the note into his tunic. "Master Holin, have his bowl tested for the powder. Alert Master Morlin what he might be treating. Apprentices, return to your rooms. Until I sort this out, you're all restricted. I'll alert your Masters."

Merek and Drefan slunk from the room. Aviva turned to go.

Master Denneth didn't let go of her shoulder. "Your room is being decontaminated. Go to my room instead. Your books and art supplies are fine, so I moved them to my room for you."

"Thank you, Master." She bowed deeply.

"I need to speak to Master Enlan. Did you get enough supper?"

"No, Master," she whispered.

"I will bring you some. Go."

Aviva darted from the room. I turned, but hesitated, and glanced back at Master Denneth. No, he had this taken care of, and I couldn't help here. She needed protection more than I needed to stay. I hustled after her, flying through the hallways. I caught up as she passed the Dining Hall. Her shoulders were curled, and her eyes darted around.

"This way. Use the courtyard. It's faster and more open if they are waiting for you."

"Thanks, Kai. Why would they do that to me?" She pushed on the door, and it swung wide, taking her with it. She got her balance back and closed the door softly. "Right, this is an open building. Lighter doors."

I'd have laughed under any other circumstances. "Merek's martial skills are advanced for his age. He wants to be Grandmaster someday. Having Master Denneth as his

Master would have almost guaranteed him the position, but Master Denneth didn't choose him."

She turned her face to the sun as she passed through the stone courtyard. I loved that little smile at the warmth on her face, even as the sun dropped through the mountains. Red and gold light painted the school in mellow colours.

"Master Enlan is acting Grandmaster, though, right?"

"Yes, he's caretaker for the school until the next grandmaster is ready. The Grandmaster trusted him to watch over the school and keep things running until that time."

She walked up the steps to the Masters' Hall, her feet barely making any noise on the thick wood. "Does that mean Master Denneth is going to be the new Grandmaster one day, or why would Merek want to be his apprentice?" Aviva pulled on the door, but it didn't move. She grinned and pulled harder, and it swung open.

"Often the Grandmaster position gets handed down from Grandmaster to his apprentice, which would be Master Denneth. He would then pass the position on to his own apprentice, and that might be why Master Denneth hasn't chosen anyone before now. He'd pick someone with impeccable character." Did she realize what I was saying? Did she know what this all meant?

She walked through the hall and stopped at the first window, her fingers brushing over the paper covering. The red tint coloured the last of the direct sunlight beaming in.

"Well, that's not me, so I don't know what he's worried about. I'm hardly Grandmaster material."

"You're young. Keep training. Who knows what you'll achieve one day? Don't underestimate the power of hard work and persistence. Come. You're under restrictions, so we need to get back."

Aviva dashed down the halls and slipped into Master Denneth's room. "But what he wants is a position, right? That's different from wanting skills."

I chuckled as I settled on the meditation cushion. "Yes, it is. Positions are often given by others. Skills are learned for oneself, and the effort can't be taken away from you. That's the difference between your character and his."

She walked to his desk, where her books and art supplies waited for her. She picked up one of her books and brought it to the cushion with me, where she settled cross-legged with her back to the wall. Masters got larger cushions so their students could join them, and there was plenty of room.

Her lips moved, and she whispered the words as she read. Her finger moved along the page, following her eyes, pointing to each word. She had improved her speed remarkably since she started. It wouldn't be long, and Master Faldor would move her up a reading level.

Master Denneth slid the door open and stepped inside, two bowls in his hands. He smiled at her deep in her book. She glanced up at him.

"Supper. Come sit." He set her bowl on his desk and moved to his bed.

"Thank you, Master." She set her book aside on the cushion and went to the desk.

Master Denneth sat on the edge of his bed, bowl in hand. He said the blessing and nodded to her. She dug into her food.

"So, what happened?"

She swallowed down a massive spoonful of veggies and millet. "I went to the dining hall like you told me. I sat in my usual place. Nobody was around." She hesitated.

"You can tell him," I assured her.

"Kai told me to change my bowl with another, so I did. He was going to tell me why, but everyone showed up, and Master Enlan started the meal. They never sit with me, though. When he started eating, he got so sick. It was scary." Her hand shook. She set her spoon on the desk and took a deep breath.

Bumping and scraping noises came through the closed connecting door. She glanced over at her room, wide-eyed. We couldn't make out the muffled voices.

"They're decontaminating everything for you." He dipped his spoon in his bowl. "They'll make sure there's no trace of the powder left, not in your clothing or anywhere."

"Thank you, Master." A tear rolled down her cheek. She brushed it away.

"You wish to stay and train?"

"Yes, Master. It's all I ever wanted, since I first saw people training."

Master Denneth smiled. "Your dedication will take you far. As long as you want to stay and learn, I will be here to teach and guide you. It sounds like Kai is looking out for you, too."

"Am I in trouble?" Her lip trembled. She gripped the edge of his desk. "I didn't do anything."

"No, child. They restricted you to your rooms while they sort this out, but that will keep you safe here with me. They need to know if Pedar was involved or another innocent target, or what role the others had, if any. There were no additional clues in your room, so this might take a little time."

She nodded, her eyes on her bowl.

"Consider this a chance to read a lot and do more art meditation. That was fun, wasn't it?"

She grinned. "It sure was. Okay, I can do this. Thank you, Master."

CHAPTER 17

I FAILED

Aviva stepped up to face Master Denneth in the cool training yard. She shivered in the early morning air. At least she slept well last night on her all-new bed and blankets. All her lessons would be private lessons with masters until further notice, and Master Denneth liked the early mornings. I curled up in a corner in what passed for the sunrise. It was getting cooler already.

"You're ready. Let's begin the next pattern.

Her eyes widened. "Yes, Master."

He turned with his back to her and stepped slightly to the side. "We begin with the same bow." Master Denneth bowed.

Aviva copied him, the motion smooth and practiced now.

"Step forward and middle block with the right hand, low block with the left."

He smoothly stepped into a bow stance, doing the double blocks as he moved. She followed along, knowing the basic movements already. She was just learning to join them in new ways.

"Rotate the arms like this." He moved his arms in a sweeping circle, each coming up towards his center in opposite directions.

She smiled and copied him. One of her forms from the guard had a similar movement. "It's a couple of blocks and a strike, or a push, right?"

Master Denneth raised an eyebrow and smiled. "Yes. The guard taught you not just the forms, but what they did, didn't he?"

She bowed her head. "It helped me remember the moves, and I watched the others train from behind bushes, but yes. He showed me."

She wiped her tear with her sleeve and stood tall, back in the starting position. Aviva flowed through the first few moves, slow and deliberate. Even as she moved, I felt her pain inside, an ache around the heart that never quite went away. Was he her only friend in this land until us? She repeated the movements a few times as Master Denneth watched.

"Excellent. After that, we close in and attack again. Each step comes at an angle, never direct in this form. By coming at them from the side, we give them fewer easy ways to attack us."

I remained at the edge of the training yard, out of the way. Master Denneth was an excellent teacher, and she soaked it all in like a sponge. She made it through to the halfway point with him. Her leg strength was being challenged, but that would come with practice. The style taught here had a few stances she wasn't used to.

"Take a break and stretch. You're doing well." Master Denneth raised his arms high over his head. "Did they give you any trouble while you fetched the water this morning?"

She dropped her upper body down and stretched out her back and hamstrings. "No, Master. I was a little late, and they were already gone, I think."

"How are you doing with making friends here?" He twisted his body around slowly, reaching as far back as he could.

She straightened up and stretched tall. "I have a couple of great friends."

"How are you doing with the other students?"

Aviva spread her legs and leaned over to one side with her hands. "A few younger boys sometimes train with me on our free day. They're nice, and helping them helps me, too."

Master Denneth smiled. "We learn the most when we teach. How are the masters treating you?"

Aviva grinned and turned to stretch behind herself, hiding the smile. I know Master Tula snuck her sweets from the nearby village sometimes, when he was down to treat an elderly woman.

"Some are really friendly. Most are polite. I avoid the others."

At some point, those last few masters would need to be dealt with. If they couldn't accept a woman warrior, and a foreigner no less, they didn't belong here. The Phoenix protects anyone, regardless of who they are, as long as they're not causing the trouble to start with.

"How is learning to heal going?" Master Denneth lowered to the ground and spread his legs, stretching out the inside of his legs.

Aviva smiled. "I love it. The people are so happy to be helped, and Eron knows so much about herbs. Not as much as Master Tula, though."

"Your reading sounds better, too."

She sighed. "It's getting better. He's giving me longer books now. I just wish it came faster. So many scrolls, just waiting to be explored."

"Time, child. You're still young. If you could be anywhere at all, where would you be?"

Aviva stopped and rubbed her chin. "I'm happy here, despite some things. I have friends and I get to train. It's not cold like the shed was. Life is better, even if it's not perfect. I don't need perfect."

"If only more students felt that way. Ready to keep going?" Master Denneth stood.

"Always." She bounced into place beside him.

***

She opened her eyes and stretched. Aviva eased her covers back and set her feet in her slippers. Her heart had its usual fire inside, but her movements were a little sluggish. Was she sore from yesterday? I smiled. Those stances could do that, if you weren't used to them, and she was so enthusiastic about learning. Even Master Denneth had trouble stopping her before she overdid things.

Aviva shuffled to her bathroom; her day clothing tucked under her arm. Within minutes, she was back and ready to go. Her little wagon sat in the corner, unused for a few days now. She retrieved the pitcher from Master Denneth's room and closed the doors behind her. Did she even notice she no longer struggled to slide the heavy doors anymore?

We were early today. The halls were nearly empty still. Dim lanterns illuminated the walls, the coloured paper shields giving the place a rainbow of light pastel hues. Sunlight reached through the windows in slivers, adding red to the kaleidoscope of colour. She brushed her fingers over a patch of light green on the walls as she passed, holding the empty pitcher in one hand with ease.

She slid the courtyard door open, silent on the rollers. There was no sign of Garin. Of course, he had a lot of additional duties as he prepared to become a master. The fountain flowed freely, clean and ready for the day. I froze behind her, staring at Merek and Drefan. Merek leaned down and took a long drink from the fountain, directly from the water streaming down. Drefan splashed him, cupping the water in his hand.

I bristled. How dare they? Where's their reverence, their respect?

She stared at them from the covered porch with the pitcher cradled to her chest.

"Well, are you going to get water, or stare at us with an open mouth like a fish?" Merek opened his mouth and closed it a few times, his eyes wide.

"Kai?" she whispered.

"I'm here. They might mock you, but you have every right to be here, and you know how to behave. They won't hurt you. Fetch your water and let's go."

"Okay." Aviva squared her shoulders and stood tall.

She walked down the steps, back straight and head high. For a moment, I had no trouble seeing her in a palace with a crown on her head. She walked over to the fountain, steady and confident, despite her insides making mine churn. Aviva stopped at the fountain and placed her pitcher under the water.

They crowded behind her.

"Step back," she demanded, her voice loud and firm.

"Sure thing." Merek smiled.

They gave her just enough room to move away. Her pitcher filled, and she hugged it to her chest. Aviva turned and stepped away. I flew down the steps as Merek stuck his foot out, catching her ankle. No!

She tumbled to the ground, the glass pitcher beneath her. The glass broke with a horrible loud crash. I sailed right over her, smashing into Merek's chest. He flew back and hit the wall many feet away. Blood pooled under Aviva, spreading out on the stones. Drefan ran, yelling indistinct noises.

I rushed to her side. Aviva lay curled up over the broken pitcher, whimpering, tears streaming down her face onto the wet stones.

"I'm here. You'll be okay."

The door crashed open. Master Ninden charged down the stairs to her side, Master Faldor behind him. Master

Ninden eased his arms under her and lifted, turning her as he cradled her to his chest. She cried out as an enormous chunk of glass slid free. Blood oozed through her tunic across her belly, staining it red. Master Faldor pulled his outer tunic off and pressed it to her wound.

"Breathe. We're getting you some help." Master Ninden marched her to the side door in the courtyard, kicking it open in front of him.

Master Holin charged into the courtyard and over to Merek, crumpled against the far wall. I ignored him and followed Aviva, staying close as they charged across the main courtyard to the healers. Master Faldor rushed ahead and held the door open.

Master Ninden took her right in and lay her on the large workroom table. He kept her shoulders and head in his arms. Tears flowed freely down her face. Her eyes were closed. He cradled her cheek in his hand.

"Stay with me, you stubborn girl. You're strong. Don't give up now."

Master Morlin rushed into the room, taking in the blood-soaked tunic and the soggy girl. He grabbed a knife and cut the tunic from her belly. "Fetch Master Tula. Now."

Master Faldor rushed from the room. Morlin grabbed a massive jar of herb and oil infused bandages. He pressed them to the wound. She cried out and her eyes opened wide. Oh, those herbs stung so badly, but they could stop bleeding in even the worst cut.

"You're doing great," Ninden murmured. "Breathe with me. Slow and easy."

Morlin picked up a needle and pulled a corner of a bandage up. Tula rushed in; his face was ashen when he saw her.

"Get another needle. This needs stitching now."

Tula grabbed a cloth covered tray and set it on the table beside her. He worked across from Morlin, uncovering another part of her wound.

I snuck beside Ninden and touched her forehead. "Sleep. You don't need to be awake for this."

She slipped into a dreamless sleep. Her breathing evened out, still good and strong. Morlin stitched quickly, probing the wound as he went. Tula lifted the bandages enough to get a closer look. Morlin had the deep part and was closing it, so he set to work on the next deepest slash.

Tula finished first, stitching up the shallow wounds around the deep gash Morlin still worked on. He spread a salve over her closed wound, laying layers of bandages over the stitches. Morlin was closing the last of the deep gash, so Tula pulled some glass shards from minor cuts with tweezers.

"There." Morlin set the needle down. "We'll wrap her up. I want her under continual observation."

Ninden lifted her in his massive hands, and they wrapped gauze around her belly. They dabbed ointment on her small slashes, removing any last shards.

Master Denneth burst into the room. He rushed to her side and took her hand. He looked as pale as she did.

"She's strong. She'll be okay." Master Tula pulled her eyelid up and peered into her eyes. "We've stopped the bleeding. She needs rest and quiet. Bring her to the first recovery room."

Master Ninden slipped his arm under her legs and lifted her, resting her head against his shoulder. She lay motionless in his arms. Not even a whimper escaped her. No, she'd sleep until I let her wake. Master Denneth remained beside him, his eyes on her, as they carried her across the hall and lay her on a cot. He set her down as slowly and gently as he could, keeping her wounds still.

"Eron," Master Tula called down the hall.

Eron appeared in the doorway. "Yes, Master?" He saw her on the cot. His jaw dropped. "What happened?"

"She's injured. I'll be by to check on her every few minutes, but I want you to watch her. Call immediately if she's in any distress at all."

"Yes, Master." Eron walked to the chair beside her bed and sat. He reached for her wrist and felt her pulse.

"I need help here." A muffled voice called from the front door.

Masters Tula and Morlin rushed from the room towards the commotion.

Master Ninden came back with another chair and set it on her other side. "There you go, old friend." He guided the stiff Master Denneth into the chair.

"Thanks," Master Denneth whispered. He lowered into the chair, his eyes not leaving her pale face.

"I'll go see what that's all about. You stay with her." Master Ninden left the room quietly.

I moved to her head and lowered myself beside her. They've done what they can. It was my turn. I couldn't do as much as I wanted, but I could still help. I brushed my energy against hers and poured as much healing into her little body as she could handle.

Master Denneth took her hand in his. Eron watched her belly rise and fall with each breath. She remained quiet and unmoving as I filled her with healing, her little blood vessels knitting back together, held by the stitches and my power.

The oil seeped down into the wound and carried the herbs, burning any microbes out. Her body would absorb it and she'd be fine. I added a touch more healing to assist. She did not need an infection as well as this wound. Finally, I settled back against the wall, spent and tired.

Her eyelids fluttered briefly. Her fingers curled slightly around Master Denneth's hand, before going still again. She was getting a little colour back to her skin, too. Eron checked her pulse again and nodded.

Master Tula walked in, a small bottle and dropper in his hand.

Eron eased from the chair and let Master Tula sit beside her. "She's doing a little better already."

Master Tula smiled. "Excellent. Pull her cheek open. I'll give her a couple of drops for the pain."

"Yes, Master." Eron reached over and slid a finger under her cheek, holding it out enough to slide the dropper in.

Master Tula placed three drops of medicine in her cheek. "This will help her sleep and heal. She can have something else when she wakes, if she needs it, and if she can swallow on her own. She looks better already." He peeled her eyelid up and checked her eyes.

Master Denneth smiled. "She's a fighter. A real little warrior. What's the commotion about?"

"They brought Merek in. He's burned from something, but Morlin has it all wrapped now. He needs rest, too." Master Tula watched her sleep for a long moment. He checked her bandages, still snug and white, so she wasn't bleeding through. "She just needs rest. The next few hours are most critical, but I think she'll be just fine."

I smiled. Of course, she'd make it. She just needs time to heal. Now we wait.

CHAPTER 18

RECOVERING

Her eyelids opened. She stared blankly at the ceiling. Her fingers twitched. Master Denneth woke and straightened up in his chair. Eron leaned down and felt her forehead. She turned her head slightly, her eyes on him.

"How do you feel?" Eron felt for her pulse.

"Hurts," she whimpered.

"I know. Hold on, and we'll get you something." Eron stood and headed for the door. He glanced back at her as he left.

"You gave us quite the scare." Master Denneth wiped her tear away with his thumb. "We're here." He rested his hand on her forehead and sent a little healing into her. It wasn't his strength or gift, but he still could help a little.

Master Morlin strode into the room, Eron following. Her eyes focused on Morlin as he sat in the chair. Morlin felt her wrist and checked her bandages.

"How do you feel?"

"Hurts," she whispered.

"I've got something for you. We'll give it to you slowly, and you can swallow it when you're ready." Master Morlin pulled a bottle from his robes. He filled a dropper part way. "Open your mouth."

She parted her lips. He let the medicine fall in her cheek and watched as she swallowed it. He gave her a little more, and she took it without choking.

"Give that a few minutes to work." Morlin placed a hand on her forehead. "It'll make you sleepy, but it'll take the pain away."

She stared at the ceiling, her eyes glassy, before her eyes slid closed. "You said they wouldn't hurt me," she mumbled. Her breathing slowed again, and her muscles relaxed.

My heart ached. I've never been so wrong in my long life, and I've had a few legendary mistakes in my time. No student has ever hurt another deliberately like that, not in the entire history of the school. I promised to protect her, and I failed. She nearly died, because I was wrong. I need to do better. This can't happen again. If I can't protect her from students, how will I ever keep her safe if she's in a proper fight?

"How is she?" Master Denneth brushed a lock of hair back from her face.

"Her wound closed well. Now we watch for infection. Once she's recovered enough, we start her on herbs to rebuild her strength and help her get her blood back." Master Morlin stood. "Thank you, Eron. You know what to watch for?"

Eron nodded, his eyes on her face. Master Morlin left. She survived her first few hours, as I knew she would. Now she needs rest. So did I, after giving her so much healing energy. I settled in for a deep meditation session. This close, I'd feel immediately if she needed me.

***

"There you are." Master Denneth set a hand on her shoulder.

I pulled myself from meditation. She blinked and turned her eyes on Master Denneth.

"How's the pain?" Master Tula took her wrist in his hand.

"Still hurts. Less." Her voice was still barely a whisper.

"I'll have something for you soon." Master Tula looked deep into her eyes.

Master Denneth looked rumpled after sleeping all night in the chair. Master Morlin left a senior healer to watch her all night, and Master Tula was doing his morning rounds, starting with her. I listened to the sounds of the infirmary all night while meditating, and she slept the night through.

"What happened?" Master Denneth took her hand in his.

"He tripped me," she whispered, her voice shaky. Tears leaked from her eyes.

Master Denneth wiped her tears away. "Who did? Which young man?"

She blinked up at the ceiling. I sensed her confusion, like a breeze inside me that tore through my essence. She didn't know. She shook her head slightly, rolling it on the pillow. Her breathing hitched, and she grimaced.

"Slow and steady. Meditation breathing. Relax and let it happen," Master Denneth urged. "They've been spoken to by Master Enlan and are being dealt with. When you remember, if you remember, you can tell me. If not, it's okay, too."

"Do you know how Merek got the burns?" Master Tula set a hand on her shoulder.

She shook her head. "Burned?"

"Yes. He's been treated and is in his rooms in lockdown, awaiting judgement."

"I don't know." She paused for a breath. "They were playing and splashing, taunting—" She gasped and winced.

"Slowly. A little at a time is fine," Master Denneth assured her.

Her fingers tightened over his hand before relaxing. "I got my water. I turned. They tripped me. I hit the ground, and it broke." She took a slow breath in and let it out again. "There were flames rushing past. Master Ninden came. Everything went black." Her brow wrinkled. "Did Master Ninden make fire?"

"Just rest. You'll feel better soon." Master Tula touched his hand to her forehead. "No one will bother you here. Sleep. You'll be fine."

"Master?" she whispered.

"Yes?"

"I'm sorry."

"Just rest. You've done nothing wrong, and I'm proud of you."

Her eyes slowly dropped closed. "Kai?" It was barely even a whisper.

"I'm here," I promised. "I haven't left. I'm sorry I wasn't fast enough."

"Kai," she mumbled, as she slipped into a medicated sleep.

Denneth and Tula exchanged a glance.

My heart ached again, this time with my own pain and failure crashing over me. Did they know I failed her, too?

***

Aviva stood across from Master Denneth in the training yard. The warm afternoon sun heated the stones, making the cool autumn air tolerable in light training clothes. She focused on her teacher. I waited in the corner, watching.

She returned to her room a week ago, after a week with the healers. We spent her training time in meditation or doing academic lessons instead, while she healed. She drank many teas to rebuild her strength and had special meals to boost her health. Aviva nearly trembled from excitement, getting back into training like this. I loved her enthusiasm.

"Today we'll begin gently. Your muscles and wounds are still healing, so instead of working hard, you will teach me one of your forms."

Her eyes widened. She grinned. "Really?"

He nodded and bowed. "Really, Teacher. No true martial artist ever looks down on other forms that are different. They all have something to teach, and each has strengths and weaknesses. Pick whichever form you feel is best with how you feel right now."

She straightened up and closed her eyes. There was a slight knot in my stomach. Why? She was good. I had to do something about that self-confidence.

"You can do this," I whispered. You're good, and teaching will make you better."

Her lip trembled.

Master Denneth reached up and cupped her chin in his hand. "What's troubling you?"

She sniffed. "I wasn't good enough to protect myself. Should I even be here?"

He tilted his head to the side and smiled. "There will always be someone better than us, bigger, stronger, faster than us. That doesn't mean we stop trying. It means we work to be better than we were, to lessen our disadvantage. Sneak attacks can get the best warriors. It doesn't mean they failed."

The corners of her lips curled up. She wiped her tear and nodded. "Okay. I've chosen a form."

Master Denneth stepped beside her.

"We start like this, clearing our mind and focusing on what we feel. Raise your arms and step out."

***

"That was excellent. Your reading has improved remarkably." Master Faldor held a small stack of books out to her. "You're ready for these. They might challenge you a little, but don't be afraid to ask for help."

Aviva grinned. She took the books and held them to her chest. While she was recovering, Master Faldor spent hours with her, reading to her and letting her read to him. She powered through the books she had and started on the next level already. She spent some of her training sessions reading even now as she continued to recover from her wounds.

"Thank you."

"You're welcome. Now, put those in your room and head to the private training courtyard. Master Denneth will meet you there. Wear your training clothing."

She bowed slightly. Aviva left the library, her eyes on the scroll beside the doors, until it was out of sight. Her training session with Master Denneth yesterday went well, but she was still in knots inside.

"You'll be fine," I assured her.

"Kai, what happened to Merek and Drefan? I haven't seen them since—since that day." She clutched the books to her chest like a shield.

"They released Merek from the school. He returned to his village, where everyone knows what he's done. Life will not be easy for a young man with no honour."

She worried her lip with her teeth. "Drefan?"

"He's working long hours of public service to make up for not protecting an innocent who was being bullied. When presented with the choice to work for the valleys or leave the school he chose to stay and work. He's mostly been in the laundry and the Healing Hall. If he comes near you again, they'll expel him."

She took a breath as she slid her door open. "Okay."

"You don't have to worry about them. Focus on training and getting better. Yesterday was fun, wasn't it?" I followed her into her room.

Aviva smiled as she set her books on her desk. "Yes, it was."

"He might have something just as fun planned for today."

She closed her door and retrieved her training clothing from her dresser. Aviva disappeared into her bathroom to change. I settled onto the meditation cushion and waited. It still took her longer than normal, but not as long as it did a week ago.

Aviva reappeared, dressed and ready to go. She walked to her door and paused, her hand on the latch.

"Come on, girl. Time to stand again. It's okay to be knocked down, remember? As long as you get back up, you're still a warrior."

She smiled. "Okay. I can do this."

We slipped out the side and down the stone corridor. Master Faldor didn't mention which training yard, so we checked the first one.

Garin stood in the middle, stretching. "Come on in. We're starting with a light warmup."

"I was expecting—"

"He's in a meeting, so I'm helping today." Garin smiled. "We'll take it slow. Tell me if you need a break or anything. Don't push too hard, or we're both in trouble, okay?"

She smiled down at her feet. The knot in my stomach dissolved, only to be replaced by little dragons flapping around, from the feel. She'd never worked with him before, despite the number of meals they shared, or times he helped her with the water. She wasn't allowed to lift the pitcher yet, and he insisted on helping. Better training, he said.

"We'll start with a brisk walk." He took off, marching to the wall. "Set a pace that feels like work but doesn't hurt."

I sank into the corner in the sun and watched. Her young age helped her heal. She moved well, no signs of pain. He led her through a complete warmup, and she managed it well.

"Now, we're going to do partner exercises, striking and blocking with no power. Only focus on technique. We're going slow so you can get a real feel for the timing. It'll ease you into sparring when you're healed enough." Garin stepped across from her.

"I'll do a high strike, a middle strike, and a low strike in that order. Do the blocks with full setup, since you have time and I'm going slow. Work on timing. No power, remember? When you're ready."

She nodded and took a fighting stance, her body bladed at an angle to him. Her hands were up and open, ready to defend. Garin stepped in slowly, his strike advancing towards her head. She tensed and flung an arm up, sidestepping. Aviva winced.

"Breathe, girl. He's not going to hit you," I reminded.

She let the air from her lungs and rolled her shoulders. Garin stood waiting, letting her shift back into her fighting stance. He struck again, a middle strike this time, even slower. She bumped his arm with her forearm, pushing it away from her.

"There you go. Nice and easy."

He stepped in again, a low strike coming at her. She slowly stepped and blocked him, moving to his side. He advanced, a high strike, keeping the slow battle dance going. I smiled as she settled into the rhythm, her body relaxing as she kept moving to his side and blocking him.

"Great. This time, I'll strike, just like I was. Block it, and use any counter strike you want. We'll do that for a while."

She bowed slightly and stepped into her fighting stance again. Garin stepped in with a low strike. She blocked low and sent a palm strike to his chest, still at the slow and steady pace they set earlier. He blocked it and struck again, another strike at her face. She dropped low and came up under him, her hands on his ribs, and gently shoved him.

Garin stepped back and lowered his hands. "Excellent. Had this been an actual fight, you would have uprooted me and sent me flying." He looked up over her shoulder.

Aviva noticed his gaze and turned.

Master Denneth stood in the archway; his arms folded over his chest. He nodded. "That's right. Use every tool and technique you have; from any style you like. We must find what's best for you and get you practice."

She grinned and bowed. "Thank you, Master."

"How's she doing?" He focused on Garin.

Garin bowed. "We started hesitant, but she quickly picked it up in drills."

Master Denneth gazed down at her. "You're not overdoing it or harming yourself?"

"No, Master. I'll need a break soon, though." Her fingers twisted around her sash.

"You have done well, and it's not time to push yet. Go clean up and meet Eron for your herbalism and healing lessons before we meditate together."

She grinned and bowed her head, her fingertips meeting at her heart. "Yes, Master."

I loved that impish smile and the way she seemed to glow with enthusiasm when she got to learn things she was passionate about.

"Master Tula will check you again while you are there. See him first."

Aviva bowed, but I felt the twinges, and I saw the grimace.

"Relax." Master Denneth held his hand up. "Your muscles need more time. Until the healers say otherwise, only bow when you are fully comfortable, not when you're tired after training. Go."

She nodded instead. "Yes, Master." She scooted from the yard, bouncing despite her tiredness.

"Thank you for your help." Master Denneth bowed to Garin.

Garin's eyes widened. "It was an honour. I'm sorry I wasn't there that day, when she needed help."

Master Denneth straightened up and looked out from the training yard. "We can't always protect everyone all the time. We can only do our best." He walked out without another word.

CHAPTER 19

TAKING HER PLACE

I sped past him and back to her room. She had already changed and was sliding her door closed again. Her eyes darted around the hallways still, her muscles tense, like a suit of armour might step from its pedestal and attack at any moment.

"You did well today." I settled beside her as she walked.

Aviva smiled. "It wasn't as scary as I thought once we got going."

We slipped out the main door and crossed the courtyard together. The sun beamed down from high overhead, warming us through as if it were still early summer. She turned her face to the sun and closed her eyes, stopping for a moment. I understood that urge.

Master Tula was in the main treatment room, waiting for her. "How do you feel today?"

"I am well, Master Tula." She bowed her head.

"Your muscles still hurt?" He waved to the bed.

"Sometimes. Not often anymore." Her fingers fumbled with the ties as she lowered herself to the edge of the bed.

"Allow me. How was training?"

She lay back on the bed and moved her hands. Master Tula unfastened the ties with deft fingers and long practice.

Aviva grinned and stared at the ceiling as Master Tula shifted her tunic off her belly. "I was scared, but it was okay. We went slow, and it wasn't so bad. Garin's an excellent teacher, and I'm not even tired, really."

Master Tula examined her wounds, his fingers gentle on her skin. "You've been careful. You're healing well. Today you and Eron will make your tea and salve, and he'll help you apply it."

She beamed. "Yes, Master Tula."

"How is your reading coming along? I know Master Faldor is most proud of you." He pulled her tunic back over her belly and slid a hand under her back. Master Tula helped ease her up to sit again.

She ducked her head and smiled. "I'm sorry for being so fidgety while I was healing. The reading really helped, and I'm on the next level now." Aviva took his offered hand and stood.

He kneeled and retied her tunic for her. "That's wonderful. Some people have more trouble resting than others, and you still did okay. How many bottles can you read in the workroom now?"

"More than half."

"Excellent. Eron is waiting. Go. Make sure you blend the salve well, and apply it to every part of the wound now."

She bowed her head again as he stood. "Yes, Master Tula."

We took the shortcut from the treatment room to the workroom, through a storage room for herbs and supplies. Eron already had bottles out and was reading the recipe on some parchment on the workbench.

***

"Kai, has the Phoenix ever bonded with a foreigner?" She picked her shirt up from her clean laundry basket and set it in the drawer.

"Yes, he has. It's not common, as few people travel this far, but there were two bonded from other continents, and more from other countries." I shifted and settled on her meditation cushion.

She worried her lip between her teeth for a moment. "Were they ever accepted fully? I mean, did they ever one day just fit in? What made him choose them?"

"The Phoenix doesn't care who you are or where you're from. All his spirit cares about is whether or not you have the heart of a protector. Both stepped in and helped when people needed them. They also found it hard at first, and both settled in just fine."

She gathered her folded socks in her hands and dropped them in the next drawer down. "Tell me about one?"

"We have a little time before the meal, as long as you keep going. That laundry won't put itself away."

She smiled and slid the next drawer open. Aviva tucked her pants inside.

"Her name was Anika, and she was a trader. This was maybe seven hundred years ago now. She led her caravan all the way to this valley. While she was on her way, an illness struck. Nobody knew where it came from. It was from the spirit world, and no physical cure was working."

Aviva tucked her belts and sashes in beside her pants. "And she kept coming? She didn't turn and go home?"

"She thought about it. A physician was making his way here, to the Healing Hall, to help find a cure. People were desperate, and the roads weren't safe, especially for a man with medicines. People were dying, and even the foods, the vegetables and fruits, those were taking sick as well."

She stopped and looked up at her drawing of the Phoenix on her wall. "Even the plants were getting sick? How?"

"The illness was from the spirit world. The Phoenix and his bonded had recently hunted down a man trying to enter this valley. They succeeded, though his bonded was incredibly old. The man they stopped, well, his son was upset. He sold his own spirit for revenge. The old bonded died, a normal death when someone is a hundred and twenty, and the Phoenix's tie to the world weakened."

She slid her drawers closed and frowned. "That's bad timing. So, people got sick and didn't have food. How did Anika become his bonded?"

"The physician needed help to get to the school safely. She sent her caravan back home and bought a donkey. With the donkey to carry the medicines, she escorted him to the school, knowing they could both get sick and die along the way. Bandits even attacked, not too far from the school, and she fought them off and brought him here."

"How did the Phoenix find her? Here?"

"He was flying over the valley, looking for a way to help, or someone to help him, and he saw her fighting, swords flashing in the sun, as she spun and whirled around the physician, defending him with every ounce of her strength. Despite being wounded, she drove them off. He patched

237

her wounds, and they walked the last bit up the mountain together with the donkey and medicines."

"She made it here?" Aviva picked up the empty laundry basket and tucked it beside her door.

"That's right. They made it up the mountain, travelling at night in the dark. She was healed while the physician got to work with the healers here. Once she healed enough, she started patrolling the paths to the school, making sure the sick made it for treatment. He liked her spirit and giving nature, and the Phoenix bonded with her."

"And that let him drive the sickness away?" She perched on the edge of her bed, her fingers gripping the blanket.

I chuckled. "Yes, with his bond restored, he helped the physicians create a cure and drive the sickness from the land. He could fly over the valleys and banish the illness from the plants himself, once bonded again."

"That must have taken time. How many people died?"

"Yes, it took time, sadly, and several people died who shouldn't have. Still, they got the medicine out to the villages, and he healed the plants they ate. Anyone who got medicine lived, and they made enough for everyone who needed it, offering it for free."

"Well, at least they got it in the end. It's still sad."

"Yes, it is. You can't save everyone, no matter how hard you try. We help who we can, though."

She smiled. "I can do that."

I chuckled. "I know."

***

She stepped into the courtyard and slid the wooden curtain closed. Aviva turned and paused. Master Denneth stood in the middle, waiting like usual, with Frewin beside him. Three masters stood nearby. Master Denneth nodded to the spot in front of him. She walked over, her eyes down at Master Denneth's feet.

"It's time. You're ready to be ranked into our system officially."

She lifted her head slowly and stared at Master Denneth with her mouth open.

I nudged her. "Close your mouth and say yes, Master."

"Yes, Master," she whispered.

Master Denneth reached a hand to her shoulder. "Do not worry. We know you've never had a ranking, so we will guide you through it. Follow our commands, just like you would during a lesson. Afterwards, the masters will have a few questions for you. Answer as well as you can. That's all you have to do."

"Yes, Master." Her legs trembled and her face paled.

"You have five minutes to warm up and prepare. Do so however you feel you need." Master Denneth stepped back. "Begin now."

"Start with a minute of animals. That always helps you focus and relax. You can do this." I moved behind her and gave her room.

She stood tall and quiet, slowing her breathing. Aviva stretched up, hands up like tiger claws, and she turned and crouched. I smiled, watching her flow through the animal inspired movements, including bear and deer, and my favourite, the crane. I didn't see any sign of soreness anymore. Master Tula had only recently given her permission to train harder again, and she was doing well.

"Are you ready to begin?"

She stood still, facing Master Denneth. "Yes, Master?"

Master Denneth smiled. "First form. Begin when you are ready and go at your own pace."

I felt jittery, like tiny dragons flew around in my stomach. I leaned against the wall and watched her, still as a statue. She bowed, showing near perfect form. In a flash, Aviva struck out and turned, blocking as she stepped. She kicked and turned, struck and moved. I had to grin at her technique. She'd thrived in the private sessions with Master Denneth and going slowly helped her perfect her form while she healed.

"Now, the second form I taught you," Master Denneth called, as she settled back into a quiet position.

Aviva bowed. She kicked out and landed, fist crashing down on her imaginary opponent. She shifted and struck with her knife hand, turned and kicked, struck again. I let myself slide down the wall and watch.

"Pick any form from your past and show it," Master Denneth requested.

She stared at him with wide eyes. He smiled and nodded.

"Yes, Master," she whispered.

Which one would she choose? Any would let her show them what she could do. She raised her arms slowly, circling around and turning. I grinned. She loved this form, a dynamic one that included both fast and slow movements.

She reached and turned, blocked and struck, all fluid and slow. Aviva kicked out quickly, stepped and kicked again, and spun and kicked without stepping down between. Her balance was strong, and her belly no longer ached, or that would have hurt. That's my girl.

"Here." Master Denneth nodded to Frewin, when she was still again.

Frewin handed her a wooden practice sword. She took it in her hand. It was lighter than her practice sword. I could tell by the way she took a few practice swings. Could she adapt? I smiled. Of course she could. She held the sword behind her arm like I taught and looked up at Master Denneth.

"Show them the sword form." Master Denneth smiled and stepped back.

Her fingers tightened around her sword and her shoulders tensed. Come on, girl, relax and do this. Just show them.

"Yes, Master."

She closed her eyes and settled. Those little dragons were having a mighty battle in my belly, smashing into each other and colliding with my insides. Come on, girl, relax. You got this. Her fingers loosened on the blade, and she lifted her arms.

Aviva turned and slashed, letting the sword tip swing through the air. She changed grips and moved the sword to her right hand, reaching out with a downward slash. I watched her crouch and come up, looking for any hint she was still sore. She rose, sword tip leading, and thrust towards her opponent.

That's it, girl, swing and sweep. Leap and stab. Doing great. This was newer to her than the bare hand forms, and she didn't get as much practice while she was healing, but I was still so proud of her. She grinned as she spun three times, sword whipping around her.

I'll need to correct that one move later, though. Her sword should come further across her body. Otherwise, she was doing great. She shifted the sword back into her left hand and slowed, settling with it behind her arm again.

"Excellent." Master Denneth stepped forward. "Frewin will take the sword. Sit and wait."

Aviva placed the sword in Frewin's open hands and sank to the stone, crossing her legs. "Kai?" she whispered.

I sped over and sat with her. "You did great. They'll discuss your progress and skill and decide what rank they should award you."

Her fingers twisted her sash, fidgeting with the tip. She stared down into her lap.

"Breathe. You're fine. You've worked hard, harder than most students here. They know that. Besides, how well do you know those masters?"

Aviva shook her head. "I don't. That one is a healer, though."

I chuckled. "Healers also defend the vulnerable. Every one of them can fight, and they're all masters. Those three will assess you solely on what they saw today."

"Aviva, rise." Master Denneth approached with the masters.

She stared up at them. Aviva put a shaky hand on the ground and pressed herself up. She gripped the bottom of her tunic.

"Aviva, apprentice to Master Denneth, we have awarded you with the rank of intermediate apprentice. Your new clothes and sash will be delivered to your room today." The healer smiled at her.

She stood openmouthed, staring blankly. Her eyes flicked to Master Denneth.

"You say thank you, Master Nima." Master Denneth nodded at the healer.

"Thank you, Master Nima." She bowed.

"Study hard, young one. Your progress is remarkable." A burly master nodded to her.

"Thank you." She bowed to him and the remaining master.

The masters left the courtyard, tall and graceful and silent.

Aviva stared at the stone floor, her eyes distant and unfocused. After a long moment, she looked up again. "Thank you, Master. Thank you, Teacher." Her voice shook. She bowed to Master Denneth and Frewin.

"You work hard, even training on your rest days." Master Denneth rested his hand on her shoulder. "Would you like to spend some time in meditation in your room? Let it all sink in. You just jumped multiple ranks, after all."

"Yes, Master. Thank you both."

"I've learned as much teaching you as you've learned from me." Frewin bowed. "You put the work in and practiced. You earned it."

"Come rest," I suggested. "You're now an apprentice fully, in rank and status."

She glanced around the courtyard again, her gaze not landing on anything in particular. Master Denneth wrapped his arm around her shoulders and guided her from the training yard. I followed them back to the Masters' Hall. She walked beside him, letting him lead. My insides felt floaty now.

"Hey, are you okay?" Garin stepped from his room as we came back, and he met her eyes.

Aviva looked up, still stunned. She nodded.

CHAPTER 20

CELEBRATE

"She has achieved a rank in the school," Master Denneth explained. He smiled.

"Congratulations." Garin bowed.

"Thanks." She smiled.

"Are you going to celebrate? You have to celebrate."

Her smile twisted. My chest felt tight.

"I don't have many friends to celebrate with," she whispered.

"I'll be there, and I know a few other apprentices who like and respect you, too. Let me know what you decide." Garin bowed.

Aviva nodded, her gaze on her shoes.

"Come, child. A lot has happened recently, and you've come so far. Let your body, mind, and emotions rest for once." Master Denneth opened her door for her.

She stepped into her room and looked around. More pictures lined the walls, more scrolls sat on her desk, and thicker blankets sat folded on the end of her bed. She kicked her shoes off and sank onto her meditation cushion.

Master Denneth kneeled in front of her. "Garin is right. When a student becomes an apprentice officially, we usually have a celebration. Would you like me to arrange it?"

Aviva nodded. "Thank you, Master." A tear rolled down her cheek.

"What's that all about?" Master Denneth wiped the tear away.

She shook her head. "So much has happened."

"I know it hasn't always been easy for you, and you've had to overcome obstacles no other student has. You earned it, though. I've never seen anyone so persistent, or who worked so hard as a student." He took her hand and gave it a light squeeze.

She nodded and closed her eyes. I felt the tightness in my throat, the pit in my stomach, the urge to cry despite her smile. Aviva was one of us now, but would she ever feel like it? She's been alone for so long; did she know how to feel accepted? Master Denneth went into his own room, closing the connecting door behind him.

I sat with her as she fell asleep, her back to the wall. Her emotions calmed and her body relaxed. This girl needed more rest. Was I pushing her to train too fast? Could I stop her from pushing on if I wanted to? I heard Master Denneth leave his room.

I slipped into his room and glanced at his desk. He had a list of people to invite to the celebration for her, partially written. I added a few names to the bottom, some boys she'd been practicing with on her free days. They liked her and treated her well, and he probably didn't know about them.

Her new clothing sat folded and piled on his bed, a pale cream for apprentices, with a border of dark green. Her new belts and sashes were dark blue. She would be a great warrior one day.

She was going to sleep for a while. I snuck into the hallway and headed for the empty Grandmaster's room. His belongings were packed in a trunk, waiting for the next grandmaster to go through. The book and sword sat behind the hidden panel, untouched.

This was my first chance to unwind and go for a stroll in a long time. I headed out into the sunlight to recharge. Young students practiced the basics in the corner of the main courtyard, Frewin and another apprentice helping them. Students working in the kitchens carried baskets of food from the storage rooms. The sun dispelled the mist, warming us all on this cool fall day. I took a moment to enjoy the fresh mountain air.

I headed back to her room to check on her. As I came around the corner, Master Denneth and Garin were talking. They nodded to each other and went their separate ways, Master Denneth to his room, and Garin towards the Main Hall.

I slipped into her room. She was still on her cushion, her head hanging at an odd angle to the side. She'd wake up stiff if she stayed there. The connecting door opened, and Master Denneth looked in on her. He smiled and shook his head. Master Denneth walked over, scooped her up, and lay her on the bed. He draped a blanket over her and turned her lamps down before closing the door behind him.

With the meditation cushion free, I relaxed on the padding and waited. She slept another hour before Master Denneth came back. He kneeled beside her bed.

"Aviva, wake up." He touched her shoulder.

She curled up, mumbling something about a sword.

"Come on. It's supper time." He pressed on her shoulder, rolling her onto her back.

"Supper?" She rubbed her eyes. Aviva blinked up at him.

"You don't want to miss this one. Wash up and we'll go."
Master Denneth rose and stepped back.

She stretched and shifted to her feet, slow and sleepy.
Master Denneth returned to his room, and we heard the
water splashing into his basin. She moved to her washstand
and poured the water in, lifting the glass pitcher with ease
again. She washed her face and hands and said the prayer,
reading it from the carved wood now. Once she was dry,
she joined Master Denneth in the hallway.

"Garin, good timing," Master Denneth greeted.

"I'm ready, Master Denneth. I wouldn't miss this." Garin
smiled at Aviva.

"Miss what? Supper?" She raised an eyebrow.

They shared a look and chuckled. I'd never talked to her
about this. She had no idea what was about to happen.

"This way." Master Denneth led her to the side door.

"Where are we going? Aren't these only the training
yards?"

"You'll see." Master Denneth smiled and kept walking.

He stopped at the far training yard and stepped inside. She
raised her eyebrow but followed. Garin walked behind her.
She froze in the doorway, wide eyes staring at everything.

"Congratulations!"

"Breathe," I whispered, beside her like always.

Masters, apprentices, and a few students gathered around some tables, all waiting for her. Paper lanterns hung from cord strung across the courtyard, giving the area a colourful glow in the fading sunlight. Streamers floated on the breeze, hanging from the cords between lanterns. A table stood along one wall, with wrapped packages on it.

"Wow." She took a slow step.

"Come in and say hello to everyone. They're here to celebrate with you." Master Denneth took her hand and led her to the group.

"Well done, you." Master Ninden wrapped her in a tight hug. "You've come so far."

She wriggled her arms free and hugged him back. "Thank you."

Eron and Frewin stepped over.

She grinned at them. "It's good to see you both."

"Congratulations." Eron bowed.

Aviva bowed back. "Thank you."

"You did great. You're one of my hardest working students." Frewin hugged her from the side, an arm around her shoulders.

"Come. Everyone will want a word at some point, and we'd all like to eat." Master Denneth led her to one chair and pulled it out for her.

Three tables had been brought out and set in a u-shape, with her at the place of honour. Master Denneth said the blessing, and carts of food rolled out for everyone. Garin set a massive pot of rice and vegetables down near her and gave her a smile. All her favourite foods were here, even those little oranges that burst of sweetness.

The sun disappeared, and we ate by lantern-light, talking and laughing and sharing stories. I felt that warm glow inside. It matched her smile, though I occasionally noticed her brush a tear away with her sleeve. Didn't she realize how many friends she had here? Nobody cared as the night grew cool, everyone wrapped up in their warmer cloaks.

"Here. Don't get cold." Master Denneth retrieved her cloak from a table and wrapped it around her shoulders.

"Thank you, Master."

"How about we all do a pattern together to warm up?" Frewin suggested.

"That's a wonderful idea," Master Faldor agreed. "How about it, boys?"

The young boys Aviva sometimes worked with stared up at him wide-eyed. Did I remember those days, when masters seemed distant, and we were in awe of them? Did I ever experience those days? It was so long ago now.

Aviva stood and moved to the open area. "That sounds fun."

Everyone stood, leaving their empty plates behind. What a sight, the students and masters all together, different heights, wearing different colours, and moving as one. Since we just ate, Master Denneth called the moves slowly, and we went at half speed, moving in unison.

She grinned and stood still afterwards, staring up at the lanterns.

Master Denneth stood beside her, a hand on her shoulder. "Thank you, everyone, for making Aviva's ranking ceremony memorable, and for joining us tonight. Young ones, you're returning after curfew, so be quiet and do not disturb your bunkmates. My apprentice has had a busy day and needs to go to bed. Now is a good time to say goodnight."

The youngest said goodnight to her first. I waited, staying back and giving her space. She seemed a little younger when interacting with them, more like a kid herself. Had she missed out on a proper childhood? Despite her ability to interact so smoothly with the Masters, did she still have a strong inner child inside?

The apprentices said goodnight next, followed by the masters. It must have been a good quarter bell before everyone congratulated her one last time and said goodnight. The bells didn't ring this late, so I wasn't sure, but even I felt tired when it was finally just us left.

"We'll bring your gifts to your room for you." Master Denneth nodded at the table of wrapped boxes. Masters were placing them in baskets. "Small tokens from us all to celebrate with you. You can open them in the morning if you want to sleep right away. Tomorrow is a day off, so rest and enjoy it. You can even sleep in. I'll take care of the water."

"Thank you, Master." She leaned against his side; her eyes closed. "Thank you for everything."

He steered her through the archway and down the stone walled corridor. "You've been an excellent apprentice. Attentive, hardworking, you learn quickly and seldom need to be told things twice, and you persevere. I'm so proud of you."

Tears streamed down her cheeks. She wiped them away.

Master Denneth slid her door open for her. "Get some rest. You earned it. Sleep well." He closed the door behind her.

She crossed her room and dropped onto her bed, not even changing into night clothes. "Kai?"

"Yes?" I settled on the cushion, my favourite spot in her room.

"Thank you, too." Her voice was muffled against the pillow.

"You're welcome. Now get some sleep. We have training tomorrow."

She yawned wide into her elbow. "Master said I have the day off."

"We still have work to do. Don't you want to learn more in your favourite style?"

Aviva rolled and went still. I detected a tiny snore as she snuggled under her covers. Tomorrow, I chuckled to myself. She needs rest, too.

***

Master Denneth slid the door open and entered, a bowl of fruit and some bread in his hands. He set them on the desk and pushed the lever up. The sunlight streamed through the open slats, shining on her face. He backed out slowly, smiling at her huddled under her blankets.

She slept a few more minutes before she stretched and rolled. The blanket shifted and sunlight shone right over her eyes. Aviva blinked sleepily before sitting up and looking around. Her gaze landed on her desk, where her breakfast sat beside her pile of presents.

"Good morning, sleepy. Have something to eat."

She wandered into the bathroom. I heard water splashing. Moments later, she was back; her face washed, and her hair brushed. Aviva moved to her washstand and blinked. Right, Master Denneth got the water this morning.

"What time is it?" She poured the water into her basin.

"You slept an extra hour."

She smiled. I waited as she washed and said her blessing. Some students might skip the ceremony, but I wasn't surprised she didn't. Aviva sat at her desk and pulled her fruit closer.

"He brought me breakfast?"

"He sure did. You can thank him later. Eat, and we can open the presents."

She scooped up some berries and yogurt. He even drizzled a little honey on them for her. Aviva smiled and closed her eyes, savouring the treat.

"How do you feel? You've been through a lot now." I shifted to her bed, where I could see her desk better.

She sighed. "I know. Maybe I'm finally settling in? With Merek gone, I feel relaxed now. All those people there last night. I didn't expect to see them like that."

"People who like you and came to celebrate with you. Sure, the youngest might also have been excited about staying up late and eating dessert and cake, but they also like you."

She giggled, every bit the young girl I caught glimpses of when with the younger boys. Aviva tore her roll apart and chewed a piece. "Did Master invite them all?"

"It was a joint effort between him and your closest friends."

Aviva stared at the packages as she ate. I took a moment to look closer at her and really tune into her. She had circles under her eyes, faint, but there. Inside, she was excited, but I felt something else. It was in how she picked at her food. She needed a full rest day. This girl was tired.

"Is it normal to receive presents?"

"It is when someone first officially becomes an apprentice. Now, most people pass their regular rankings and are chosen and accepted in a special ceremony before the entire school, but you came here on special invitation instead."

She reached out and touched a box, her fingers brushing over the paper. "It's been so long since I've had a present."

"Wash your hands and let's see what they gave you."

She set her bowl aside and wandered into her bathroom. I heard the water as she washed the fruit juices from her fingers, and the towel sliding on the bar as she dried herself. Aviva appeared in the doorway, staring at the gifts.

"Open them, Silly."

She took a slow step, her eyes on the pile.

"You don't need to stalk them. They won't run away," I teased.

CHAPTER 21

Rest Is Important, Too

A viva grinned and shook her head. She sank into her chair and reached shaking hands to the closest gift. Her fingers trembled as she tore the paper away, revealing a carved wooden box, stained and shining. An envelope fell into her lap.

She set the box down and picked up the envelope. Aviva unfolded the parchment and stared at it. "Help, Kai?"

I looked over her shoulder.

"For a friend," she read aloud. "From Master Ninden, right?"

"That's right. You're not used to seeing their names, are you?"

She shook her head. Aviva set the parchment aside and picked up the box. Tiny pieces of dark and light wood created a mosaic set into the lid. It was the waterfall and

259

trees on this very mountain. She flipped the delicate little catch and lifted the lid.

I almost gasped with her. Sitting inside on a velvet cloth, a polished carved necklace of a wooden bird stared up at her, its fiery feathers glittering with little metal flecks embedded in the polish. She picked up the bird and held it up in front of her drawing of the Phoenix. It was nearly a perfect match.

"Wow. That's an amazing coincidence."

I watched the little bird swing from the chain of corded wooden beads. I smiled. How young and innocent. "Why don't you put it on?"

She slipped the wooden beads around her neck. The carved bird hung just below her collarbones, under her tunic. Aviva touched the bird through the cloth and smiled. "It's warm against my skin."

"Open the next one."

She picked up a long and flat package from Master Denneth. When she peeled the wrapper off, she had another carved box in her hands, the width of her hands and about a foot long. Aviva popped the catch and opened the box.

"Oh, my."

"That's going to be fun." I peered over her shoulder.

She picked up the paintbrushes in her hands and ran a finger lightly along the bristles. Bottles of ink were lined up along the back of the box in a row, black and gold and red and blue and more.

"Those are all made with plants from this very mountain, and are highly sought after for their quality," I explained.

"It's wonderful." She carefully set the brushes back in their slot. "I can't wait to try it."

"This one is from Master Faldor. I'll bet you'll love it, too."

Aviva grinned and picked up the heavy package. "I bet it's books." Her eyes shone in the lamplight. Her grin was wide with delight.

She tore the wrapper off and added it to the growing pile of paper. Her eyes widened as she saw the cover of the top book. Aviva spread the books on her desk and pressed her hand to her heart. I couldn't read some of them, but I smiled as she wiped a tear away.

Two books were storybooks in our language, longer than what she'd been reading, but still within her abilities. The other books were brightly illustrated and colourful, not our style at all. She picked one up and opened it, reading the first few pages with a speed I'd never seen before.

She closed the book and held it to her heart. "I haven't read this in ages."

"What is it?" The picture on the front was of a forest, but with different trees than what we had here. A girl faced the reader, her hand raised, with a ball of light shining above it. Her other hand held a sword, shining in the imaginary sunlight. She wore clothing like I'd never seen before, covered partly by a long cloak. A golden pony stood next to her, staring off into the distance.

"It's a story I told him about. He asked me about things I've read and enjoyed. We talked all meal about books one day, back when I was new. This was one of the books I told him about." She placed the book on her desk and piled the others with it.

"He loves it when people read. He likes your thirst for knowledge and stories."

Aviva went through the rest of the pile with delight. Master Tula and Eron got her more sweets and some teas she enjoyed while healing. They even gave her a scroll about the teas from around the country, and any medicinal or health benefits each had. She pored over the scroll for a few minutes, devouring every word she could.

"I'll help you read it fully later, if you like."

"Thanks, Kai."

Garin and Frewin got her training tools, including weights she could wrap around her wrists and ankles, and sand filled bags to squeeze and increase her grip strength. Other people gave her salves for sore muscles, meditation tools like candles and a thin cushion for extra padding, and some spark sticks.

Master Denneth knocked on the connecting door and waited before sliding the door open.

She set a bottle of liniment down and dashed over, wrapping her arms around him in a tight hug. "Thank you, Master. Thank you so much."

He stood frozen, his eyes barely blinking, before rubbing her back as he hugged her. "You work hard. You deserve some things to help you relax and enjoy life, too."

She let go and backed up a step. "Thank you for breakfast, too. I haven't slept like that in ages."

"Make the most of those days. None of us get them often. Now, it's a rest day. Have you any plans?"

She opened her mouth and stood there; head cocked to the side. She closed her mouth again.

He laughed. "Perfect. It's good to do nothing, sometimes. Everything in balance. Too much training is bad for the body, and so is too much sitting. You work hard, so enjoy doing nothing."

Master Denneth turned and left, sliding the door closed behind him.

She took slow steps back to her bed and sat with her eyes on the pile of gifts. "Wow."

I sank to the mattress beside her. "You've worked really hard. Rest. This afternoon we'll go for a walk or something. There are still new things for you to discover."

***

I perched on a rock and looked down the mountain. The school spread out before me. Everything was quiet, only the chirping of birds and the ever-present crash of the waterfall to keep me company. The forest was vital and healthy, and there was still no sign of that feeling from a while ago. She was almost ready to come up this way. Almost.

She'd be done her lunch any time now. I sped back down, enjoying the breeze on my face. I was certain she'd be safe in the library all morning, so I finally came up here to bask in the sacred part of the forest. Master Faldor even gave her a book about the Phoenix and the sacred pool. I sat by that very pool this morning, meditating.

She was in the hallway just outside her room, her hand on her door.

"Ready to go? We'll walk slow, since you just ate."

She tilted her head and tapped her fingers against the door. "Sure."

"We'll go out the back gate and into the upper forest."

She weaved among the masters and apprentices to the side door, slipping among them like a ghost. Instead of walking towards the training yards, she walked to the outer wall and around the back of the buildings to the back gate.

"What are we doing today?" Aviva opened the gate and stepped through.

"We're going to enjoy the beauty of nature."

She pressed her hand to her mouth, covering her laugh. "Okay, what are we really doing?"

I chuckled. "Have I lied to you yet?"

Her brow wrinkled. "Not that I know of." Aviva headed up the path leading to the waterfall.

"I love your faith in me. Remember the path with the little wooden bridge over the river?"

She smiled and her step quickened. "Sure do." Last time, she stared down at the little fish in the stream for nearly an hour, laying sprawled across the bridge.

"That's where we're going."

Aviva marched up the path, passing under the hanging branches with ease. "What are we doing there?"

"We'll enjoy nature, just like I said. Quiet meditation lessons, just the two of us. Oh, and the mountain. I guess that's the three of us."

She walked along the rising path, her fingers brushing over the trunk of a tree occasionally. Aviva wrapped her cloak closer about her, warding off the thickening mist in the cool autumn air. The little bridge came into view, and she darted ahead to it.

Aviva kneeled on the smooth boards and peered over the edge. Little fish swam in the strong current. Frogs and tiny insects played in the pools at the edge of the stream, protected by the rocks that created calm areas. Algae and plants clung to the rocks and soil. Fish swam up and grabbed a mouthful of algae and insects, before darting back into the current again, tiny flashes of silver in the clear water.

"Sit with legs crossed or stacked. If you can relax your mind, you can keep your eyes open. Otherwise, close them. Ready?" I settled beside her on the bridge.

She straightened up and shifted to her backside; her legs crossed in front of her. "Ready."

"Now, breathe slow and deep, but relax and let it happen. Don't force it. See if you can feel the fish. Don't seek them, just let their spirit touch yours."

She looked down at the water, her eyes not fully focused. "Is this like a master feeling spirits?"

"Yes, this is how they start, too. Now be quiet and focus."

Aviva sat quietly for a few moments. "I only feel you. You're like a blinding light beside me, and you overwhelm everything around me."

"Really?"

She blinked and rubbed her eyes. "Really. Why?"

"I've trained a lot. That could be it." Well, that was all he was sharing just now. She wasn't ready for the full truth. "Just meditate quietly and feel what you feel. We'll go back soon."

***

"Are you ready?" Master Tula smiled; his eyebrow raised.

"Uh, maybe? Sure. I guess?"

He laughed. "It's not that scary. Well, usually, anyway. We won't be helping with anything you're not ready for. Come. People need help."

"You got this. I'm here. Besides, you might find this useful in the future, too." I brushed my energy against hers, sending her warmth.

"Follow me." Master Tula turned and led her to a storage room.

She hustled to keep up, staying right behind him. Aviva stared up at all the shelves full of baskets, bottles, and jars. Sheets and bandages sat folded and stacked neatly on some, beside simple tunics and pants. Some jars held cloths and bandages, soaked in oil and herbs. She and Eron made some the other day, and I saw her handwriting on a few jars.

Master Tula pulled rolls of bandages from two separate baskets. He held them out for her to look at. "See how these are different?"

"Yes, this one is tightly woven, and this one is a loose weave. They're both bandages, though, right?" She blinked up at him.

"Right. You can touch them. Hold them. They'll be boiled and sterilized soon. That's what this symbol means." Master Tula pointed to a symbol on the baskets.

She stepped closer and scrutinized the symbol. Aviva took the bandages and ran her fingers over them. "The ones in the paper wrappers have been sterilized?" She nodded to stacks of paper packages beside the baskets.

"That's right. Can you think why there might be two separate types of bandages?"

She chewed lightly on her lip and scrunched up her nose. Aviva gazed down at the bandages in her hands. "Well, you used these when I was still bleeding." She held up the tightly woven roll. "You switched to these later. They're less absorbent but let more air through."

Master Tula beamed at her. "That's right. We also used the oil-soaked cloths over your wounds, and we use them over burns, always under the tightly woven bandages. Anything we want to keep moist and protected, use the tight ones. Anything you want to breathe well, like wounds in later stages of healing, or damp skin issues, we use those." He nodded at the loosely woven bandages. "Ready to learn to use them for real?"

She handed him the bandages, and he tucked them back in the baskets. "Okay. What if I mess up?"

"I expect you will mess up. That's part of learning, and we all make mistakes when we start. We get better and keep trying, and over time we master a skill. Grab a basket." He waved his hand toward a stack of baskets beside the door. "We need a few things before we go."

She retrieved the reed basket and held it against her body. Master Tula selected some paper wrapped bandages, and some rolled bandages and set them in the basket. He chose a jar of oiled cloths and added it as well. Finally, a couple of packages that made a metallic clink joined the other supplies in the basket.

"That should do it. Now, let's go help people feel better. Is it too heavy?"

She grinned. "Nope. I've been training hard and being careful. I can lift more now with no problem."

Master Tula took something cloth from the shelf and unfolded it, holding it up in front of her. He shook his head and selected another one. "Maybe these? Those were way too long. Try it on over your clothes."

Aviva set the basket down and took the healer's robes from him. She wriggled under it and threaded her arms up through the sleeves. He helped ease the neck opening over her head.

"Those will do nicely. Come with me."

He swept from the room, his robes floating out behind him. She picked up the basket and followed, jogging to catch up. Master Tula disappeared into the front treatment room. I smiled and stayed with her. She wouldn't see anything too horrifying in this room.

I settled in the corner as she followed him along the room. A man sat on a bench against one wall, near to the door. He held his hand to his chest. The other wall was lined with beds, and a few were occupied.

Master Tula kneeled in front of the man. "You can set the basket on the bench here for me, thank you." He nodded to a spot beside the man. "Aviva, this is Siko. Siko, she's starting her first shift in the infirmary with me, and she'll be helping me today." He reached for the man's hand.

Siko held his hand out for Master Tula, the angry red burn covering most of his palm. Aviva paled, but stayed steady.

"Breathe," I reminded her. "You're fine." I felt a burst of fear, a tightness in my chest. Was she afraid of fire? Wait, during the revolution, they burned the palace to the ground. Was she there for that? I'd have to ask later. If she's afraid of fire, I needed to know.

Master Tula examined the damaged skin, turning Siko's hand slightly to see his swollen fingers. "What happened?"

"My apprentice set metal down when it was still hot, on the bench for cold metal only. It wasn't glowing anymore, and I picked it up. Foolish boy. Foolish me." Siko scowled at his hand. "Is the damage permanent?"

"I doubt it. You got here quickly. If you left it, it might be. Aviva, this is a burn, so what do we want first?" Master Tula looked at her, a slight smile on his face.

She pointed at the jar. "The lavender and herbs will heal the skin and ease the pain, and the oil will keep the skin from drying out and tightening."

"That's right. I'll hold his hand still. Use those tongs and lay bandages over the burn. It's okay if they overlap. We want two layers everywhere. Make sure you get it between his fingers." Master Tula nodded to the basket. "It's the thin package. Try not to touch the thin ends of the tongs, as they're clean. You can touch the thicker part."

Her hand shook as she unwrapped the paper from the tongs. Aviva gripped the thicker handles. She unscrewed the jar and fished for a bandage with the tongs.

"Don't worry about the oil dripping on things. It happens. That's why we wear the robes."

She smiled and let her breath out. Her hand steadied.

"I remember the first time I picked up hot metal with tongs." Siko stared out the window opposite him, his eyes distant and misty. "I was so scared I'd disappoint my Master. Hammer metal wrong and you can ruin it, you know."

"Did you do okay?" Her voice was quiet and steady. She draped a bandage over his palm, moving it with the tongs.

Siko laughed, his head back against the wall. "No, but I learned and got better. I left the metal in the fire too long and damaged it, right in the middle of the bar. He knew I would, but it's all part of learning."

She slipped a bandage between his fingers, laying it partly over his palm. "He wasn't mad?"

"He yelled, but he yells when he's happy, too, so that wasn't new. No, he ruined many bars when he learned, back when he was but a lad. He was the finest blacksmith in the valleys before he died, so he learned his lesson well." He looked down at his hand. "That's magic stuff. Doesn't even hurt where the bandages are now."

She kneeled straighter, her hand steadier. She even had that slight smile she got when she feels confident with a new skill. I had to admit, Master Tula chose an excellent first patient for her. Blacksmiths were used to apprentices and new learners and understood what it felt like.

"Excellent. One more piece between those longer fingers, and a second layer now." Master Tula nodded.

"Do you know blacksmith Harrid?" Aviva covered the last of the red skin between his fingers.

Siko threw his head back and laughed. "We were apprentices together. He took after me old master and stayed at the forge when the old man died. You know him?"

She ducked her head and hid her smile. "He yelled at everyone else, just like your master, but never at me. He taught me to polish weapons and oil tools. How did you end up in another village, if that was your master's forge?"

"We both grew up in that village with our Master. Harrid finished his apprenticeship first, so he stayed on and got the forge. I left for another village when I finished my apprenticeship, as they needed a blacksmith."

Aviva finished the second layer of oiled bandages and glanced at Master Tula.

"How does the hand feel now?" Master Tula looked carefully between his fingers, searching for any uncovered burn, and found nothing.

"The ache is gone."

"The skin is fragile, so I will wrap it this time. Pay attention, Aviva. I'll talk you through it, and you'll do one on someone else."

She nodded and moved closer, watching like a hawk as he picked up the rolled bandage.

CHAPTER 22

GONE!

"Ugh." Aviva moved away from the doors, into the sun.

"You did really well. Your bandaging is smooth, which is more important than being fast right now." I moved beside her into the bright light, soaking in the warmth.

She closed her eyes and smiled; her face turned to the sun. "How can people find so many unique ways to injure themselves?"

"People are creative. Sometimes they channel that into making works of art or useful things, and other times they suffer for it. You helped ease that pain, and that's a spiritually powerful thing to do."

"What?" She blinked, her gaze dropping to the Masters' Hall doors.

"Every time we help someone, we strengthen our own spirit. We're helping ease suffering, or we're adding to it, with each action we choose."

"What if I do nothing?" She stretched her arms up high overhead.

"You're still contributing to suffering, by not helping ease it, if you could. People with powerful spirits work hard, either to help or hinder."

Aviva dropped her palms to the stone, stretching her back and legs out. "Not all spirits are good?"

I laughed. "Are all people good?"

She cocked her head to the side and smiled. "I guess not. People are just people, mostly, a mix of selfish and helpful."

Blackness clouded my vision. My chest felt squeezed. My stomach rolled and flipped. "It's in danger. Get moving."

"Where? What is?"

My vision cleared, and I felt less unsteady. "Grandmaster's room." I flew across the courtyard. "Hurry."

Aviva dashed across the courtyard, dodging Master Foril.

"Come back here, now!"

She was right behind me as we charged into the Masters' Hall. I pelted down the corridor to the back corner, the still empty Grandmaster's room.

"Arg." I hurled myself at the intruder.

He flew back into the wall. My eyes fixed on the sword in his hands. I smashed into him, hit after hit. He grunted and curled up. Where was she? She was right behind me at the doors. He staggered to his feet, an arm over his head.

She appeared in the door, casting a shadow across the room.

"Stop him," I growled.

She raised her hands and shifted, turning to her fighting stance. He charged at her. She spun low and kicked his ankle. CRACK! He leapt over her and charged through the door, down the hall, and out of sight. What? How's that possible? I heard her snap his bone.

The secret panel stood open, the compartment empty. "No. Not now. Not after all this time."

She stepped in front of the hidden space and touched the sword stand. "Now what?"

"We go after him. Quickly now." I raced into the hallway.

She followed me as fast as her legs could carry her. He shouldn't get far on a badly injured ankle. He shouldn't be running at all, though. We reached the first intersection. No sign of him anywhere. He'll need to leave through a gate. There's no way he can climb the wall like that.

"He'll head into the forest. Let's get outside and start looking." I sped towards the main doors.

We darted into the sun.

"Ask the watchmen at the gates if they saw him leave. I'll start looking ahead."

She ran to the main gate. I headed to the seldom used side gate, behind the Students' Hall. The heavy and thick wood door stood ajar. Footprints led into the trees, one deeper than the other. He was limping. How was he still moving?

Aviva raced around the wall and towards me.

"Learn anything?"

She looked down at the footprints as she came to a stop. "Someone saw a shadowy figure run into the trees here. We follow?"

"We follow. First, we grab a few things."

"How many people know about this gate?" She scanned the ground, seeing only the fresh footprints.

"Only people who live here, usually."

"It's an inside job?" She tilted her head and peered back through the gate at the Students' Hall beyond.

"A what?"

"Someone from the school did it?"

"It looks that way. Now, he has a sword. Get yours. Swiftly, now."

We snuck back through the gate and around the walls, back to the Masters' Hall.

"Leave a note. Tell Master Denneth you're helping a friend and will be back as soon as you can. It's true, and an honourable reason to leave on a moment's notice."

Her clothing was damp with sweat, and she was breathing hard as she slid her door open. She knocked and opened Master Denneth's door, but he was elsewhere, as expected. I waited as she scratched out a quick note for him.

Master,

A friend needs help. Be back soon. Thank you.

Aviva

She left the paper in the middle of his desk, under a paperweight. Aviva slid his door closed and grabbed her sword from the corner.

"Leave that sword. It's dull. We'll get a sharp one from the armoury. Get your cloak and let's go. Don't get chilled. Don't forget boots. They'll support your ankles better on the uneven ground."

She set her sword on her bed and slipped her boots on. Aviva swung her cloak on and met me at the door. "Where's the Auxiliary Armoury?"

"This way." I sped from the room and down the halls.

Her feet made little noise as she ran behind me. We ran through the back passages to a guard tower in the corner of the main wall. It would be empty. A single watchman up above would look out, not down.

"In here and be quiet."

She slipped through the door and into the dim stone room, the only light from narrow slits in the walls. They lined the walls with weapon racks, all sharp and battle ready, oiled and cared for.

"One of these. Try this one." I stood beside some worn scabbards holding sturdy swords. The hilts were plain, but the blades were strong, lasting many centuries with care.

She pulled the sword from the rack and drew it with a metallic hiss. Aviva swung it close to her, testing the weight in the cramped room.

"That'll do nicely. Let's go. We're leaving your sneaky way."

She darted back out, staying in the shadows from the stone walls. We slipped behind the Main Hall and back of the kitchens. Under the untended guard tower, she bounced up the walls, using the corners to push up. Aviva dropped to the other side into the soft earth below.

"You do that too easily." I chuckled. "Now, let's go find him."

She dashed into the trees and towards the footprints. "The tracks?"

"Partly. I'm tied to the book and sword, and I can feel them, too. If he's headed where I think, we'll catch up before it's dark, if we don't catch him sooner."

Aviva jogged over the damp ground. She spied the footsteps and stopped. "Kai, what about these?"

I frowned. More footsteps, at least four more men, were travelling with him now. "Okay, we'll be even more careful now."

"He is injured, though. Look at the uneven steps, and he's putting more weight on this side of his left foot." She followed the tracks up the hill.

"Where did you learn to track?"

"I didn't, but it's common sense, right? I read a scroll about it with Master Faldor's help. The fact his footprints are on top means he's coming after them. Otherwise, their tracks would cover his."

"Right. Keep moving. What else can you tell me about his track?" I peered through the trees ahead, trying to feel our surroundings.

"His boots have no tread or heel. They're completely flat."

"Good. What does that tell us?"

She shook her head, still following the tracks through the trees. "I have no idea."

"You might not know this, because it's unique to here. Only one group in history used that type of boot. The pointy toe is reinforced. See the deeper impression it leaves?"

She kneeled and looked closely, her face near the ground. "Here?"

"That's it. They can dig that into the cracks of walls or rock and climb with it."

Her clothes rustled softly as she brushed the dirt from her knees. Aviva picked up the pace again. "Do they sneak places a lot?"

"Yes. They're thieves and bandits. Power hungry, and greedy. Want to stop them?"

"I'm only one girl. What chance do I have?" She scanned the forest ahead.

"You are one resourceful girl who can sneak in and help me steal my book and sword back. Once we have those, you have all the chance in the world of stopping them."

Aviva pulled her cloak tighter around her head, protecting her neck from the cold mist. "Does the book have special powers or something? What makes it so important?"

I stayed beside her as we scrambled up some boulders. "The book contains all the knowledge of the Phoenix. It won't help the bandits unless they figure out how to read it. It's in code. The bonded will need that book to complete the Phoenix's rebirth, though."

She wiped her forehead, smearing dirt across her skin. "The Grandmaster, he was the last bonded, right?"

"Right. He protected the sword and book for the Phoenix. He used the sword for decades, keeping people safe."

Aviva slipped between low-hanging branches, back among the trees and under cover. "How many times has he bonded with someone?"

"A great many times, and each one adds to the knowledge in the book. The Phoenix is eternal, but without the bonded to tie him to the physical world, his powers to protect are limited to the mountain. When he's tied to his bonded, he can go anywhere they go, including out into other countries and across the sea."

"So, without the bonded, only the mountain and school would be safe?" She ducked down behind some bushes and listened.

I felt ahead, but it was only empty forest where we were. "Right. Even the valleys around us wouldn't be fully protected. They also help protect the book and sword, and wield the sword in the protection of others, with his strength and abilities."

She crouched and scanned the damp earth for the footprints. They were getting faint and harder to follow. "Is the bonded changed?"

"Yes, but only on the inside. As much as he gains their connection to the physical world, they gain his connection to the spirit world. They also become stronger protectors and better warriors. Aviva?"

"Mm-hmm?"

'Don't forget to look up, too. They could lurk ahead or above us, and if you only focus on the tracks, they can jump out and surprise you."

She stopped and leaned against a boulder. Aviva closed her eyes and breathed slowly. "I barely know what I'm doing out here, like this. How am I supposed to do this?"

"I'll teach you. This is just one big lesson in bandit hunting. You'll learn as we go. I'll keep you safe. I'm keeping watch, too."

Aviva turned and peeked over the boulder. "Promise?"

"Promise."

She pushed up and crept around the boulder, searching for the tracks. "Okay, let's go. So, mighty teacher, how do I spot an ambush?"

I chuckled. "There are different signs, depending on who's doing the ambushing. Bandits need somewhere big enough to hide their forces. On an uneven mountainside, we have the advantage. Stop and listen regularly. Excited lookouts often breath harder and fidget or whisper. Bored guards might not be careful, and you'll see them. Feel for them. They're not disciplined like a trained warrior."

"What if we catch up? There's, what, five of them?" She stopped and cocked her head. The river roared up ahead, not too far from us.

"We only move as fast as we feel safe. If we spot them, we assess their real number, and any chances we have." I felt ahead. Still nothing. He moved awfully fast for an injured man. Were they carrying him?

"Has the Phoenix ever hunted bandits here before, as man or spirit?"

"Yes. His very first scuffle with bandits where he had to give chase, they rode into the town and stole everything they could carry. They even kidnapped children. He went after them."

"What could they possibly want with children?" She stopped behind a cluster of trees and leaned against a thick trunk.

"Slaves, maybe, or to sell. Might even raise them up to be more bandits. The bigger your group, the more you can steal. Either way, they needed rescuing. He tracked them down, just like we're doing now." I peered closely at the track. "They've slowed down. If he took something to numb the pain, it's wearing off."

"They didn't, though, did they? Those tracks are just as deep." She crouched and touched the tracks under the uneven one.

"That's a good catch. No, it looks like they're going on ahead. They have left him behind." The uneven tracks were closer together now, and the right foot imprint was shallower than before. "Get down. Hide." I pressed back into a bush.

She tucked and rolled into the bushes under a tree, disappearing completely in her brown outdoor cloak. The bushes closed around her and went still. I could barely see her tucked under the leaves, down against the tree trunk.

Footsteps vibrated through the soft soil, a quiet thudding getting louder as they approached. Four pairs of feet moved in front of me. I could just see the whites of her eyes past a pair of boots, down low in the shadows. The boots shuffled about.

"Where'd she go?"

"Keep searching. She's here somewhere."

"Maybe she gave up and went back down the mountain?"

"Make sure. Find her. I don't care how."

The boots turned and kept going down the mountain where we came from. She remained still, not even her breathing gave her away. I followed them with my senses until they were gone, well out of sight.

"That was close. Come on out."

"Thanks Kai." She wriggled from the bushes. "What now? They're behind us as well as ahead."

"We keep going, hiding when we need to."

Her eyes darted around; her body crouched low. "Can you feel them if they get close again?" Her voice shook.

"Yes. I'll keep an eye out for you and keep you safe. Just keep watch as well, and we'll make it."

She darted between the trees, not rustling a single branch. Aviva followed the tracks, crossing it occasionally as she zigzagged her own path. The path grew steep, and she scrambled up over rocks, grasping trees and bushes to pull herself up. Aviva wriggled up onto a flat rock and sat.

"What's wrong?" I settled beside her.

"I've been thinking." She stared down the path behind her. "You can feel where we're going, at least a bit. Why are we tracking them when they're along the path, trying to stop us? Aren't we safer on a parallel path until we get closer?"

CHAPTER 23

HIDING

I smiled to myself. "That's an excellent thought. I bet that's why the Phoenix renews regularly, with a new bonded."

She leaned back against a tree and gazed down into the valley below. "What do you mean?"

"Well, legend says when the Phoenix dies, it's reborn from the ashes. That's all true, but there's more to it than that. It releases the spirit from the bonded, like you saw at the funeral, in flames. It's born again into full spirit form. Each time the Phoenix bonds, he gains memories and thoughts and experiences from the bonded. They bring in fresh ideas, if you think of it that way."

"Even after all those bonded people, all those centuries and more?"

"Yup."

Aviva giggled. "You sound like a student when you say things like that."

I chuckled. "I love watching the young ones. They're so full of hope and potential. It keeps me young, too."

"What happens to the bonded person? If the Phoenix gets their memories, I mean."

"It's not one-sided. They get access to all his memories through the centuries, all his experiences. The two spirits blend and they temporarily become one."

She pressed herself down against the rock and pointed. "We should go."

Down below, shadows moved among the trees, people coming up the mountain.

"Find a different path among the boulders. There aren't many places to hide, so find one, and we wait. They'll pass."

She scrambled over a large boulder and into the bushes. Aviva dropped over another boulder and clung to the rock, edging her way along a narrow rock ledge. A few more yards and she'd be safe, back in the trees and away from the edge.

"I hate this part of the path," a voice growled above her.

Aviva glanced up to where she just came from, her fingers gripping the rock. Boots moved above her and hushed voices whispered.

"Then shut up and walk. You'll be through quicker."

She shuffled slowly along the ledge; her body pressed against the rock wall. I glanced down at the crevasse behind us. It was a heck of a drop, but it hid us on this narrow ledge. Hand over hand, she shimmied her way along. Her toe dislodged a rock. It clattered down the crevasse, echoing as it banged off the rocks.

"What was that?"

A shadow fell across the rock face behind us. She held still. Her legs shook.

"Nothing. Get moving."

Their footsteps faded as they moved on in the direction we were heading as well.

The instant they were gone, I was beside her. "Come on, girl, you can do this. A few more feet. Let's go."

"My fingers are cramping," she whispered. A tear fell against the rock beside her toes.

"You can do it. Just another few feet. Left hand first."

She shuffled her fingers along, not lifting them from the rock. A small streak of blood covered the rock face. We needed to get her across now, while she could still grip the rock.

"That's it. Left foot now. You got this."

She shifted and moved, a slow hand and foot at a time. "What happens to the person?"

"What person?"

She sighed. Her hand moved again; another streak of blood left on the rock. "The bonded. Do they die of old age, like the Grandmaster? He was really old."

"Great question. Get to the other side and I'll tell you."

She stared up at the sky, a sliver above her, and shimmied her way over. Her arms gripped the boulder. One more climb up and out, and she'd be safe.

"Yes, they age, though slower than normal. Many live to be a hundred and twenty, some live longer."

She panted and shifted her toes to the wider ledge around the boulder. "Don't they get arthritis and such?"

Aviva reached up and pulled herself onto the top of the boulder and rolled under a tree just past it. She shimmied away from the crevasse under the branches. Aviva lay quietly, breathing hard.

"They do have a few aging related issues, like everyone else, but they keep fit. The Phoenix can lend them strength when they need, a bit at least. Despite their age, they still die before they can no longer fight."

She held up her hands and looked at her palms. Her skin was streaked with blood and scraped. She frowned.

"Let's get off these rocks and get you some healing. You remember which herbs to look for?"

Aviva nodded. She closed her eyes and slowed her breathing, slipping into meditation. I gave her a few minutes to recover, since the shadows covered us, but she needed to get moving.

"You're doing great. Now, let's find those plants for you."

She rolled and sat. "Just a quick break?"

"Real quick. We need to think about sheltering. It'll be dark soon, and we don't want to run into them in the dark. You also don't want to be caught sleeping, do you?"

Aviva shook her head. She cradled her hands in her lap, bloody palms up.

"Wait here. I'll go look for the herbs."

She closed her eyes and curled up on her side. I sped into the thicker trees. The herbs grew best in sunny patches where rocks sheltered them. I should find some close by. Still, they wouldn't be flowering this late in the year, and I could miss them if I wasn't careful.

There, not too far away, I found a patch. I rushed back to her. She slept, her hand under her head. There was blood on the soil where her palm must have shifted.

"Wake up, girl. You need care first."

"What—?" She blinked and shook her head.

"Come on. I found some, not far away. There's water nearby. You can put all that herbalism to good use. Now, just over the rocks and down a bit. There's a patch of herbs near the boulders."

She pushed herself up, whimpering at her hand in the dirt. I wish she complained more. I could probably run her through with a spear without her making a fuss.

"This way." I guided her to the herbs.

She kneeled beside the little plants, low and sprawling, as they covered the soil beneath them. Aviva plucked a few plants and picked a few extra flowers from what she left. "I don't have anything to mix them in. Hmm." She glanced around.

"Take some bark from that tree. You can scrape it off with the sword. Bend it along the length and you can make a paste on it. Just add water slowly, so it doesn't run off."

She pulled her sword and set the blade against the trunk. "How'd you learn all this?"

"Wisdom of the ages. Always learn from those who have seen and done more, and you'll get new ideas. Also, listen to the young, as they are open to possibilities that older people no longer consider. They innovate freely."

The sword bit into the tree and she pulled down, peeling a slab of bark off, a thick oval chunk falling at her feet. The stream was incredibly close, the trickling water just ahead through some bushes. We slipped through and she kneeled beside the shallow water.

Aviva bent her bark into a curved shape and set it on the rock. She crushed the flowers with her hands and placed them in her makeshift bowl. She gasped as she scooped the cold water up in her hand, her eyes going wide. The water trickled from her hand onto the flowers.

After a quick glance about, she picked up a rock. Aviva added the rest of the herbs to the flowers and water and mashed them with the rock. The plants and water blended, making a thick and dark paste that coated her rock and bowl.

"That should do it." She set her rock down.

"I know it's cold, but wash your hands first. Once that's done, spread the paste on your scrapes and leave it on overnight. We'll wash it again in the morning."

She stared at the cold water flowing past her and sighed. The water washed her palms clean, and she gently rubbed the dried blood off. Aviva shook her hands as dry as she could before scooping up the paste and rubbing it between her hands.

"That's so soothing." Aviva smiled, her eyes closing.

"How did it feel to hold the sword? Painful?"

"A little. Not too bad."

I glanced at the sky. "There's no way we'll make it tonight, with it this late now. Let's find a safe place to spend the night."

"You've been here before, right? You know anywhere?" She scanned the forest, trees and boulders in all directions.

"Well, yes, but we need to keep you warm and dry." It had been a great many years since I'd come this way or this far. Even mountains changed, trees grew, and others died. "This way."

She looked up at the sun, dropping towards the mountains below us. We had an hour of safe light left, maybe. Her clothing would help her blend into the shadows, but wouldn't keep her as warm as she needed, though her cloak would help. Aviva followed me across the mountain without a word.

"There, under that cluster of trees. Shelter there, against those rocks. They'll hold some heat longer for you."

"This group here?" She pointed at a cluster of trees and bushes below a boulder outcropping.

"That's it. The thick plants will keep the wind from you. The rocks will help shelter you. Now, what can you eat around here?"

She turned on the spot, slow and steady. I spotted a half dozen different plants she could eat. Would she see them?

"Those." She pointed at some tender herbs with delicate white flowers. "Just not the roots."

"Good. Gather some before you settle for the night."

I slipped into her shelter as she kneeled beside the herbs. The rocks were cool, but not cold yet. I brushed against the rocks, focusing on them and pouring energy into them. The rock grew warm. I pressed more energy inside, driving more heat deeper into them.

"Got some." She crawled in under the trees, the herbs in her gooey hand.

"Great. Huddle up against that rock and wrap your cloak around yourself. Eat your supper and relax. We're below the path, so if you're quiet, no one will know you're here." I shifted and let her settle in against the rocks.

"They're warm?" She smiled.

"They hold energy from the sun for a while." She didn't need to know the whole truth. Not yet. "Eat. Get a little sleep. We'll keep going soon."

She nibbled the herbs, her back to the rock and her cloak tucked around her curled up body. It would need a good washing later. She needed warmth more than cleanliness. When she was done, she rested her head back against the rock, her hood cushioning her from the hard surface.

A gentle snore, tiny and almost inaudible, came from her. I smiled and settled nearby, keeping watch.

***

"Up and at it. Time to go."

She blinked and rubbed her eyes against her cloak. "What?"

"How do your hands feel?"

Aviva held her hands up and flexed her fingers. The herb paste flaked off. "They don't hurt, and the scratches are healing over." Even in the gloom, I could see the fresh pink skin on her palms. "I'm okay."

"Let's get you more food. I won't let you starve."

Aviva crawled from her shelter. "I trust you."

"Where would you look first?"

She glanced around, the bright moon giving plenty of light to see by. "Near water, first. The river and stream are behind us, so do we go back?"

"Where else might you look?"

"In sunny patches near boulders. Mist collects there, and plants absorb the water. There should be some good places above us, right?" She stared up at the boulders.

"Right. You pay excellent attention, despite your fear. That'll save you one day. Let's go look."

Aviva stretched. She closed her eyes and yawned, her mouth open wide. "The rocks are still warm. How's that possible? How long did I sleep?"

"Maybe the rocks like you. It's just after midnight. Are you hungry or what?"

She grinned and looked up at the rock face above her. Aviva scampered up, her hands gripping the boulders as she climbed the sloping surface. Her stomach growled. "You're not helping. Now I'm even more hungry."

"All the more reason to find food quickly. Quietly, now. The path is just up ahead."

Aviva stayed low on the rocks, her belly to the slowly cooling surface. She stopped on a ledge just below the path, resting among the ferns and grasses growing here. Her hands still looked good, though she was breathing hard from her climb.

"There's some." She pointed to some herbs close to her, on another section of soil across a small gap.

She crawled over and lay flat, stretched among the plants. Aviva reached her arm across the gap and wrapped her fingers around the woody plant stem. She tugged sharply. Her body shifted closer to the gap.

"Careful." I leapt the small gap and landed beside her plants. Peering down over the edge, I only saw darkness. Her ledge wasn't that wide, either. I worked at the roots, loosening the soil for her, though I couldn't do much.

She tugged again. The plant slid free, dirt spraying as she dislodged it. She shimmied back from the edge, feeling her way, and sat with her back to the boulders. Aviva shook more dirt from the roots and wiped them with her fingertips.

"I guess there's no getting these clean later, huh?" She looked down at her pants, streaked with dirt and damp soil. Aviva sniffed the roots, leaving a streak of dirt under her nose.

I chuckled. "You'd be amazed at what they can do in the laundry. If not, though, they'll turn those into cleaning rags or something and get you a new pair."

A tear rolled down her cheek, shining in the moonlight. "Master Denneth gave me these. I wanted to take care of them. Show him I was thankful." She wiped the tear with the back of her hand, streaking more dirt across her cheek.

"He'll understand. Besides, the dirt will help you hide better. It's better to be dirty and alive than immaculate and dead, right?"

She nibbled the root. "It's watery inside."

"If we can find a couple more like that, it should fill you up and give you energy for now. That milky substance is good for you. Eat the whole thing if you can."

"The leaves are bitter. If Eron hadn't told me about this, I'd never eat it." She wrinkled her nose and took a bite. "Bitter usually means poison, or at least I have to cook it first."

"Good. What else can you tell me about the plant?"

She chewed another leaf and swallowed with a grimace. "It's best blended with berries, or eaten when in flower, but that was a month ago, right?"

"Right. You're doing a great job staying quiet, so just keep your voice low like this. Let's have a look around."

Aviva finished the plant. She shifted into a crouch and peered around. Her eyes focused across the gap, where more plants grew. If she missed, the drop would kill her. Her body tensed.

"No, we can sneak up and back dow—"

She launched herself across the gap, her body stretched out. She sailed over the gap towards the boulders. I winced

at the thud as she landed, her body flat against the rocks.
She lay motionless in the ferns.

CHAPTER 24

STILL HANGING ON

I flew across the gap and to her side. "Talk to me."

"Ow." She curled up on her side, her arms around her ribs. "Hey, another plant." She tilted her head back, her eyes looking past where she landed.

"Can you move? Are you hurt? That sounded horrible."

She pushed herself up and sat. "I'm okay. I spread it out over my whole body, using my hands like the break-falls they taught. It aches, but I'm okay."

"Don't you ever do that again, you hear me?"

She curled up and rested her head on her knee. "I'm never trying that again. Haven't you ever done anything stupid before?"

I glared at her. "More times than you could count. I was young once, too. If I say don't do something, it's because I know better you foolish girl."

She shimmied over to the plant and gripped the woody stem. "Oh, my skin aches. That wasn't good for my hands." She tugged, her other hand digging around and loosening the roots. "There." The plant pulled free, and she shook it.

"I'm going to check the trail. Sit, eat, and don't get yourself killed; you hear me?"

Aviva nodded. Her mouth was full of roots. I sped up to the trail, listening closely for any sound at all. An owl hooted nearby. Nobody was close. Moonlight shone down between the trees, spaced farther apart this high up. We didn't have as much cover up here, but neither did they.

I scampered back down the boulders. She sat right where I left her, another plant in her hands. Aviva chewed the leaves.

"We can go now. The trail drops back lower into better cover ahead. Let's get there before the sun comes up."

"If we cross a stream or river, I'm getting a drink and washing."

I laughed. "Fine. Stick with your girly ways," I teased. "The drink is important, though. There's water ahead once we drop with the trail. Get moving."

She scooted up the boulders. Now and then, I caught a small wince as she pulled herself up. She'd need her hands tended to again soon. Silly girl.

Aviva poked her head up to trail level. "It's clear," she whispered.

"Are you up for a brisk walk?"

She pulled herself onto the trail and popped to her feet. Aviva set off, marching down the path, following the slope down. She darted from each tree and bush patch to the next one, using what cover she had. Was there a lookout below watching us?

"Almost there. Hurry."

She dashed into the trees, following the trail among more boulders. We were back in the shadows, away from the brightest moonlight. She stopped, her back to a tree, and took some deep breaths. I gave her the time she needed. If I guessed wrong and rushed her, we'd get there, and she'd be too tired to help me.

The path rose and fell among the trees, crossing the side of the mountain. She kept a steady pace, not once complaining or slowing. What caused this small girl to willingly brave the dark and unknown just to help me? She had no reason to. Then again, that drive to help is exactly what the school needed right now.

The moon passed overhead, marching across the night sky, changing the shadows we passed through. We were close, I knew it.

"It stopped moving, just up ahead."

She crested the small rise and tucked behind a boulder. "Wow."

I followed her gaze, knowing what she'd see. On the next rise ahead, they built an old compound into the mountainside. Torches and fires reflected off the walls and metal roofs, giving the buildings a warm glow that was visible over the high wall that surrounded it all. How long has it been since I've been here?

"What is this place?" she whispered.

"This once belonged to a warlord who controlled the valley and protected the residents many centuries ago. It's been occupied on and off many times since then." I scanned the walls. Everything still seemed intact. They built it to last, and it was standing up to time well. "There are guards on the walls. See them? There's only one way in, aside from the front gate."

"We're going inside that?" her voice trembled. Her fingers gripped the boulder.

"That's where the book is. Please, Aviva. I need your help."

She lowered her forehead to the boulder and closed her eyes. I sat patiently as she took a couple of slow breaths.

"I'm scared, Kai. I'm no warrior. How can I do this?"

"I'm with you. I'll help you, just as you help me. We can do this. You're brave. Look at the way you came into the school and tackled every challenge thrown at you, proving so many masters wrong."

She stared up at the compound. "What's the way in?"

"Thank you. If we cross the river and climb above the compound, there's a cave with the secret passage leading right into the main bedchambers and suite."

"Wait, we're breaking into the most protected part of the compound? That's crazy. Isn't the biggest, scariest guy going to be in there?"

"And my book and sword."

Aviva frowned. "Isn't it convenient to have a secret passage right where we want to go?" She watched the guards strolling along the compound walls, between watch fires.

"The warlord had a family, a wife and children he adored. He wouldn't run from a fight, but he wanted them safe."

She scrunched her nose up and stared at the moon. "Weren't warlords bad people?"

"Life isn't so simple as people being good and bad. No, he wasn't a bad guy like you're thinking. It was a different time, and they had a different way of doing things. We can't judge the past by our values without considering what they valued as well. He protected his people. Some warlords were better, some were worse, but nobody is all good or all bad."

"What about the Phoenix?" She sat on a rock behind the boulder.

"He sometimes killed to protect others. Some people steal because they're desperate and need to feed their family. Life is complicated, and we should remember that before we judge others."

She peeked around the boulder at the compound. I could feel the war going on inside her, my chest feeling tight and my stomach churning.

I brushed my energy against her and gave her warmth. "When you need to fight, remember why you're fighting, and who or what you're protecting. This will help you decide what the right thing to do is. You can do this."

She worried her lip between her teeth. "Who or what are we protecting by getting your book back?"

"That's an excellent question. We're protecting everyone who ever needs the Phoenix again. Remember, the Phoenix is timeless, as long as there are people who stand up and defend others, but the book will make that easier for them. The sword has his spirit imbued in it, and the Phoenix can wield it like no one else, doing great good."

"But as himself, or through his bonded?"

I smiled. "When a bonded person picks up the sword, the spirit of the Phoenix within him interacts with the sword, and the sword gains power."

"Or her, right? Sometimes the bonded is a woman."

"Right. Some of the fiercest protectors he's ever bonded with have been women. Now, are you ready to go?"

Aviva nodded. She stretched. "You really think we can do this? Wouldn't you have been better off asking Garin or a Master for help?"

I scanned the surrounding forest. "You're small and sneaky. We can be in and out before they know we're there. You can do this. I know you can."

She took a deep breath and let it out. "Let's go."

"Stay low and move fast. The moon won't help us hide."

I slipped among the trees, moving down towards the river. We darted from bush to bush, staying as deep in the trees as we could. Did they know about the traps in the complex? Had they activated any? I had to get her to the secret passage before sunrise. The sun would beam down on the mountainside, giving us away for sure.

She stayed right behind me. I smiled at the way she passed under tree branches without rustling them. The river ahead covered any noise of our passing, but she was so quiet, I had to feel for her sometimes to be sure she was with me.

I moved around the boulders, looking for the wide part of the river. The water rushed past, fast and deep. The boulders hid us from the compound above. This was the safest place to cross, but my heart still skipped a beat. Could I really keep her safe from this? The water was high right now, with this year being so wet.

She moved beside me and crouched at the edge of the river. The dark water splashed up on her toes, dampening her boots. Moonlight shimmered off the surface, making it hard to tell boulders from rapids. "I have to cross this?"

"It's about knee deep here. We can do this."

"Kai, I'll get washed away. Look at it." She dipped a hand in the water and shivered.

"There is a way. Find a couple of branches. Something as thick as a staff, and as tall as you, if we can."

She turned and walked a few steps, focused on her task. There had to be some here. This was the right time of year to look, at least.

I moved along the riverbank, under the trees, and away from the rushing water. "Aha. This one will work. It's a little thick, but that's better than too thin."

"How about this one? Will the twigs and branches matter?" She held a branch up, as long as she was tall.

"No, that's perfect. Hold that in your right hand, and this one in your left. You'll walk across the river, digging these into the riverbed as you go. It'll help you balance. The water will push against you hard. Always keep both feet and one branch, or both branches and one foot planted at a time."

"Like this?" She planted the branches in the soil and shuffled along, one slow step at a time, using the branches like walking sticks.

"Yes. Keep your legs wide for balance and lean slightly onto those branches. Just like that."

Aviva stepped to the edge of the water and stared down. The spray soaked her pants. She shivered.

"I'm with you. You can do this."

She planted the branches in the riverbed and stepped from the boulder. Water rushed up just over her knee. She gasped. Aviva shifted the branches further out and brought her other leg into the rushing water.

"This isn't so bad. It's strong, but I'm okay."

"It'll be strongest in the middle, where the riverbank won't slow it down. Focus on each step. Ground yourself in the river, just like in a fight. One step at a time, now. Look ahead. It's not far."

Aviva lifted a branch. The water pulled at it, tugging the end downstream. She planted it and moved a foot, followed by the other branch. Her legs shook. Water splashed up her thighs. She clenched her teeth and took another step, and another.

"Almost halfway there. Come on, girl. You can do this." I perched on the rock, waiting. Make it. A dozen more feet.

She reached a branch out and plunged it down. It sank deep. She toppled forward, under the rushing water. The water closed over her head.

"Aviva!"

I dove into the icy water, speeding to her. She was gone. I stretched out and kicked, the water carrying me fast downstream. Moonlight filtered down, but I couldn't see well. I felt her, though. I pushed around a rock and propelled myself down river.

Something bumped against me. It was her. I slipped under her and lifted, focusing with all my might. Her head broke the surface, and I felt her gasp. I grabbed a boulder, and she clung to it, hanging on with all her energy. I shoved, lifting her higher, and she scooted up the rock until she was perched above the river. Aviva panted and wheezed, coughing water.

"See, I knew you could make it." I laughed, grateful to see her sitting there, even looking like a half-drowned cat.

She stared at the river, wide eyed. Her hair and clothing dripped. "How did you do that?"

"I told you I'd be there for you. It takes a lot out of me, but you're worth it."

Aviva shivered. I had to get her moving. "Come on. We're almost across, and it's shallower here again. We'll jump. You can make it."

Her jaw trembled. She nodded. The breeze stripped the warmth from her. It had to be now.

"Just jump this last deep bit right here. See the shallow section? You can see the bottom in the moonlight. We've done this on balance exercises before. Let's go."

She struggled to her feet, perched on the small boulder. Her boots slipped on the wet surface.

"One big jump. Big as you can."

She coiled her body and bent her knees. Aviva fixed her gaze on the shallows. She took a breath and her muscles tensed. Water dripped from her hair and clothing. Aviva launched herself at the riverbank, tucking her body tight for distance.

Water splashed around her. I launched myself across behind her. She kneeled in the shallows, her hands on the riverbed. She crawled across and collapsed in the grass.

"You did it."

She shivered hard. Her breathing was ragged. We wouldn't make it far tonight, but we couldn't stay here. There was no way they didn't hear all that. She needed shelter and warmth and needed it now. Somewhere their patrols wouldn't see her, if they were even looking.

"Come. We have to go."

"So tired."

"No, don't close your eyes. Get up, Aviva. Dig deep into that stubbornness and use it. You don't give up, so don't give up now. Get up or die."

"So cold." Her teeth chattered.

"Yes. Moving will keep you warm. It's not far. Get up."

She staggered to her feet.

"That's it. Move. Right foot. Good. Now left. Keep going."

I moved ahead, searching for shelter. The mountain was full of caves and crevices, nooks and outcroppings. She followed behind, slow and steady. Her hunched shoulders and curled up body told me all I needed to know. There, that spot will do.

"Right here. This spot will do just fine."

She curled up between the boulders, out of the wind.

"I'll be right back." I had to be. She didn't have long.

CHAPTER 25

WAIT A MINUTE...

She leaned against the rock, propped up in a sitting position. I darted back to the riverbank and searched. Gathering and carrying grasses and leaves took focus. She needed me more than ever, though. I sped back with them and tucked them around her, giving her insulation for the night. Her shivering slowly eased, and she slept quietly. I stayed beside her, giving her what warmth I could.

We needed to go. She needed rest. Did I make the wrong choice? She has what it takes, but she's so young. I always thought I had more time. No, I knew the moment I saw her through the trees, she was the one.

Leaves rustled. Branches moved in the distance. Was someone coming? A patrol? I glanced at her. She slept peacefully, quietly, not moving. I poured what warmth I could into the surrounding rocks. The rustling came closer.

I snuck into the bushes, towards the approaching intruders. They weren't hard to find, honestly. They bumbled past me, crashing through the undergrowth, as I crouched in a bush. I waited until they were a dozen feet away. I rustled the bush.

One man spun. "Over here."

I darted across the path and into the trees, away from her and the river. I rustled leaves and branches. They followed, tripping and scrambling behind me. I slipped ahead and circled back, quiet and unnoticed. They kept going away from her.

She hadn't moved when I returned, except to press closer to the warm boulder. I settled beside and waited. How long should I give her? I watched the moon slide down towards the mountains. Night was almost over.

She stirred within the hour. It mustn't be all that comfortable, sleeping sitting up among the rocks. She shifted and sat straight, blinking up at the moon. Aviva rubbed her bleary eyes. At least she wasn't shivering.

"I found some food right nearby. You'll recognize some herbs, too."

She smiled. "I am hungry."

"Hey, look. Your clothing is clean, too. You were worried, and now you don't have to be. Come. Let's get that food."

She crawled from her shelter and followed me into the trees. Aviva grinned and sat, her fingers digging into the soil around the plants. She wiped them off and nibbled them, ignoring the last of the dirt clinging to the roots.

"Can you still feel them? The book and sword, I mean," she asked, between mouthfuls.

"I can."

"How old are they?"

"The book goes back to the first bonded, many centuries ago. The sword was made a couple of lifetimes later."

"I read about a Phoenix, a mythical bird, as a little girl. It was in stories from distant lands and other myths." She tore another mouthful of roots and chewed them.

"You think it's a myth?"

She shook her head. "I don't know what to think. I know spirits are real now, and never thought they were, either."

I chuckled. "Yes, spirits are very real."

"He's real. The sword and book are real, so he must be real." She nibbled on some more leaves. "Swords need hands to hold them and people to wield them. Real sword. Real person."

"What is the Phoenix, if not the spirit of a warrior and protector, living on to keep the peace? You know spirits are real."

She stared off into the forest. What must it be like, learning childhood stories of mythical creatures was not just stories? I couldn't even imagine. Maybe I'd seen too much to know. I felt her wonder, her amazement, even a bit of disbelief still, deep inside me.

"It's a hard climb and we don't have long left. Ready to go?"

"What if I fall?" She stared up the mountainside, steep and high above them. Her lip trembled.

"Hey, I'm here. You're never alone again. We'll do this together."

She chewed the last of her herbs and stood. Aviva brushed her hands off on her pants, streaking fresh dirt across the cloth. We gazed up at the compound, and past it to the rock face we'd climb to get there. She looked at her palms, pale pink streaks stretched across as new skin. Aviva balled her hands into loose fists and nodded.

We crept through the trees, following the river part way. Her eyes widened at the bridge ahead of us.

"You didn't tell me there was a bridge."

"You don't want to use it. There's a reason we avoided it. Come, and stay quiet."

I led her through the bushes, down below the bridge. She tucked herself lower as a sentry paced the trail above us. At least the rushing river hid any noise we might make, moving through the bushes like this.

"Don't go right under it yet. It's not safe," I whispered. "Look up at the supports."

She peered up in the moonlight. "Those pins don't look normal," she whispered.

"They're rigged to collapse."

She frowned up at the bridge. "How did they all get across?"

"See the extra holes?"

Aviva nodded.

"They add special pins in those, and the bridge will support a heavy wagon. Without those pins, it's not safe. Now, quickly, cross under, and stay against these posts. Fast as you can, and don't touch anything."

She scurried through under the bridge, stopping in the shadows until the guard on the other side turned and paced back and away from us. We darted into the undergrowth and deep into the trees. The bridge disappeared below us as we snuck through the forest.

"If the Phoenix is a firebird spirit, what happens when he touches water?"

I chuckled. "The Phoenix is a firebird, but so much more than that. He's spirit, so it's more a spiritual fire. It burns in his heart. When joined with a warrior like the former Grandmaster, he can take the form of an actual bird, feathers and all."

"Does he like bird baths? Most birds like bird baths I've seen."

So many questions, but at least she was moving, and at a steady pace behind me. "Yes, he can bathe and fly in the rain without being extinguished, just like any bird."

"What about when he's not bonded to anyone, like now? What does he look like then?"

I laughed lightly. "All the questions? What makes you think I have the answers?"

"You know so much," she whispered. "You're really old and wise."

I scrambled up the rocks and headed for the base of the cliff. "The Phoenix exists as pure spirit. He can't act directly like with his bonded, and anything a spirit does to interact with the physical world takes immense concentration. That's why the sword and book are at risk without a bonded to help protect them."

She scampered up the rocks beside me. "You said the book contains all the knowledge of the previous hosts, but doesn't the Phoenix also know it all? Can't he just share again if something happens to the book?"

I paused on the rock.

She stopped and closed her eyes. "I'm not saying I won't help. I just want to understand."

I smiled. "I know. The book helps the bonding finish and can transfer the knowledge quickly. Imagine needing to sit and listen to every story of every bonded since the beginning. It might take several lifetimes to record it all again."

"Oh. I see. Magic?"

"Spirit. It's not the same thing, though people might think it is, if they don't understand it. It's a spirit transfer." I started climbing again. "Magic isn't what most people think."

"Spirits exist. Does magic exist? It was in my story books, too."

"It does, and I hope you never have to see it. Spirit is powerful and takes a powerful person to use it. Magic changes a person, and not for the better. Only people who can't use spirit use magic. Now, we're almost on the trail. Keep going."

"How much farther?"

"Just up ahead."

She giggled. "You said that two 'just up ahead's' ago."

"See the base of that cliff face to our left?"

"Mm hmm."

"Look a third of the way up and directly above us. See that?"

"The shadowy spot?"

"Yes. Get there before the sun goes up. Hurry."

She peered over her shoulder at the horizon hidden behind the surrounding mountains. The sky was glowing a faint red, outlining the mountains. We had little time. Aviva grabbed a rock and propelled herself up faster without me urging her on.

Did they know about this entrance? Would they be guarding it? I doubted it, but we wouldn't know until we got there. I stayed below her. If she fell, I needed to be ready. It might be the end of me saving her, but I'd sacrifice myself for her. She could bring the Phoenix back, just off her belief and stubbornness all on her own.

"Did the Phoenix know the warlord?" She pushed off and grabbed the next rock.

"Yes, the Phoenix was here, back when he was still just a man." Hey, if stories helped her climb, I'd tell her any tale she wanted.

She boosted herself up onto another small ledge. "What was he doing here?"

"The warlord called him. He'd been trying to protect his people, those who weren't able to fight, but worked in his fields or made pottery and such. Another warlord kept sending troops and invading the edges of his land and was building up an army. This new warlord killed people who were old, weak, sick, and whatnot. He needed to be stopped."

"The Phoenix fought for him?" She scampered up the next section of rock, using the shallower slope to get higher quickly.

"No, not in his armies. The Phoenix helped with traps, like the bridge, and picked places for watchtowers. He also insisted a squad of soldiers stay and protect the villagers, and that they form a plan to evacuate if the army got too close."

She scrabbled up to the next ledge. "The warlord wasn't angry?"

"He was disappointed, of course, but the defenses worked. The plans he helped make defeated the invaders. The warlord pressed on and took the next valley with the Phoenix's help and plans, and he only had to treat the people well in return."

Aviva shimmied up a spot with fewer handholds. She banged her knee on a rock and muffled her whimper in her shoulder.

"Are you okay?"

"I'm fine. It just stings." She blinked back tears. "Did he keep that promise? The warlord, that is."

"He did, as long as he lived. He died one day, and his son took over. The boy was not the man his father was, though, and things got worse for the villagers."

"What did he do? The Phoenix, I mean." She pushed up onto the next ledge. The rock took a reddish hue from the growing dawn.

"He marched through the doors, the ones in the main hall, and confronted the warlord right there in front of everyone. It was during a banquet, so anybody with any power was there. They spread the tables thick with food the warlord stole from the villagers. I'll tell you about the rest at the top."

She sighed. Aviva looked over her shoulder. "Wow, look at that."

I looked down below us, across the valley. A town sat distant over the next ridge, just visible by the lights glowing below in paper lanterns. The river shimmered in the fading moonlight, sparkling like fairy lights. The call of the wolves and the hooting owl were the only sounds.

Aviva wriggled onto the final ledge and rolled away from the edge. "Well, we're here. What happened next?"

I settled onto the ledge beside her and glanced at the cave, dark and silent before us. "The warlord was upset at the challenge, in such a public manner. He ordered the guards to arrest the Phoenix."

"How many guards?"

"So many they surrounded his hall, all there to keep his rich guests safe. A few dozen guards in all. The hall was also full of tables of guests, so it wasn't an open space to fight like a training hall. Servants also cowered against the walls, scared to run and get cover, in case the warlord killed them for leaving their posts. He didn't want to harm an innocent person in a crowded area like that."

"What about the guards? Was he worried about them?"

"Come into the cave entrance. Don't stay in the light." I tucked back into the shadows. When I felt for anyone around, the cave seemed empty. Only insects lived here now. "You are who you follow. The guards followed the warlord. Many left when the old warlord died, those with honour in their souls. They roamed the valley still or found a new leader to serve."

"Am I following you or are you following me?" She tucked into the shadows and peered deeper into the cave.

"Neither. We walk together as friends. Hopefully, we'll change each other for the better."

"What happened next? You can't leave the story there."

"Come on. I'll tell you as we walk." I started down the cave.

Aviva hesitated a moment, glancing back at the moonlit night, the red and purple hue colouring the mountain from the rising sun. I brushed my energy against hers. She turned and followed.

"The guests all ran. Servants scurried to cover in the commotion, hiding in passages and the kitchen. They knew his reputation and trusted he'd save them."

"The guards?" She walked down the dark tunnel, her hand on the wall.

"They surrounded him. The thing is, they had to be careful about attacking, or they could hit each other. He could strike in any direction and hit an opponent. He dodged and weaved, ducking and parrying, and they missed him each time, but they slowly fell, one by one, from the blows of the other guards. When there were only a few men left, he leapt on a table and ran for the warlord, leaping from table to table. He quickly outran the guards."

"What about all the food? Could he really just run along tables without tripping or slipping?" She stumbled in the dark and regained her footing.

I slowed down for her. "I'm telling you about this epic sword fight, a tale for the ages, and you're interested in the food?" I laughed.

"Well, the villagers could have used it, right?"

I smiled and shook my head. She was always concerned for the little guy. She was perfect. "Remember how you worked in the cave, balancing on the pillars?"

"Mm hmm."

"He started in that cave, doing the same thing, and he's taken every bonded there to train, without exception."

She stumbled as the tunnel dropped, catching her balance in moments. "What did the warlord do? If a sword fighter ran at me over tables, leaping with inhuman balance, sword swishing through the air, I'd be scared."

I chuckled. "Yes, he was. He ran. Lost all credibility with his men right then. He knew about the secret exit, saw it as a boy, and headed for it. The Phoenix helped build it, though, and he gave chase. He stopped the warlord from opening the tunnel and made him promise to step down."

"Who took over? Was he any better?"

"She, actually."

Aviva stopped. I heard her breathing, quick in the dark.

"The warlord's wife was from the village, and she knew what the peoples' lives were like. She was intelligent, and the Phoenix backed her claim. They found the old warriors to serve her, the ones with honour who left, and she took control. By now, warlords were losing power anyway, but she brought peace for a decade before everything changed."

Her hand brushed over the rock at the end of the tunnel. I focused, and a torch flared to life. She cried out and shielded her eyes.

CHAPTER 26

SNEAKING IN

"**S**orry. Take a moment."

She curled up and sat, her eyes squeezed tightly shut. I waited beside her as she slowly blinked a few times. She shielded her eyes with her hands and looked around, back down the tunnel into the darkness. After a few more moments, she lowered her hands and looked around.

"Pull that lever right there. The panel will open, and we'll be in the bedroom. Be quiet, as we don't know who's waiting, if anyone."

She grasped the wooden lever and pulled. A click echoed in the tunnel. Wood slid on wood. She reached out and stepped forward, her hand stretched out to whatever was blocking the light. Aviva tumbled forward and disappeared. A tapestry flapped closed behind her, hiding her from sight. The breath fled from her body and she grunted.

I sped through the tapestry and to her side, scanning the room as I entered. It was dark and empty, only the light from the windows to see by. She lay on the dusty rug by the fireplace she tumbled through, staring at the ceiling.

A cloud of dust rose around her hands as she pushed herself up to sit, her fingers pressing into the rug. "Kai, I don't think anyone's been here for ages."

Cobwebs clung to the furniture and filled corners. They shone in the dim light. Dust blanketed everything, thick and undisturbed, except the outline of her body where she landed. Aviva was coated in a layer of dust.

She stood and tried to brush herself up. She coughed hard and stopped. "They're not here. Now what?" Her shoulders slumped. "Do we have to search the whole compound?" She coughed again; her voice sounded hoarse.

"No. We just need to find the parts they're using, right? Wherever their leader is, that's what we want. We'll go slowly, but I have some idea where to look. Do you remember which buildings were lighted, when we looked from the distance?"

Aviva nodded. "The big one in the middle, and the two smaller ones on either side."

"We're in the main quarters, near the hall. They're not directly connected, since the warlord wanted privacy. We can sneak over and check it out. Stay low and in the shadows. You're good at that."

She smiled and crept to the door. Her muscles tensed as she reached out to the dusty and faded red door.

"Aviva?"

"Yes?" she whispered.

"Breathe. You've got this. It's just like the training and games in the forest."

She rolled her shoulders and wiggled, loosening her muscles. Aviva took a deep breath and let it out slowly. "In the games, I didn't have people willing to hurt me." Her hand trembled on the door handle.

"I'm with you. Take a moment and breathe."

"Has anyone ever stolen the sword and book before?" She leaned against the door, ignoring the cloud of dust she stirred up.

"Twice. It can happen when the bonding doesn't occur right away after a death."

She rubbed her eyes. "Ugh." Her eyes watered from the dust, and she blinked furiously.

"Here." I touched her face. The dust fell away.

"Thanks."

"Ready?"

She nodded. "I still think you should have picked some-one more capable." She pressed the door open and snuck through.

"You're fine as you are. Low and slow. We're losing our night cover, so let's make the most of what we've got left."

Aviva tucked low against the wall and moved under the windows, deep in the shadows. I barely saw her sneak along. We sped to the door at the far end and paused, lis-tening. This building was silent, not even a creak or settling of the timbers.

She pulled the door open a crack and peered through. Massive windows flooded the hall with light. The tattered curtains crumbled from age, joining the dust on the floor. She snuck to a window and peeked out the corner.

"There?" She pointed at the next building over, a massive hall with light flooding through the windows.

"There."

"How will we get there without being seen?" She looked as far as she could while staying low. "There's a ledge up there, below the second tier of windows."

I followed her gaze up the wall. It was a good fifteen feet or more up, but there was a wide ledge under the second level of windows. She wasn't thinking of—

She darted for the double doors at the end of the hall.

331

"They'll see you. This way. Over here." I willed her to listen, to trust, and to feel me.

She stopped and turned. I guided her down a side hallway, back around the bedchambers. We went up some stairs and back down, over the hidden tunnel, and to a thick wooden door. This was a servants' passage, no fancy furniture or wall hangings, just plain walls and a few small windows. We stopped at the door.

"This will put us out of sight, in shadows behind the living quarters. From here, it's a quick dash to the kitchens, and hopefully to the ledge you're determined to use."

She smiled. "You know I can."

I couldn't help my grin. "Yes, you've proven most adept at scaling heights and going unseen. I'll let you know when the guards are away, and you run for the shadows. Now, get closer, and get ready."

She slipped through the door, silent as any assassin. I passed through. She was already tucked in the shadows, the morning light not reaching this far in the compound yet. I peered around the corner and felt for the guards. A guard approached from the far end of the hall, a torch burning in his hand.

"Duck down low and wait. He'll pass soon enough."

I didn't hear her move, but I glanced back, and she was gone. I felt her there, though. We listened to the boots on the stone, steady, getting louder. The footsteps stopped, and when they restarted, they faded. I peeked out, and he was heading away.

"Now. Be quiet," I whispered.

She darted across to the kitchen wall across from us, a flash in the light and gone again. Aviva stayed low as she passed among the deep shadows, tucked down low near the ground. She paused where the smaller kitchen and large hall met in a corner. I raced to her side.

"Is he looking this way?" she whispered. Aviva examined the stone corner blocks, her fingers gripping in the gaps.

I peered around the corner. "No, you have time.

She scrambled up the corner, her fingers and toes finding space in the cracks, gripping the rock as she climbed. Like a flash, she was up on the ledge and tucked against the windows. I couldn't see her from below at all, except for the toe of her boot. Her foot moved, and she was gone from sight. I sped up, following her path, and crouched beside her.

The massive room was full of light, flickering flames from candles and torches and a fire roaring in a massive fireplace on the wall beside the kitchen. Long tables filled most of the space, with benches on either side. Bandits sat and ate or slept along the walls in bedrolls. At the end here by us, there was an ornate table on a raised area. A grizzled man with grey strands in his hair sat in a gilded chair with precious stones inset, at the middle of the table looking down at the others.

"There are so many of them," she whispered.

"It's there. That end table, near the middle. My book and sword." Energy surged through my body. I was so close.

"We wait? There's too many of them. I can't get in and out without being seen."

"Yes, we wait. It looks like they've been up all night celebrating, doesn't it? He looks ready to fall asleep, just like most of his men."

Her fingers pressed against the stone wall. "I might have to sneak in there, right?"

"I'm hoping he'll take the sword and book to a quieter hall to sleep."

"Wait, isn't that—" She pointed at a long table near the main doors.

"What's he doing here?" I narrowed my eyes at him.

"Did we just find our inside man?"

"Excuse me?" It took a moment to remember what she meant. I would not tell her, but her expressions from her home sometimes were darned cute. It reminded me how young she really was, that she hadn't lost them yet. "Yes, I think we found our inside man."

The man in the fancy chair yelled and waved. Merek shifted off the bench, moving unusually slowly, and limped down the hall.

"I don't think they're using any other rooms, Kai. Everything else is dark, and there are people sleeping everywhere."

I frowned. "There are legends of a curse on the compound. Pure nonsense. Those stories were started to protect the compound, not because anyone actually placed a curse here, though. Well, let's make a plan."

"These windows don't open. There's immense doors down there, and one from the kitchen." She surveyed the room. "How will we get in?"

There were a couple of side doors, but we'd be seen getting to them.

"What about that?" Aviva pointed down at a serving girl, entering from the kitchen, staggering under the weight of the platter. "Can we get in that way?"

"Let's check the kitchens. There may be more servants than bandits, for all we know, and they might be loyal to the bandits."

She waited for the guard to turn and scampered back down the wall. Aviva was back in the shadows before my feet hit the stone floor. She darted towards the corner, her hand on the wall. Aviva stopped part way and drew her hand back.

"Chimneys," I explained, feeling the heat. "Massive fire-places for cooking."

We crept to the corner and glanced around. The back area was like a miniature courtyard, with a well out in the open. Red and pink sunlight, with the first golds, blanketed the stone. There was no cover. There were also no guards.

"Stay here. I'll check it out." I moved around the corner, staying low.

I felt around me, but there were no other guards here. We knew about one, and another patrolled the opposite side of the hall, but no one was watching the kitchens. Odd. I sped back to her.

"Let's be quick. Get a look around, see what you can learn."

She followed me around the corner. Aviva snuck to the nearest window and peeked inside, staying low in the cor-ner. A few women moved around inside, preparing food and filling pitchers with frothy dark liquids. A couple of young women in grease-stained clothing came from the hall and picked up platters. They left again, straining un-der the weight of the food.

"With so few servants, they'll see you right away. Especially with a sword on your belt."

Aviva sighed. "So, what? We wait a day and hope they all fall asleep sometime?"

We needed a proper plan. I watched the women moving around, each working at a task and focusing on it completely.

An old woman at the fires pointed at a bucket. Was she scolding a young woman who just came back with an empty platter? The young woman set the platter on a table and picked up the bucket, her arms straining with the weight. She staggered to a door near us.

"Hide."

"No, I have an idea." Aviva snuck to the shadows around the corner and watched.

The door swung open, and the young woman stepped out, letting it bang closed again. She walked past the well to a pit and poured a greasy mixture down it. Aviva wrinkled her nose. I didn't blame her. The young woman walked to the well, dropped a bucket down, and hauled it back up.

Aviva stood, squared her shoulders, and snuck over to the woman's side. "Hello," she greeted, her voice quiet. She slipped into the shadow from the well.

The woman's eyes widened, and she gripped her shirt over her heart, dropping the bucket back down the well. "Who are you?" she whispered.

"They stole something important from my friend, and I'm here to get it back. Are you related to them?" Aviva nodded to the hall.

Her eyes teared up. The woman shook her head. "No, we live two valleys over, but they came to our farm at night. Grandmama and I were taken. They needed cooks and servants, they said. They'd pay us, they said, but we were dragged out here without a chance to say no."

"Would you like to get out of here? I can get you back, but I need your help."

She shook her head, eyes wide. "They'll kill us. I just know it. They said if we try and leave, they'll hunt us like wild deer."

"They'll never know. All I need is your clothes, so I can blend in. I snuck in through a secret passage over there." Aviva nodded to the bedrooms. "There's all kinds of clothing you can wear instead. If I can get you dressed, can I take your place?"

Aviva hauled the heavy water bucket up, barely struggling after all her time training. She set it on the stone pavement beside her. I saw her eyes widen, and she tucked behind the well.

"What're you doing, hanging out here when you should be working?" A guard appeared around the corner and swaggered over, his hands on his hips. "We were told we could punish you if we found you not working, and we got to choose how." His lip curled up into a sneer.

The young woman trembled and backed against the well, her hands up in front of her. Aviva circled the well, staying low, and darted out. A kick to his knee brought him to the ground. She pulled him close and got him in a choke hold. Hey, I didn't teach her that. Her guard friend? The bandit went limp in her hold, slumping to the stone.

"Help me drag him over here," Aviva whispered.

The woman stood frozen, trembling like a leaf in a hurricane. Aviva grabbed his ankles and hauled him across the stone, glancing quickly down between the hall and the bedrooms. She ripped strips from his shirt and tied his wrists and ankles and gagged him. Aviva rolled him to his side and propped him up against the building.

The door opened and an old woman stepped out. Aviva stayed back in the shadows, watching. The old woman shuffled to the younger woman and wrapped her arms around her. She peered into the shadows.

"Come out. I know you're there."

CHAPTER 27

DISGUISED

Aviva stood and stepped back into the light. She walked over with slow and confident steps. Would they help or call the guards?

"Thank you for protecting her, but what are you doing here?" Her sharp grey eyes held Aviva's gaze. "You can't stay. They'll punish us, too."

"No, they won't, because you're leaving. Come with me and hide until I am done. I'll come back for you, and I'll get you out of here. It might take a little time. If things go badly and they spot me, stay hidden until I come back. I will come back. I know somewhere safe." Aviva's jaw clenched.

She narrowed her grey eyes at Aviva, cold and hard as steel. "May you be cursed if you break your word."

Aviva nodded. "Come. Quickly."

"This way. I know a shortcut," I promised, guiding Aviva back to a new section of wall.

I got them back to the bedchambers, sneaking through back passages. We stopped at the wardrobes and Aviva rifled through them. The first one was all silk clothing, fit for a warrior. We tried the second one. Colourful dresses and robes filled the hangers and shelves.

Aviva picked up some dark grey silks. "These should help you hide in the forest. Ever worn silk before?"

The young woman looked at the shining fabric, her eyes still teary. The old woman wrapped her in a firm hug.

"I haven't in a while. It'll be fun. You'll look just like a princess. A princess that can hide in shadows and who's strong enough to get home again." Aviva smiled at her. "Now, can I have your clothes?"

She handed the silks to the young woman, who took them in shaking hands.

"I hope you know what you're doing." The old woman reached up and untied her granddaughter's tattered tunic.

"So do I," Aviva muttered. "Kai, privacy?"

I smiled and shook my head. "I'll wait outside the door. Leave the sword in the tunnel. There's no way to hide it in those clothes."

I slipped from the room and waited. Her plan could work, but she'd need to hurry. The women had been missing for a while. We might still have enemies among the servants. Worse, if the bandits overheard the servants talking, we might all be in trouble, enemy or not. I paced the hallway, waiting for her.

Aviva stepped from the bedroom, dressed in the tattered and grease-stained clothing. "Let's do this before I lose my nerve."

"Pull the headscarf a little closer to your face, and you actually look like one of them. The hall is illuminated by candles and fire, which will help us. Look down a little more. There, that's it." We actually have a chance, I think.

She shifted her headscarf. "Just like that, huh? Sure, we can do this. Why not? I love it when the odds are against me."

I followed her the fast way back to the courtyard. "I can't tell if you're joking or not."

Aviva paused, her hand on the door latch.

"I'm with you. You'll be fine." I let my energy brush against hers.

She smiled. "That other time, it didn't go so well for me when you said I'd be fine."

"I know, and I'm so sorry for that. I saved you on the way here, though, right? We know there's trouble this time, so

I won't delay. First sign of trouble and I'm in there like a wet blanket over a fire."

Aviva cracked the door open and listened. Birds chirped in the nearby forest. There were no human sounds beyond the muffled noises from the hall, so we were probably okay. I hoped. We hustled to the kitchen door. She paused, her hand on the wood. Aviva took a breath, stood tall for a moment, and gathered herself. She huddled slightly and pushed her way inside.

"About time, girl. Get that platter in there now. Ori's been run off her feet without you." The old woman by the fire peered at her through the dim light.

Aviva moved to the platter, her back to the woman, and slid her hands under the edges. She grunted under the weight, despite her training. They loaded the platter full of meats, animals taken from the mountain, no doubt. She wrinkled her nose. I boiled with fury. Animals on the mountain were in a sanctuary. Nobody dared take them. This can't go unpunished.

She staggered through the door and into the noisy hall, the weight of the platter making her tip back for balance. Aviva glanced around, like a deer before a fire. Where was she supposed to go? Her heart raced and her stomach clenched.

The platter slipped in her sweaty palms. I ducked under and focused, lifting with all my effort. She waddled to-wards the stairs down to the long tables, staying close to the wall, her head ducked as much as she could. Where was Merek? Would he recognize her?

"Over here, girl. What's wrong with you?" a gruff voice called from the head table. A man stood and pointed down the table towards the man in the ornate chair.

We turned together, and she shuffled down the table, her head down and the platter balanced against her. Meat juice slopped up against her soiled shirt. She slid the platter on the table a third of the way down. We both glanced at the sword and book, sitting in front of the grizzled old man in heavy armour.

"More drink, girl." A man thrust a jug into her arms. "Now."

Aviva scurried back to the wall and through the door. "Kai, it's so close," she whispered.

"I know. Get the drink while I make a plan. At least we're close. You did it."

She dodged the other girl in the kitchen, her arms loaded with another platter. Aviva darted to the kegs along the wall. She clutched the jug to her chest. Which one?

"I'll distract her. You figure this out." I sped across the kitchen and to the nearest fireplace. With a nod, the fireplace roared to life, the flames shooting up four feet high. Oh, it felt so good to be this close to flames.

The flames engulfed the meat, turning on spits over the fire. The woman dunked a cloth in a water bucket. She beat at the roast, the fat sizzling and spattering with her efforts.

Aviva was still standing at the taps. Oh, there were three different varieties, I realized. I set the next fireplace ablaze as well. The other girl was back, and she pointed to the left barrel. Aviva nodded, her head still down, and filled the jug. Dark and frothy liquid splashed and gurgled. A bitter grainy smell joined the burning meat aroma.

She turned the tap off and held the jug in one hand, easy after all those mornings of chores. I waited until she was at the door before I let the fires go and sped after her. My little stunt consumed the logs, so they'd need to rebuild the fire. That would keep them busy.

"Okay, this time we want to get closer if we can."

Aviva nodded. She walked to the table, jug in hand, pretending it was heavy. I waited by the wall as she walked along the table to the demanding man, and she slid the pitcher in front of him. A man walked towards her, so she turned and headed back to the wall. Nobody seemed to pay her any attention. We had a chance. Next time, the book was ours. She passed the last man at the table end.

He reached out and grabbed her wrist. "What do we have here? I don't remember those pale eyes."

She cried out. Her knees hit the floor. A tear splashed on the stone.

"A different girl?" The bandit leader stood, his chair scraping on the stone floor. He walked down the table and towered over her, glaring down. "Tell me, what would a young woman like yourself be doing all the way out here?"

She glared back up at him through tear-filled eyes. Her hand was white from the man's grip. Hold on, Aviva, I pleaded silently. I'm coming. Rage flowed through me. Her fear beat at my chest, distracting me.

The bandit leader reached out. She cried out as his hand hit her cheek, the slap ringing through the silent hall.

"What are you doing here?"

Her eyes darted around the room. Our stomachs rolled.

"Answer me."

She clawed at the hand on her wrist.

"If you won't tell me, maybe I'll let the men get answers however they want, huh?"

"It's her." Merek hobbled over, his eyes blazing with fury.

No, he was not hurting her again. Fury rolled through me. I focused. The candles, torches, and fireplace roared to life, flames turning into an inferno. The doors blew open with a gust of wind. I rose on the wind and was at her side in an instant.

Bandits scattered, yelling. They crowded through the doors.

"This place is cursed!"

"What's going on?" the bandit leader roared above the commotion.

I slammed into him, knocking him from his feet and into the man holding her. She yanked herself free and ran for the nearest window. I charged ahead, smashing into the glass, bursting through with the shards. She launched herself through the opening behind me and into the court-yard.

She skidded around the corner and to the hidden door in the shadows. I sped through behind her and hovered over her as she lay in the dark on the stone stairs.

"Let me help you."

She whimpered; her wrist held against her chest. Aviva curled up in a tight ball. Her cheek was bright red still. Her wrist was turning a deep purple. I had to stop the bruising. He sheared some blood vessels, and I wasn't about to lose her now.

"Be at peace. I'm here." I let my essence show. My love and care for her gave me extra strength. I lowered myself over her face and wrist. My essence showed as sparkling lights that floated together as I soothed her body and soul.

Her whimpering stopped. Her tears slowed. She pushed herself up with her good hand and sat with her back to the wall. Aviva blinked in the light.

"Is that what you really look like?" Her voice shook, but she was speaking, at least.

"No. It's all I can manage right now. We have much to do before I have my full strength again, but it's enough to care for you. How do you feel?" I hovered before her face, warm soft lights glowing yellow in the darkness.

"I failed you. I'm sorry."

"We haven't failed yet. I didn't protect you as fast as I wanted, and I can't say sorry enough for that. Still, the book and sword are unharmed, even if we're not the ones in possession of them right now, right? We'll get them back."

"They know we're here. It's only a matter of time before they find us now. What do we do?"

"They don't know why you're here, though, do they? We still have that going for us." I settled a blanket of warmth over her, surrounding her in the only way I could hug right now.

"You need a better warrior. I'm not skilled enough or strong enough. I can't hope to win for you." Tears rolled down her cheeks, and she closed her eyes.

"You don't have to win for me, you'll win with me. You'll win because of who you are." Girl, you need to snap out of this. I can't do it with an emotional mess.

"Kai, ever since I started training at that school, it's been an uphill battle. From the first day, I've had to work harder and longer than anyone else just to keep up. You should have picked someone more capable."

"That's enough." I bristled, my lights going red. "You've worked hard, showed your determination, and you have a genuine passion for the martial arts. You've overcome odds already that most of them will never face, and until now you've done it with a genuine smile. I felt your confidence grow with each achievement, no matter how small. How many of them can say that?"

She ran her fingers over the stone stairs under her, the smooth wooden wall behind her. Her emotions flopped all over inside.

"You've had to fight for it and work hard. You know what it's like to face great odds. You know who else knows?"

She wiped her eyes. "Who?"

"All those farmers in the villages we protect. All the people who take their products and turn them into things like clothing and baskets. The blacksmiths who turn raw ore into tools and hope nothing goes wrong. Every one of them must face the weather and they wish and hope for the best, just like you. They work hard, just like you. That is actual strength."

She stared at the stone at her feet. "Garin would have been a better choice."

"I seriously considered him," I admitted. "He's a good man who cares about people, and is already a powerful warrior. I chose you for a reason." I felt my anger mellow, and the light turned back to a cool yellow. "It wasn't because you were a warrior who could defeat anybody. It wasn't because you were the smartest, or fastest, or most confident. That doesn't matter."

"I don't know how we're going to do this." She blinked back tears.

"You know, when the Phoenix was still a young man, he was in a situation where he felt overwhelmed, too. It was just him, a cave full of bandits, and some children who needed rescuing. If he failed, they'd take the children to another country and sell them."

Her heart calmed and her shoulders relaxed. "But he was a warrior, right?"

Good, she loved stories. I could get her back. "He had practiced fighting, just like you, but hadn't used his skills in actual combat much. He was going against bandits who were stealing and raiding for decades and knew how to fight."

"How did he manage?" She perked up, sitting straighter.

CHAPTER 28

IT CAN BE DONE

"He had to be smart about it, like we'll have to be. Since it was only him, and a dozen of them, he needed to fight in areas they couldn't surround him."

"He could fight in narrower tunnels, so they couldn't get around him," she mumbled.

"He sure did. He snuck in, moving low and slow. Each sentry he got to, he knocked them out. It was a risk, but most people don't wake up quickly or well. After taking out four sentries, he only had eight bandits left to deal with, and two children still to rescue."

"What happened next?" The light he gave off reflected from her eyes.

"He found the main cavern where the bandits kept the children. The kids were on a platform over a chasm, and they rigged it to drop into a river down below. If the bandit leader saw him, he could get rid of the children, just like that. Tied up as they were, they'd drown if the fall didn't kill them."

"He had everything set up? Was he a slave trader?"

"Back then, nearly all bandits traded in anything for a coin, including people. He was worse than most, though, taking a few children every year from the towns. With such a well-armed group, he was hard to stop."

"But he got the children out, right?"

I chuckled, my lights twinkling brighter with my mood. Good, she was out of her funk. "You want the short version?"

She shook her head. "No. How did he overcome the bandits?"

"He kept to the shadows, getting as close as he could to the platform. He needed to keep the children safe and do it without being seen. The platform had to be jammed, or the lever did. The Phoenix ran back to the last man he had disabled and grabbed his sword and dagger. They were fine steel blades, good and strong."

"Using the weapons he finds there. Smart."

"That's right. He returned to the main room, keeping low and staying in the thick shadows. Caverns are dark places, as you know, even with some torchlight. He got within a couple dozen yards of the platform, though the lever was still out of reach."

"He has to jam the platform, then?" She shifted to the edge of the step, her hands gripping the stone.

"A simple frame held it, attached to chains that connected to the lever. If anyone pulled the lever, the frame rotated, and the platform fell. He took the dagger and held it in one hand, feeling the weight and balance of it."

"As soon as he throws it, they'll know he's there, though." She brought a hand up over her open mouth.

I shimmered, casting brighter light around us. My colours shone whiter. "Yes, but he can't leave them. He focused and threw the dagger. The point embedded through a link of chain, right into the platform, with a dull thud. They knew he was there."

"He still has eight bandits to deal with. What did he do?"

"He was among the stalagmites near the chasm, still deep in shadows. He weaved among them, keeping out of sight as long as he could. They came after him with torches, though. He didn't have long."

"If he was close to the edge, so were they." Aviva straightened up. Her eyes were dry again. Her wrist no longer pained her, with the way she pressed down against the stair she sat on.

"That's right. The space you fight in can be your biggest ally, if you use it. He leapt onto a stalagmite and hopped to another, out of their reach. All that pillar training paid off. He dropped and swung from the stalagmite, kicking a bandit off the edge."

She pressed her lips together. She'd learn life was seldom simple, and some choices were between bad outcomes.

"He pulled himself back up and moved away from the edge. His sword slid from the scabbard, flashing in the torchlight. The Phoenix fought like his life depended on it, keeping their backs to the chasm. One by one, they fell, sometimes from slipping or bumping into each other. Soon, he was facing the main bandit, and in a flash and clang of swords, the bandit lay motionless on the ground. He grabbed the kids and ran."

"So, if I use the banquet hall to my advantage, keep out of reach, and keep calm, I can do this."

"We can do this. Fully together, and not like this. You're coming with me first."

She stood. "Where are we going?"

"Up the mountain. It's time."

"Up—up the mountain?" she rubbed her chin. "What's up the mountain?"

"Something we should have done before we came. I thought we had more time. You're ready now, though. Get up. I'll lead you."

She followed me back to the bedroom.

"Get changed. You'll be more comfortable, and you can grab your sword again. I'll wait over there."

Aviva grabbed her clothing and began stripping the rags off. I waited in the hallway. The sun shone brightly across the valley. Men ran around the compound. Footsteps in the dust told me they'd already been and gone in the hall and never went into the bedroom.

The door opened a crack. "Coming?"

I slipped through the opening, though I didn't need it. "I'll hide myself like before until we've got the women through the tunnel. I'm still with you, like always, and we'll climb the mountain together."

Aviva pushed through the secret tunnel. The women huddled in the torchlight together on the rock floor. They looked up at her with wide eyes.

"This way. I'll show you the back route." Aviva waved at them to follow.

We moved down the tunnel together. She kept the pace slower as the old woman walked with short steps. The sunlight welcomed us back out into freedom.

"I have something more to do before I leave," Aviva explained. "A friend told me that path there will take you down to a village where you'll be safe. They can help you get home from there." She pointed down a path partially hidden by a boulder. "Do you want to go, or wait for me?"

The old woman smiled and took her hand. "We'll go. We can make it. I've lived in these valleys my whole life."

She placed her hand on the old woman's shoulder. "Be safe. I don't know how long I'll be, but I'll check up and make sure you got there."

"Of that, I'm sure." The old woman winked. "There's a pass close to here that takes us home. I have relatives in villages along the way."

They bowed in parting, and the women headed down the path.

"I hope they make it," she whispered.

"They'll make it. I doubt many bandits know about that path."

"Did you?"

I appeared beside her, faint lights in the sunlight. "Yes. It only leads to some more secluded villages, though. There's nothing down it a bandit would want. This way."

I led her around some boulders behind the ridge, and we headed up through the forest. The trees were smaller and there were fewer of them, but the rocks were large and impressive. She climbed without complaint, scrabbling over boulders occasionally and darting among the trees. We came to a river, wide and swift.

"What's this doing here? Where does it go down the mountain?" She stared at the river with her arms crossed over her chest.

"It doesn't go down. It circles the sanctuary. Feel that? Open yourself to it."

She closed her eyes and took slow breaths. "It feels like you. It's all bright and glimmering." Aviva opened her eyes and watched the water flow past, sunlight shimmering like my own lights in all the colours.

I led her to a spot where the rocks were flat. "Ready to work as a true team?"

Aviva nodded.

"Trust me. Place your hand on that boulder. I'll place mine over yours."

"You don't have hands, spirit." She smiled.

"I sure do. Go ahead."

She reached out and set her palm against the boulder, flat on the massive rock at the water's edge.

"Don't worry. I won't harm you. Stay still and trust me."

"I trust you. The way you repeat that, I wonder if I'm doing the right thing, though."

I laughed, a sound like tinkling bells and gentle wind chimes. "You're fine. Some people get scared when they see me."

Calling on the power in the water and my sanctuary, I shimmered and called my full spirit form. She's only ever seen pictures of me. Those couldn't capture the way the light and fire shone from my feathers and radiated from my essence. I reached a wing out and lay it over her hand, my flames flickering harmlessly on her skin.

"Her heart is true, and she is me." My voice didn't come from my long slender beak, but from my heart and my fire. I felt my flames pulse and flicker as I spoke.

Her eyes grew wide as she stared at the river. Flames flickered and rose from the water, rising to create two arches across the river. Fiery spirit essence filled in the space between, creating a bridge deck. The railings were tiny tendrils of flame reaching for the sky.

"I will wrap my wing around you, and you can pass through my flames without harm. Once we're fully joined, the flames will never hurt you. Fire will do your bidding, like it answers to me."

"Once we're joined? What about my feet? Won't they burn?" Her legs shook and her face paled.

"No, you'll be fine in the protection of my wing. You can touch the railings with your hand and not burn, as long as I have you wrapped in my embrace. Come."

I stretched out my wings, catching the sunlight in my feathers. Oh, the sun felt good, warming me through. I curled a wing around her and pulled her close.

"Walk with me. It's not far now."

She hesitated, her foot hovering over the flaming bridge. Aviva straightened up and stepped, her eyes closed.

"See, you're fine."

Aviva opened her eyes and stared at her foot. The flames curled around her foot, but her clothing remained undamaged. I held my other wing up over her, shielding her eyes from the brightness of the sun, magnified here in my sanctuary. We crossed together, step by step, and stopped on the other side. I let her turn and watch the flames sink down into the water once more.

"This way."

A path of shining stones appeared at her feet, extending a few feet beyond where she stood. Aviva took a step, and another stone appeared beyond the last. She moved along the path with me, watching new stones appear before us, and others disappear after we passed.

"Are you doing that?"

I laughed, giving off more music. "It's responding to my presence. Once we're joined, it'll do the same for you."

"Joined? Like bonding?" She stopped. "Are we about to bond?"

"Yes, we are. You'll gain access to my knowledge and experience. You'll have thousands of years of warriors and guardians behind you, hundreds of forms and techniques at your disposal. They have lost some of them to time, except within me. You will be my voice in the world."

"What about my training?" She gave in to my gentle pressure with my wing and began walking again. "Is it done, then?"

"Oh, Aviva, it's just beginning. You'll have the knowledge, but you need to practice and learn to use the skills. If you allow it, I can temporarily control you, and we fight as one. You need to allow it, though. I won't just take over your body without our permission."

"You're limited by my strength and speed, though, right?" Her eyes fixed on a cave entrance ahead as we rounded a rocky outcropping.

"Yes. You're strong and agile. It'll be fine. Your basics are excellent, and that's all I really need. The fancy stuff looks impressive, but the basics will save you every time. Let's go inside."

She stopped at the entrance. I gave her a moment to look. The light stopped at the entrance as well, and she couldn't see anything past the opening.

"Don't be afraid of the dark. I am the light."

I stepped into the cave. Stretching out my wings, I filled the cave opening. With a strong beat, I sent a burst of wind down the tunnel. Torches flared to life along the walls, not with flames, but with a glittering ball of white light. I made them of my essence and they glowed like I did.

"No matter where we go or how dark it is, my light is always with you. You'll learn how to control it for yourself one day."

"You're not going to keep me from stargazing, are you? You're brighter than the moon, you know. It almost hurts my eyes."

I laughed, loving the small smile on her face. "I can dim myself and hide within your heart if you want to experience the dark. I love watching the stars, too. Ready?"

"Is anyone truly ready to walk into a cave on top of a sacred mountain and bond with a magical spirit of martial arts?"

"Actually, yes," I teased. "Most of my hosts look forward to it immensely. Mind you, they grew up on my tales and legends, and I just sort of appeared to you."

Aviva ran her fingers over the rock beside her. "How did I do?"

"Other than fearing you were mad, you did great. No hysterics or anything. You nearly fainted, but you didn't. I was proud."

She stepped into the cave with me. The path outside disappeared. I wrapped her in my wing and walked her deeper into the mountain, guided by the glittering torches. We walked together through the still and quiet air, not a breeze to disturb the magical torches.

We rounded a corner and entered a cavern. Aviva stopped and stared up with her mouth open. Two massive statues stood on either side of a doorway on the far side, glittering with their own light. Both were of my full bird form, just like the picture in the library. Their wings were open and raised, spread across the massive cavern, their beaks crossed over the doorway, blocking it. Braziers burned at their feet.

"In there. That's where we do the bonding."

"What will this mean? How will it affect us? I know you told me, but I'm not sure I understand."

"It started back when you cut your hand on the sword. From that moment on, I felt your emotions. Now, when we finish the bond, I'll sense your thoughts, and you'll sense mine. We'll have access to each other's memories. If you clear your mind, we fight together as one. If you're over-matched, I can even things up for you, if you trust and don't give in to fear. I'll live in your heart as long as you're alive."

"So, when we go back for the sword and book, you can help me defend myself?" She fingered the hem of her tunic, her hands shaking.

I nodded, keeping my beak close to my chest. "Yes. I have centuries, millennia of experience defending people. Once the sword is in your hand, you'll get its power, too."

She strolled to the doorway, the statues towering over her. I stayed beside her, my wing against her back for contact. She couldn't see beyond the statues' beaks, through the door. It was dark inside.

"What's through there? How does the bonding work?"

CHAPTER 29

TOGETHER

"All you have to do is walk forward. Just keep walking, no matter what. I will do the rest. Just trust me. It's a test of bravery and trust. Feel as scared as you want, but know I will not let you fail or fall. My wings are powerful."

She swallowed hard. Aviva nodded. "I trust you." Her hand trembled as she reached up and touched the beak of a statue.

"Hey, you stayed at the school when most people would have left. You followed me into the woods, simply because I asked for your help. You entered a bandit infested lair, despite being outmatched. This will be easy in comparison."

She nodded. "I'm ready, I think."

I felt my insides roll and churn. She trembled, scared near to death, but I felt the resolve, too. "Breathe. Fear can't hurt you. When you're ready, walk forward. I'll be right behind you the whole way."

Aviva straightened up and squared her shoulders. She took one last slow breath. The bird statues turned their necks, the beaks sliding aside to reveal the doorway. She stepped forward, into the darkness.

"Great. Keep walking. I'm here. Close your eyes if you need."

I held my wings up and open around her. The surrounding area glowed with my light. It shone from my feathers. She followed her shadow, stretched out long in front of her.

Shadowy beings moved around us, at the edges of my light. A clawed hand reached into my light and slipped back into the darkness. Aviva shivered but kept walking. A large black shape prowled the edge of my light, glowing red eyes fixed on her.

Aviva walked to the edge of a cliff and stopped, the shadows still lingering at the edges of my light. Without movement, my radiance started growing smaller, the shadows pressing in.

"Keep moving," I urged.

"But the cliff? I'll fall."

I laughed. "I have wings. You'll fall, and I'll save you. Take the step."

She took a slow breath. Shadows crept closer. The glowing red eyes approached from behind. A claw reached along the ground, stretching to grasp her foot. Move, I urged inside my head. I can't make you jump. A claw snatched at my tail. I whipped my feathers around, smacking it with my fire. The claw disappeared into the darkness with a wail.

Aviva stepped from the ledge and plunged into the darkness below. The gigantic shadow pounced, reaching for my tail. The glowing red eyes fixed on me. I threw myself into the air and let myself fall after her. The creature flew past me and hurtled down, faster than she could fall, deep into the abyss. I tucked my wings and streaked down towards her.

She rolled in the air, her arms and legs flailing. "Kai!" Her hand reached out to me. Terror burst through me.

I swooped down and wrapped a claw around her, cradling her. My wings stretched out and caught the air. I flapped my wings and soared back up across the canyon. She shook and trembled in my claw, tears flowing freely. How could someone so adept at climbing be so afraid of heights?

I set her on the rocks and landed beside her. My wing folded against me, my other wing wrapping around her again. I sent as much warmth into her as I could, though it was hard when I was in a physical form. I couldn't just touch her heart yet when I had form. Not yet.

Her trembling slowed, and she calmed her breathing. Aviva leaned into my feathers, and I pulled her close against my body.

"You're doing so well. I told you I'd keep you safe. Just breathe."

"What—what else?" Her teeth chattered and her voice shook.

"We're almost there. We keep walking."

She glanced up over my wing. "Where did the sky come from? Aren't we inside the mountain?" Her hand on my feathers felt less shaky. She blinked at the sky above us.

"We passed through into the Realm of the Divine. Spirits live here, in this outer layer. Creatures you think are legends live here, too. You see it through human eyes, but once we've bonded, you'll see it as I do. You see sky because your brain can make sense of sky."

She nodded, her head resting against my chest. I opened my beak and breathed slowly, sending soothing and healing over and into her. Her muscles relaxed, and she sighed.

"Ready? Walk with me?"

Aviva curled her legs under herself and pushed herself up. She stood beside me, still held in my wing, her head barely at the base of my neck. Aviva closed her eyes and breathed, slipping into a meditation. I waited and felt my insides slowly unknot themselves.

"I'm ready." She began walking, slow steps at first.

I moved with her, keeping a wing around her. The cliff disappeared behind us, and we walked through grasslands, blue sky above us. I heard the rushing of water as we climbed the rise. She stared at the raging river, deep and wide.

"We walk across. I will keep us up, and it'll feel just like walking on the grass. Don't fear what's below us. You won't slip beneath the surface."

"Okay." She gripped my feathers, and I winced.

"You don't have to hold so tight. I'm with you. Don't pluck me like a chicken. That would be embarrassing."

"Sorry." Her hand relaxed, and the tugging stopped.

I pressed gently, and she stepped onto the water. We set a steady pace together. The water was clear, and we could see all the way to the bottom, shallow and rocky at first, dropping quickly many feet down, and deeper still with each step.

A massive fish swam under us. Its tail slapped up from the water. She gasped in the cold as her clothing got soaked. Steam rose from my feathers. I let my warmth pour into her and her clothing dried.

She glanced down and tensed. The fish charged us from below, mouth gaping wide. She fixed her gaze on the riverbank and marched on, her hand tightening on my feathers but her steps not slowing for a moment.

Tentacles rose from the water and slapped down on the surface in front of us. I lifted my wing and carried her over it, touching gently back down on the other side. A tentacle reached for her. I opened my beak and breathed fire, and the tentacle jerked away from her.

"What? How?"

"I am hope and light, a spirit of the will to survive. They are from despair and darkness. Both live here in the spirit world, connected to and reflecting your world. They can't withstand my strength, though. Not here. Keep walking. We're so close now."

She stepped up onto the riverbank and collapsed to her knees. I lowered myself to the grass beside her and waited. Shimmering lights formed an outline in the grass ahead, rising to form solid walls of golden fire. She shielded her eyes with her hand. The whole temple glimmered and glowed as it formed from the fire. Two more statues stood on either side of the door. This pair had their wings lowered across the doorway.

"When you're ready, it's in there. You're almost done."

She pushed herself up. I walked her to the doorway.

"She is worthy. Let us pass." I stretched my neck up and stared into the eyes of the statues.

"As you decree." The wings raised and pointed at the sky, open fully upwards.

The inside shone bright gold and red and blue, oranges and yellows and every colour she could name. We walked inside together.

"Right there, that's the last step." I nodded at the fire blazing in the middle of the room. "Step inside and trust that you won't burn up or die."

She stared into the flames. "Just like that, huh? Are you coming, too?"

"This last step is for you to start. I'm here, but you need to transform, too. I'm not the only one who changes here."

"I won't burn?" The flames reflected in her eyes.

"If you believe I won't let you burn, you won't burn. I can protect you, and you will be completely unharmed."

Aviva walked over to the fire and stopped beside it. She reached a hand out towards the flames.

"Don't test it. Step in with confidence. You got this, and I'm here."

She closed her eyes and stepped into the flames. Aviva turned and faced me. The flames licked up her body, covering her skin, hair, and clothes. Her thoughts flooded into me. I felt her fears and doubts burning up and blowing away like ash, uncovering an inner confidence we now shared. Her deeper traits, her kindness and compassion, and inner strength joined with me now.

I felt her pain, the ache of losing those she loved. I had felt it many times over the centuries, myself, and I hugged the pain before letting it go. She'd always acknowledge it, but it would no longer be her constant companion.

She smiled at me through the flames. I stepped into the flames with her and sunk inside her heart, my physical form dissolving into her body. Our spirits blended, joined as one now.

"I can feel you," she whispered.

"We're joined and bonded now. I rest in you instead of walking with you. Can you feel my inner fire?"

She nodded and smiled. "I can."

"Let it feed your own inner fire. We're one, but still two. Now, let's go get our sword and book."

The fire died around her, vanishing flickering flame by flickering flame. "Now we go back?" Flames still danced in her eyes, visible only to me. Well, me and a few masters, but they hadn't seen her yet.

I nodded. "Now we go back. Hang on to me, right down at the base of my wings, and I'll carry you."

She stared at me; wide eyes fixed on mine. I turned my back to her and stretched my wings out. I willed my body to grow even larger until she had to reach up to my wings. Here, in my sanctuary, my powers were full and strong. Changing size and shape was nothing to me. I glanced back over my shoulder.

Aviva stepped around my long tail feathers and stood at my back. Her hands were gentle as she grabbed my wings, though I winced at the odd pain as she wriggled up onto my back. I'd smooth those feathers later. I leaned forward, and she nestled into place.

"Hold on firmly. I'm taking us straight out through the barrier between spirit and physical world, right into the forest. You might want to close your eyes and press close to me. Until you're more comfortable with heights, don't stare down at the ground."

Her teeth chattered. She pressed herself close to me and squeezed her eyes shut. Her fear and trust were both there, grappling in her heart, but trust was stronger. I stretched my neck up and breathed out. The temple dissolved around me.

I pushed up and beat my wings. We shot up into the sky, coiling up and spiraling in the wind. I carried her through the fiery barrier of my domain and into the void between worlds. We shot through the darkness of the void, and I floated down into the night sky, back in the physical world and mortal realm.

"Have a look. Just glance around quickly. What do you think?"

She peeked through cracked eyelids for a moment. Aviva's eyes popped open, and she stared at the stars above us. "Why can I see them in the daylight?"

"You see them because I can. Amazing, isn't it?"

"Wow."

"Wow does sort of cover it." I chuckled, filling the surrounding sky with the musical tinkling of bells. I folded my wings a little, and we soared down towards the mountainside.

She shut her eyes tight and hugged herself against me. I felt the trust clearly between us, a warmth that filled both our hearts. With time and practice, she might even come to enjoy our flights. I grinned to myself as I felt the wind in my face. How good it felt to stretch physical wings again.

We shot down through the sky towards the mountainside cave. They would see me as a fireball streaking through the sky, a shooting star or the like. Daylight would help hide us, but not enough, sadly.

My feet touched down on the rock, my mighty wings beating to soften the landing. I folded my wings in, partly covering her. She still clung to my back. I turned my head around and rested it beside her.

"You're safe. We're down."

She peeked out through barely cracked eyelids and glanced around. Her hands unclenched and she straightened up. "That was—"

I chuckled softly. "Fun? Freeing?"

"Insane." She stroked my head gently, her fingers running through my feathers. "Amazing, though. I flew," she whispered.

"As you grow stronger, we can fly more. How do you think the Phoenix gets around the valleys to protect so many people in a place with rugged mountains?"

Aviva shrugged. "I guess I never considered it. I didn't know how big and wild this place really was." She stared out at the valley below us, one of just many for miles.

"What about when your parents came with you? You're not from this land, so you came by ship, right?"

She nodded. How could a smile be so sad? "I was little, though. I played with the sailors and other children on the ship, and time passed quickly for me. Everything seems big when you're little."

My chest felt tight, the ache of loss. Over the centuries, I'd felt so much loss. It was just part of me, but for her it was still so fresh.

"Are we better sneaking in, or should we make a proper entrance? Show up on the doorstep, flames burning brightly, and walk in like we own the place?" She fidgeted on my back, shifting her weight.

"We're bonded, so they'll be able to see me if I will it. Legends run strong here and many bandits might flee. Those that don't though, they'll stay and fight. Until you read the book, my memories of combat will be limited for you, and I can only do so much right now. Get the book and it changes everything."

"Book first. Got it."

"Ready?"

She nodded, her hands gripping my wings. I pushed off and soared up, not hiding myself for a moment. We circled the compound, high in the sky, and I surveyed it. People moved around in the hall, visible through the windows. People still packed the head table, gathered around as if they were planning something.

"Hang on. This might get dramatic."

CHAPTER 30

GOING IN

I folded my wings and dived towards the front hall doors. Sentries pointed and gasped. A few feet from the ground, I opened my wings and flapped. My feathers burst into flames. I let out a cry, harsh like an eagle, loud like a whale. Her heart pounded as she clung to my back.

My wings beat again as I touched down on the steps. The sentries ran past, covering their heads with their arms. Men scattered, darting for the compound gates, not looking back. I felt them go with my senses and kept my eyes on the doors.

"There. That's the casual followers, and the superstitious gone. All that's left are the battle-hardened warriors with discipline."

"You're not helping," she whispered.

"I've got your back, and I can do more for you now, though they won't see me. You know I'm here, and I'll protect you, even when invisible. Let's make an entrance."

"I can't believe that worked." She stared through the gates, at the men who scattered into the forest.

"They grew up with my legends, too. If they stay, they know what awaits them. They were probably desperate if they became bandits in the first place, especially here."

She frowned. "Nobody should have to steal to live."

"You're right. Soon you'll be able to change that. Worry about it after. We have a job to do."

She slid from my back and walked to the doors. A small door nestled in the larger pair, big enough for a single person to pass through.

"Oh, girl, let's really make an entrance." I nudged her with my beak, pulling her back against my chest.

She pressed against me. I lifted my outstretched wings and flapped hard, buffeting the doors with the air. I pulled my wings back, sucking the doors open with them. My feathers burned brightly as I screamed at the hall, though only I saw it. I could appear to them, or I could channel my energy into protecting her. Until she read that book, I knew which was more important.

'I'm with you. Go.'

Aviva smiled. She marched forward, drawing her sword. Grizzled bandits, older and scarred, turned to stare at her, but her eyes were on the chief. She strode towards him, covering the ground with surprising speed for one so short. If I didn't sense her fear deep inside, I'd never know she was afraid.

"I've come for my sword and book. They don't belong to you, and I'll take them back now." Her voice was powerful, filled with the confidence I poured into her through our connection.

"Do you know why we took the book? Do you know what's inside it?" The leader walked forward a few steps, hands on his hips. He stared down at her from the dais.

"It contains knowledge."

"That's right. Knowledge that could benefit everyone. So, why's it hidden away? What does the school keep from us?"

She hesitated. Her mind was spinning, and I caught glimpses of what tumbled through her head. She only got into the school because of the Grandmaster, because of me. How many others were denied the right to learn?

'Hold firm, Aviva,' I whispered directly to her heart.

'What if he's right, Kai? Can the book really help people?'

'It can and will, but this is not the way. He can't understand it. It needs you. It's hidden because it's useless without me and who I bond with.'

Her brow furrowed. She kept her eyes on him. "You can't read it, can you? What has it helped you with so far?"

"It brought us hope." He smiled, a wide and toothy grin. "Once we unlock its secrets, we can take the place of the school. We will be the peoples' new hope. They'll look at us instead."

"Why does it matter who people look to, as long as they have peace and a chance at life? They loved the Grandmaster," she yelled. "I was there. I saw the funeral. I lived in the village. They had order and security. All you brought was fear and suffering. You kidnapped the women and made them work. That's not fixing things. That's no better than what you accuse the school of. You denied them choice."

"You'll return the book to the school and things continue as they are, then? You'll let favouritism continue, denying so many people the chance to learn and better themselves, the way the masters do now? If everything is so wonderful, why did your little friend Merek help us?"

"He's not my friend," she spat. "He's a bully who picks on people, just like you. There's no place in the school for bullies."

I felt a breeze. I held my wings around her. An arrow flew at me from behind. I shimmered and called my protective fire. The arrow bounced off my flames and landed on the ground as ash.

"I'll take my book and sword back now." Aviva held her hand out.

He threw his head back and laughed. "Why don't you come and take it from me? Are you afraid of a fair fight? You best me, you get your belongings back. You win, and we'll leave the valley."

'You're not ready, and it won't be a fair fight,' I warned. 'Decline. We have another way.'

She walked down the hall, stopping a few feet from the dais and the table where the book and sword sat. I stayed right behind her.

"You can't use it, can you?" Aviva smiled. "It's just a regular sword for you, nothing special, and no magical powers."

He sneered down at her. "I'll learn."

"You want a fair fight, but life isn't fair. Some people thrive while others lose families, or homes, or their freedom. Only the powerful speak of fair, but they don't want it, because they'd lose their power. I don't accept that. I'll change it."

'Read the book,' I urged through our bond. 'We're a team now, and I've got your back.'

Aviva leapt up, grabbed the book, and darted under the table. She scooted across the dais and leapt back to the floor, pelting for the main doors. A sword swung inches from her back, slicing the edge of her tunic.

I let my power out and the flames grew and burned, twisting from every candle and torch in the room. "Run."

I swooped over her, covering her with my body. My beak opened, and I cried out. Guards shivered and paused as we ran past, my heat spreading out and threatening them with burns. Arrows whistled through the air and bounced off my flames. She slipped through the doors and around the corner, out of their sight.

"This way." My flames faded, and I sailed towards the bedchambers, leading her through the halls and doors.

We stopped in the bedchamber, and I flapped my wings. The dust blew around, hiding all traces of our passing. She darted into the tunnel and the panel closed behind her. Aviva leaned against the wall; the book cradled in her arms. She slowly slid down to the rocky floor, her back to the wall.

"One down, one to go. Now what?" She smiled up at me, shimmering before her.

"Now you read it." I chuckled.

She closed her eyes and took a slow breath in. Her fingers brushed over the cover. The gold lettering curled and twisted like little flames when she touched them. "I can read this now," she whispered.

"It's an ancient script. You'll understand it now because of me. Read."

Her fingers shook as she opened the cover. The pages seemed to glow. She slowly turned the pages, the book balanced on her knees, as she looked at all the symbols and pictures that floated across each page.

The book trembled in her lap. It slipped to the rock before her and opened to the middle pages. She reached down and grasped the book. Bright light shone from the book and engulfed her. I waited patiently, watching, as the book shared my knowledge with her in moments.

She dropped the book and grasped her head. "Ah, it aches."

I opened my beak and breathed over her. She lowered her hands and looked up at me. Sweat beaded on her forehead. Her body shook, calming slowly as my breath washed over her.

Her eyes were distant as she stared across the tunnel at the rock wall. I rested my head against her shoulder as she let the information seep into her soul and rest in her mind. It was a lot to take in all at once. I knew that, and she needed a few minutes.

"I understand now," she whispered. "I see it all. We can help so many people, but the book can't be read like he wanted to. It's like their experiences are now mine. So many lifetimes—"

"Now you know." I lifted my head and met her gaze. "So, how do we make the most of what you know?" She hadn't soaked in all of it, not by a long shot, but the martial knowledge and healing information was there for her. It was enough. She'd need to read more later.

"Okay, I have the knowledge, but how much use is it?"

"You know how to do the techniques. You can use the techniques; just know it won't feel natural yet. You're also limited to your own speed and strength, but you're more than strong and fast enough. Trust in yourself, and in me."

"I can feel it. I know you." Her eyes glowed red as she looked at me, before fading back to their usual pale colour.

"Ready to retrieve our sword?" I burst into flames. She was excited, the energy burning through our link, and I felt it, too.

"Absolutely."

She picked up the book and set it back in her lap. Aviva pulled her tunic off and wrapped the book inside, tying it to her back with the sleeves. She shivered in the cool air, her light undertunic not giving her much warmth. I moved forward to her and settled into her chest, around her heart. Her shivering stopped.

They were scouring the area, checking the compound for us. She felt it, too, sensing what I sensed. She wasn't afraid, though she shared my caution. We waited until they left the living quarters before sneaking back out to the main courtyard.

"Now, walk like you own the place, because we do. This is my mountain, my valleys."

Aviva straightened up and marched from the shadows to the main hall. The doors still hung open, blasted back and damaged from our earlier arrival. She marched inside, not slowing for a moment. The room went silent, except for the hiss of swords being drawn. Most of the guards were gone, but not all.

The leader turned from the table and looked up, his mouth hanging open. His moustache twitched. "Come to bring my book back? Couldn't open it, could you?" His lip curled up, exposing coloured teeth.

"I read it just fine. I'm here for my sword." She strode down the room towards him, down the center between the tables.

He grabbed the sword from the table and drew it from the scabbard. "You can have it back when I stab it through your pesky little heart."

Aviva smiled. She knew how the sword was forged, knew its secrets. She knew because I knew. I was there.

"Guards!"

The closest guard lunged; his sword outstretched. She sidestepped and kicked his wrist. His sword clattered to the stone, and he fell to his knees, cradling his wrist to his chest. Two bandits lunged, one on each side. She spun and stepped. A bandit cried out as the other man ran him through.

I felt their energy, knew what they were going to do. With me in her heart, she knew it, too. The last three bandits circled us. She stood calmly between them, staring up at the leader. Someone lunged from behind us. She tilted her head; the sword missing us by inches. Aviva dropped and spun, sweeping her leg out and knocking another man to the floor. She rolled and stood, facing the remaining men.

They lunged, swords out, trying to trap her. Aviva turned sideways and slipped between the swords. She cartwheeled away, dodged under a table, and ran for the dais. We could feel them behind us. It didn't matter.

She leapt onto a table and ran for the dais, sidestepping dishes and leaping platters. Aviva jumped to the dais and faced the leader. She walked towards him, one deliberate step at a time.

"I'm here for my sword. Hand it over, leave the valley, and don't come back." Her voice was like ice, cold, hard, and emotionless.

He threw his head back and laughed. "This is the most prosperous valley in the entire country. Why should I do that? I have the sword. You haven't even drawn yours." He pointed the tip of the sword at her.

Aviva grasped the blade and held it firm. "Because you can't win. You can leave and never come back, or you can return with me to face your crimes."

He stared at her hand. He tried to twist the blade. She stood calmly, not flinching. No blood dripped down her hand, no sign she was holding something razor sharp.

"How's this possible?" His eyes flicked between her and her hand.

"That's my sword. It won't hurt me. It already knows my blood." She held her right hand up, palm open to him. The scar crossed her palm, shiny white skin still unmistakable and easily visible. "You can't hurt me with it, but I can hurt you." Aviva twisted her hand and yanked the blade from his grip. She held it out, pointing at his chest.

I poured my essence into the blade and flames roared to life along its length. The room glowed with orange and red light emanating from the blade. Any remaining bandits fled. She kept her focus on the leader.

His eyes widened, and he stared at the sword. "This can't be. The Phoenix died."

"I was reborn." Our voices united. "I protect this valley, and the next, and the next, as far as I can reach."

His boots skidded on the stone, and he scrabbled away, around the table and into the kitchen. She stood quietly, watching as he passed outside the windows, heading for the main gates.

"Do we follow?" Aviva leaned against the table.

"Do you feel up to rounding up the bandits and bringing them to justice right now?" I appeared, perched on the edge of the table beside her. The flames merged back into the sword blade.

"Honestly, I'm exhausted. I need a proper meal, too. I guess we can track them down after a nap, right?"

I chuckled. "Right. Besides, maybe you and I aren't the only ones keeping the valley safe. We don't work alone. Peace is too big a task for any one person, no matter how powerful. Let's go back."

She picked the scabbard up from the table and sheathed the sword. "Do you suppose the other bandits left? What about Merek?"

"We'll find out. He won't get far on that injured leg. Whatever narcotics they've given him must have worn off by now. You need to rest first. You're not used to channeling my power and I can feel you are ready to drop. Let's get those remaining women out of here and head back."

CHAPTER 31

READY TO DROP

Aviva shuffled to the kitchen and stopped in the doorway. The old woman stirred a pot of stew over the fire. Fresh wood sat beside the fireplace. She seemed oblivious to the commotion, or that everyone had run. A middle-aged woman and the other young woman huddled in a corner. They stared at Aviva with wide eyes.

"Ma'am?" Aviva called.

"The stew is nearly done. Grab some bowls. Quick, girl." She moved the massive metal ladle with both hands, ignoring everything around her.

Aviva raised her eyebrow. "The bandits are gone. We can all leave now."

The young woman burst into tears and buried her head in the other woman's shoulder. She held the girl, rocked her gently, and stroked her hair. Mother and daughter? I felt my chest tighten, and it got hard to swallow. I poured warmth into Aviva's heart, where I rested, soothing her, too. Images of her parents, the guard, and Master Denneth flashed through our connection.

"The bandits are gone. I'm going home. If you want an escort down the mountain, follow me. If you can find your own way home, go ahead." Aviva turned and left the kitchen.

She walked down the long hall between the empty wooden tables loaded with food. I stayed nestled in her heart, a warm presence to keep her going.

"Miss?"

Aviva stopped and turned. "Yes?"

"We're coming. Please wait. Mom's leg isn't the best, and Granny's nearly blind. That's how they got us." The young woman leaned against the doorway to the kitchen, her hands clasped in front of her.

Aviva nodded. "Get them ready."

I shimmered and slipped from inside her, perching on the table nearby. "You know, it would be a shame to waste food when you're so hungry. Have some fruit while you wait, at least. You need the energy. I can only keep you upright for so long. I can heal, but it's not my strongest skill by any means."

She laughed. It was great to see a genuine smile again. "Sure. It looks fantastic."

Aviva settled on the bench and grabbed a pear from a bowl of fruit. She nibbled it, sucking the juice out. I sat in silence with her as she finished her pear and picked up an apple.

The women walked into the hall, the young woman guiding her granny. Her mother had a bundle on her back. A loaf of bread stuck out from under the top flap.

"We're ready." The young woman smiled at Aviva. "I'd like to go home now."

Aviva stood and bowed. "This way."

We walked through the main doors and out into the courtyard. Aviva let the older women set the pace. We hadn't taken the path yet. Would the bridge be crossable? How would we get them to the other side? We headed through the main gates and down the wide path, the smooth dirt track making walking easier.

We stopped at the edge of the bridge. It no longer hung between the supports, but lay in pieces in the river.

Aviva eased down the riverbank to the edge of the bridge. "We can still cross, if we're careful."

She glanced down and her stomach heaved. Aviva pressed a hand to her mouth and dropped to a crouch, facing away from the river, her hand on the ground for support.

I wrapped a wing around her as I investigated the water, turning my long neck to see. What had she seen?

A dark shape lay under the bridge, partly visible as the sun glinted off armour, the water scattering the reflected light. A dark boot stuck out from under the end right near us.

"I'm here. Just breathe. He won't be hurting anyone else again. You'll be okay."

The old woman gripped the edge of the bridge deck and slowly climbed her way up onto it. Her granddaughter helped boost her up. They didn't look down, but ahead to the other side.

"Come on, girl. They're crossing. We don't want to leave them without a guard, do we?" I sent soothing into her.

Aviva wiped her forehead and stood. She helped the mother up onto the bridge deck and followed them across, she and the young woman helping at each spot the bridge broke. They got the older women across safely, going from deck piece to deck piece, and down onto the riverbank on the other side.

Her mind was spinning as we headed down the path. 'Kai, how can I protect people if I can't handle death? Am I still any good to you?'

I felt her thoughts clearly flow between us. 'If anything, it's a good thing,' I assured her. 'It means you'll never be too quick to kill. Our goal is to defend, ideally without destroying life. Some of my bonded went their whole lives without killing. I bet you can, too.'

Aviva let out a breath and wiped a tear from her cheek. We followed the path down together.

'Don't forget to look and listen,' I reminded her. 'There might still be bandits around.'

The path was quiet. I sensed nobody. A sword lay abandoned at the side of the path. Further down, we passed a bloody tunic. A boot lay in the path over the next rise. We kept walking.

Aviva stopped, holding her hand up. The women stopped with her. I heard it, too. People were talking up ahead, around the bend. Many people, from the sounds of it.

'Have the bandits regrouped?' She sounded tired. 'Who's leading them?'

'I don't know. You're small and sneaky. Let's go find out. See the boulders? Use them for cover and get off the path.'

She pressed her hand over her heart. "Wait here. I'll be back once it's safe. Tuck into the trees and hide."

I remained inside her, letting her do her thing. She was small and sneaky, and she didn't need me for this. We crept up to the boulders and peered around the edge. Voices grew louder as we approached. Aviva strained to listen, and we started understanding words, then sentences.

"Masters, spread out, and take the others in small groups. We'll stay and guard the prisoners."

Masters? Her heart raced. She grinned. She knew that voice. Aviva peeked around the boulder. Her fingers gripped the rock, ignoring the discomfort as her new skin scratched against the rough surface. She leapt the boulder and raced to the group.

Master Denneth walked towards her; arms outstretched. Aviva ran into his embrace and hugged tightly. Her heart burst with joy, filling me with heat.

"What are you doing here?" she whispered. Tears streamed down her face.

Master Denneth kneeled and brushed her tears away. "Someone I care about needed help, so I followed as quickly as I could. I encountered bandits and needed help myself, so I brought some friends."

She looked over his shoulder at the masters and students milling about, some guarding a group of bandits sitting on the ground, bound in ropes.

"It's good to see you safe. Are you okay?" He peered into her eyes.

Aviva smiled. "I'm okay. My friend is, too. I'm so tired, though, and still starving." She dropped her head to his shoulder.

Master Denneth looked over her shoulder at the sword strapped to her back, and the book bundled in her outer tunic. Would he know what they were? Of course he would. He's seen them before.

Master Ninden returned with a group of senior apprentices, leading three bandits bound in rope. He glared down at the bandits, scowling deeply. "Sit, or it'll be the last thing you do." He looked over and his mouth dropped open. "Aviva, you're safe!" He darted to her side.

She opened her eyes and smiled. Aviva straightened up. "I am. Thanks for helping. There are three women on the trail behind me. I'm escorting them back. They could use some help."

Master Ninden waved his hand, signaling the others. A master led some apprentices down the path.

"Anyone who threatens family will learn. We live in peace until they bring war to us." Master Ninden grinned at her, showing teeth.

Aviva wobbled and gripped Master Denneth's shoulders for balance.

"How about we get you back and let Master Tula give you the once over? I know how you feel about Master Morlin." Master Denneth winked at her. He wrapped an arm around her waist and steadied her.

Aviva glanced at the bandits. The masters seemed to have everything under control. She nodded.

"Allow me to carry your burdens?" Master Denneth nodded at her sword and tunic.

'Kai?'

'Yes, if you trust him, and I can feel you do. He's a good man. We can let him help.'

Aviva nodded. Her fingers fumbled at the knot in her tunic sleeves. Master Denneth eased her sword belt from around her and slung it over his shoulder. Master Ninden swiftly untied the knot with deft fingers and let Master Denneth take her book, still covered by and wrapped in the tunic.

"Allow me to help." Master Ninden took her hands and turned his back to her. He pulled her forward, and she wrapped her arms around his neck. He looped his arms around her legs and stood, holding her on his back. "If we go now, we'll be back before supper."

Her stomach growled, drowning out the noise of chattering students nearby. Master Denneth unwrapped a fruit bar and handed it to her. Aviva scarfed it down one-handed, holding on as Master Ninden started down the mountain.

'Doing okay?'

'Yeah, Kai, I am. Tired.'

She finished the bar and wrapped her arm back around Master Ninden's neck. I rested around her heart as she dropped into a deep slumber.

***

Master Ninden lay her on her bed, stretched out carefully. Master Denneth draped a blanket over her.

"Let me know how she is." Master Ninden set a hand on Denneth's shoulder.

Master Denneth reached a hand up to Master Ninden's shoulder. "I will, old friend. Once she has rest and food, I'll let you know. You can visit when she wakes."

Master Ninden left. The room felt bigger without the mountain of a man in here, and somehow emptier, too. Master Tula slipped in through the door behind him, a medical kit in his hands. Eron followed close behind, his brow furrowed when he saw her. Master Tula sat on the edge of the bed beside her and lay a hand on her forehead.

"She slept the entire way back." Master Denneth sat in her desk chair, turning it to face her. "Had a snack, too, but she's still probably hungry."

Master Tula felt her pulse at her wrist. "I'll check her over and see to her health. Once I'm done, I'll let you know how she is."

Master Denneth stood and bowed. He left through the adjoining door. Eron closed the door to the hallway. Master Tula pulled her blanket back. She stirred and blinked up at him.

He felt for her pulse again, with her awake. "How do you feel, child?"

"Hungry, but okay." She smiled and glanced around. "What time is it?"

"Two bells from nightfall. He said you slept the whole way back. Open your mouth for me."

Aviva did as he asked. Master Tula examined her. She followed each instruction without protest or complaint, laying quietly and letting the healer work. His hands moved over her lightly, checking for any injuries she might not mention.

"Eron, a half packet of the recovery blend, mixed with a teacup full of water, please. Our little friend here is a bit dehydrated."

Eron took a packet from the medical kit and walked to the connecting door. After a quick knock, he disappeared inside. We heard muffled voices through the door.

Master Tula placed his fingers at the collar of her undertunic, his fingers on reddened skin. He pulled down slowly, exposing the upper part of her chest at her breastbone. She pulled the blanket tighter around her chest, but let him examine the skin above it. Did she know it was there?

A marking over her heart, like a tattoo in light blue and red ink, an image of the Phoenix was etched into her skin. The stylized bird was a few inches across and high at most.

"Does that hurt?"

Aviva looked down. She reached up and touched the skin. "No. That's new."

Master Tula pulled her tunic up fully as the sliding door between the rooms opened.

Eron entered with a teacup cradled in his hands. He walked over and kneeled beside her bed. "I cooled it for you, so you can drink it now."

"Let's sit you up." Master Tula slid a hand under her back and helped Aviva sit. "This will help you feel better. Food is coming for you, too."

She smiled and took the cup from Eron. "Thank you, both."

"Finish that quickly. Once you've had a meal, you can sleep again for the night. Take tomorrow easy, and I'll be by to check on you regularly." Master Tula stood. He walked to the connecting door, his robes flowing behind him. "Eron, once you're packed, return to the workshop. I'll meet you there."

Eron bowed his head. "Yes, Master." He smiled at Aviva. "Rest up. We'll have more herbalism lessons for you soon."

Aviva sipped her tea. Eron moved to the desk and packed up the medical kit, tucking the rest of the packet back inside. He tucked the kit under his arm and left.

"Kai, what's the mark on my chest?"

I slipped from her body and perched on her knee. My feathers glowed, casting a red and gold light around the room. "That's the sign of our bonding. You'll carry it for life."

"Do they know what it means?" She sipped more tea, draining the little cup.

"The Masters will. Don't be concerned. I formed the school to help train warriors to aid us. They'll help you grow your skills, and keep you fighting fit, while training themselves as well. Just stay humble. Remember, we serve the people. They don't serve us."

"You're smaller now."

I chuckled, my musical laugh creating music in the air. "I'll grow as you and your skills grow here in the physical realm, and I can always make myself bigger or smaller. When you're at your fighting peak, I'll be big enough to carry you far across the mountain range with a single flap of my wings. I'll still be able to shrink down to fit better, too. Think I'd fit well in here, with a few dozen foot wingspan?"

She laughed. "No."

The door opened, and Master Denneth walked over, followed by Master Tula.

Master Denneth bowed. "Kai. It's been a while."

"Too long." I let my musical voice project, so they could hear me, too. "The energy of youth has certain advantages."

Master Tula took the little teacup from Aviva and set it on the desk.

Aviva lay down and pulled her blanket up to her chin. "They can see you?"

"They can, now that we're bonded. Normally, people only see me when I allow it, but they're different." I flapped my wings, stretching them out. "It feels good to manifest so easily again."

Master Tula kneeled beside her. "We've been training for decades and are in tune with both the physical and spirit realms, to some extent. We can see some spirits. You'll find only some masters can see Kai."

Her eyelids drooped. She blinked slowly. "What happens now?" Aviva looked up at Master Denneth.

Master Denneth smiled down at her. "You eat and rest. Tomorrow, we focus on meditation, as that will strengthen your bond with Kai. After that, the actual work begins."

"Actual work?"

I laughed and curled up on the end of the bed. "You need to learn to tap into my full powers and potential. We've only scratched the surface of what we can do. We also need to meet with the masters and decide how to keep going."

She frowned. "Will they accept me? Some masters will, but the others?"

Master Denneth kneeled beside her and took her hand. "You bear the mark, right? They will accept you. Change might not come easily to everyone. Along with martial skills, you'll start diplomacy lessons, too."

A knock on the hall door pulled her attention. Master Tula slid the door open. Garin stood there with a tray of food. He smiled at Aviva. She sat up and smiled back. Master Denneth helped her sit fully.

"Thank you, Garin." Master Denneth nodded to him. "You can leave that on the desk."

Garin stepped inside and set the tray beside the medical kit. "How are you feeling?"

"I'm okay." Her cheeks burned red. "Just tired."

"I'll see you tomorrow." Garin backed from the room and closed the door.

Master Denneth and Master Tula helped her ease from the bed and walked her to the desk. She inhaled the steam coming from her tray, her favourite blend of rice and veg-etables.

Master Denneth pushed her chair in for her. "Eat, child, and rest. Tomorrow's tasks will wait for tomorrow."

She picked up her spoon and tucked into the food. I flew over and perched on her shoulder. We'd be together nearly constantly now. I will watch over her as she trains and sleeps and learns. She still has a lot to learn, but tomor-row would come soon enough. Each new day was a new beginning, and I got to see life anew through her eyes. Tomorrow.

DEAR READER,

If you enjoyed my book, please consider leaving a review. It helps other people find my books, so they can enjoy them, too.

You can find more information on all my books at www. aliings.com. Sign up for the newsletter for bonus content and scenes, tips and facts, book information, and more.

ALSO BY

Legends of the Mountain

Phoenix Rising

Other Books

Rogue Magic

A Flash Of Light

ABOUT AUTHOR

Ali spends her days with her horses and ponies, dreaming of adventures and magic. She enjoys martial arts, especially swords and edged weapons, though she practices for self-improvement. She also practices meditation, both sitting and moving varieties.